BETWEEN BLOODE AND WATER

BETWEEN THE SHADOWS

MARIE HARTE

BETWEEN BLOODE AND WATER
ISBN-13: 978-1642920697
Copyright © March 2022 by Marie Harte
No Box Books
Cover by Moonpress Design | moonpress.co

For exclusive excerpts, news, and contests, sign up for **Marie's newsletter**. https://www.subscribepage.com/betweentheshadows

BETWEEN THE
SHADOWS

BETWEEN BLOODE AND WATER

THE NIGHT BLOODE: A BRIEF INTRODUCTION

Varujan—patriarch (leader), strigoi tribe, known for his savagery, ability to seduce, smarts, and powerful magic, can shift into a raven; direct descendant of Ambrogio, the very first vampire

Duncan—revenant tribe, known for his power of seduction, speed, and intelligence, shifts into a raven

Orion—*vrykolakas* tribe, able to swim like water-folk, very strong, employs hypnosis on prey, shifts into a raven

Kraft—*nachzehrer* tribe, has a rage form that cannot be stopped until he tires himself out; super strong, shifts into a wolf at will

Khent—reaper tribe, with an ability to bring back the dead, arrogant and magical, shifts into an owl

Rolf—draugr tribe, steeped in magic, able to shift into a wolf, only blond vampire in existence

—

Mormo—clan magician and servant of the goddess Hecate, both human and not human, powerful

Hecate—clan patron, in charge of the rowdy bunch though they choose not to see her as anything but an inconvenience; goddess of witchcraft, death, and crossroads.

—

1. **Bloode Empire** (every vampire in existence) 80,000+ members
2. **Vampire Tribe** (vampires with defined characteristics) 1000-10,000 members
3. **Vampire Clan** (vampire families within their tribe) 6-60 members

—

Bloode—the essence of a vampire, made of (vampire) blood and magic

—

Vampire: beautiful, lethal, unfriendly, top predator
Lesser beings: everyone *not* a vampire, to include: humans, magir (creatures of magic who are not human,) monsters, fae, gods, and demons

Sunday, January 2nd
Mercer Island, Washington

Orion had seen a lot of things in his two hundred and forty-six years of living, but the reanimated raccoon racing from the reaper while also being chased by a battle cat, two obnoxious kittens, and a wolf was an all new level of weird.

"Damn it. Get back here!" the reaper commanded.

Despite his ever-present arrogance, everyone alive and dead ignored him as they raced around the basement's main living space, hissing and barking.

Smoky, Orion's kitten, grinned as he passed by, the little jerk never so happy as he was while annoying Orion's kin.

The other three vampires in the house, not counting the reaper and draugr (running around in wolf form), watched with him, as did the crazy dusk elf they'd all been forced to accept.

Truly, Orion was living in momentous times. Vampires from different tribes living together, when normally they'd have killed each other by now, had to be a first. Especially since two of the idiots had mates, which normally caused vampires to act even *more* territorial. For sure, the apocalypse had to be right around the corner.

Even the goddess Hecate, the owner of the large house they all lived in, agreed.

Kraft, the only vampire among them to match Orion's strength, looked at him, grinned, and in a light German accent said, "Your demonic feline taunts the reaper yet again. I'm beginning to like him." He paused and added with deliberate menace, "Perhaps I'll allow him a few more months of life before I eat him."

Orion flipped him off, which had the younger vampire laughing and making lewd comments about Orion's lineage.

Before Orion could pound the giant bastard into the floor, a deep, melodic voice accompanied the arrival of a creature no one wanted to deal with, as evidenced by them all slinking away into the shadows. Hell, even the raccoon, battle cat, and kittens darted away.

"Where did everyone go? Oh well. You, Orion. I have a job for you." Mormo, the freaky bastard who served the goddess they'd been unwillingly pledged to, pointed at him. Neither young nor old, Mormo had long white hair, a face with delicate features more suited to the fae than to other magir or humans, and an arrogant attitude not belonging in those not vampire.

Orion and his kin considered those not Of the Bloode to be lesser beings, and as such, he thought Mormo's conceit misplaced.

Even if the bastard had the ability to make his bloode boil, freeze, or explode on a whim.

Orion groaned. "What do you want? I'm supposed to have off tonight."

"Says who?" Mormo arched a brow, his red eyes glowing.

They'd all speculated on what Mormo might be but hadn't come to a consensus. So they called him a magician, which fit well enough. Who else but a magic-user could gather six vampires from different tribes to serve a goddess none of them worshipped? Without Hecate's power and Mormo's magic, Orion and the others would have killed each other by now. Cursed long ago to only exist in small groups, his kind were driven to kill vampires outside their own clan.

And speaking of family... "You know, you should pick one of the others for this chore. I've been doing *a lot* since Samhain. I've been working hard all through the holidays."

"Which you don't celebrate."

"I saved Christmas from a heretic."

Mormo sighed. "You broke Santa's leg and managed to scare a small group of children."

"He was an imposter ready to eat young humans!" Shouldn't Orion have been rewarded for that?

"You mean a department store Santa plying children with candy canes to put them at ease for pictures on his lap in a special evening celebration at Nordstrom's?"

"Monstrous!" Orion barreled on. "And creepy. Why were they on his lap? Why is his suit such a beautiful color if not to tempt the young to gather closer? Why fatten them up with sugar if not to sweeten their blood?"

Mormo pinched the bridge of his nose. "Never mind."

"Exactly. I made an effort to celebrate stupid Christmas for Macy's sake. And what thanks do I get? More work."

Their only human and the clan's Bloode Witch, Macy had recently mated their revenant, a decent vampire who acknowledged Orion's superior strength and fighting prowess. Thanks to that pair, Orion had adopted his best fur buddy, a feline of estimable power and treachery.

He grinned, wondering who would win in a battle between his gray kitten and Kraft. Honestly, it could go either way. Smoky had the art of treachery down to a science.

"I don't even want to know why you're smiling."

Orion shrugged. "Eh. Leftover cheer from your Christmas."

"Not mine." Mormo sniffed. "Stop changing the subject. We need you to investigate reports of a suspicious island that comes and goes. It was spotted by a few magir up north."

"Just magir?"

"Yes." Mormo sighed. "If the humans aren't seeing it, that means the island has to be magical in nature, yet Hecate hasn't gotten word of anyone claiming ownership of this new land mass. Neptune claimed a section of the waters north of the city years ago. He should know who's trespassing but doesn't."

"I'll stop you right there. Keep your gods and god friends to yourself. Just tell me what you want me to do." He spotted Smoky peering at him from around the couch, the kitten's brother, Nightmare, sneering before taking off again. Now *that* feline Kraft could devour and Orion wouldn't mind.

The little fucker kept leaving live scorpions and venomous centipedes in his shoes. Orion had no idea where he'd been finding them.

Mormo gave him specifics for what seemed like hours yet hadn't been more than a few minutes, the magician keen on dragging everything out, unnecessarily. Orion finally left the house for the dock in the backyard, pleased at the surprise he found. Instead of a three-person skiff, he spotted a pretty little yacht, maybe thirty-five feet in length, with a hardtop shaded cockpit and deep stateroom for hiding from the sun.

Having a goddess at their disposal had one or two good points. Money didn't seem to be an object of contention when they needed supplies and tools. And... Well, that was pretty much all he could come up with on good points.

At least able to enjoy the outdoors away from the house, Orion pulled out of the dock and didn't look back.

. . .

THE TEMPERATURE and weather kept most people inside, though the lateness of the hour could also be attributed to such a quiet night on the water. The dense clouds overhead let loose a flurry of snow, the cold just enough that though the white stuff wouldn't stick, the streets would likely ice over before the sun rose. Roads would become treacherous, the freezing air making it more difficult to find prey out and about.

The snow did have a huge plus though. Orion appreciated the lack of boats around as he steered his craft through Puget Sound.

The unidentified land mass had been reported south of Whidbey Island, rumors of rogue magir fighting then disappearing on its shores. A white castle, not the good kind filled with burgers, but an actual castle giving off magic vibes, had also been sighted.

As a vampire of the *vrykolakas* tribe, Orion thrived in the water. His clan—his *old* clan—had talents in that lovely, wet, alien environment that others could only dream of possessing.

An odd homesickness struck. He missed the crisp scents and warm feel of Santorini, his birthplace. A volcanic island located between the Ios and Anafi islands in Greece, Santorini was famous for its dramatic views, in particular the town of Thira and the sunsets from Oia, which he'd often likened to flame cleansing the sky safe for his kind to thrive. Hell, he even missed the black pebble beach of Kamari, not to mention the leagues of merfolk and water-magir his kind often played with and fed on.

The spray from the Aegean sea never failed to satisfy, such a different place and feel than the dark, cold waters of the Sound.

And that made him angry. Orion didn't do sadness. He hated, he envied, he killed. And he found joy in battle, in amusement with his new kin, typically at the expense of another. Regret was a waste of time.

Annoyed at an unwelcome melancholy, he snarled, the sound taken by the wind. He continued speeding up, uncaring of disturbing a few merfolk and water-shifters on his way who swore at him.

"Yeah, screw you too," he shouted back.

The magir, those non-humans who lived in this plane of existence, only lived here because humans didn't know about them. Like they didn't know about the island that appeared out of nowhere before him. He throttled back on the engine and drifted closer.

Personally, Orion didn't like all the secrecy. He wouldn't have minded outing magir and the Bloode Empire especially, engaging in an all-out bloody war for supremacy with weak humans. But he'd been outvoted the many times he'd suggested the notion.

And so, as Mormo nagged earlier, in no way was Orion to gain the attention of the Magir Enforcement Command (MEC) on this assignment. MEC, the magir and witches used to enforce laws on non-humans, could be super annoying.

He'd dealt with them back in October. Though they'd been scrappy and no real threat, a bunch of them together against one of his kind might be able to do some damage.

No one could best a vampire one on one but another vampire. Lesser beings had their place, but rarely could those *not* Of the Bloode best those Of the Bloode. Everyone knew vampires remained at the top of the food chain.

But in an effort to play nice with their new Bloode Witch—a member of MEC who had family also working as agents—he'd refrain from involving them.

It was too bad Orion couldn't have at least brought Kraft with him for entertainment, because Kraft lived to brawl.

Though a younger vampire of the *nachzehrer* tribe, Kraft amused him. Not partial to water, nachzehrers turned into wolves at will and were known for their fighting prowess, savages in battle. Only Kraft could physically match Orion in a fight. And maybe Varu, their patriarch, but that fight would be less about brute strength and more about strigoi savagery and power.

A longing for blood and battle descended, and Orion hoped against hope he'd find something to kill while on this boring errand.

After tying up the boat, he bounded onto the beach, his hair soon slick with snow, his sweater covered in the stuff. Dense with trees and an intriguing scent—a mix of blood, steel, and fire—the island felt magical, definitely not something a human would detect.

Uncaring of the weather and unaffected by its temperature, he moved through the falling snow and cocked his head, hearing some groans, a grunt, snarling, and then a woman's voice.

"Please, stop," she begged. "You're hurting me."

Hmm. Prey? Orion sped a short distance into the woods, following the scent of blood. He saw a few wolves torn apart, one an injured lycan trying to drag himself toward a fallen packmate. He could tell them apart because the wolves looked mundane, but the lycan was in his much larger, direwolf form, and he saturated the area around him with the scent of magic.

Orion followed the sound of weeping deeper into the trees, tracking the scent of fear and broken pine.

A dozen lycans battled amongst themselves while two of them nipped at a gorgeous woman in tattered clothing. Her pale breasts heaved and her long, muscular thighs pushed past her torn gown as she tried kicking them away.

Intrigued at the smell of her rich blood trickling from a bite at her thigh, he hurried to dispatch the lycans bothering her. As he killed the two, he noticed a large structure just behind her, past the trees. The castle loomed over them like a white mountain, stern and forbidding. Distracted by the feel of pressure on his wrist, he looked down.

A lycan was trying to rip his hand off, but Orion had tempered skin, his frame toughened by the rush of adrenaline-fueled bloode hardening beneath his epidermis. He shook the lycan free before ripping his—no, *her*—head off, then handled the others.

Once he'd taken care of disabling—not outright killing them all because where was the fun in not giving lesser beings the chance to try to kill him again—he followed the enthralling scent of sweet blood to the woman clutching at her dress, trying to hide her pale skin.

"You smell good," he growled, hungry and curious, because her scent didn't taste human on his tongue as he licked at the air.

"Did you kill them all?" Her voice shook, and though she appeared young, her eyes held the knowledge of someone far older. "They wanted to eat me."

"A few of them are still alive." He thought she looked annoyed, but she blinked, and the smell of fear wafted from her like a fine perfume.

"Y-you're not like them. D-do you p-plan to eat me too?" She blinked bright blue eyes at him, her long, dark hair whispering over her shoulders, as if caught in a breeze despite the lack of wind in the trees. The snow had stopped falling, and a spear of moonlight bathed the woman in a glow, highlighting her loveliness.

He smiled, mesmerized by the strange blue light around her. "You plan to offer me a sip?" He looked her over, focusing on her neck. "Trust me, it'll feel good."

She blinked, her eyes wide. "You want to drink my blood?"

He stalked her, pressing her back against a nearby tree. "I do." Ready to hypnotize her if necessary, he wasn't prepared for her to tilt her head and close her eyes.

Supplicant, she whispered, "Then drink, vampire."

Too bemused by the call of her blood to realize she should have been more alarmed, he leaned close and bit. A burst of power exploded in his mouth and traveled throughout his body.

So sweet. He drank more, gulping her down, and the sweet turned bitter. A choking thickness made it hard to swallow. Then fire, boiling his bloode, caused him to fall to his knees in agony.

A throaty laugh accompanied his pain, a hiss of black magic licking his bloode.

Then the world turned dark.

Three days later
Lake City (Seattle), Washington

K aia clutched the cell phone held to her ear and did her best
not to roll her eyes, but dealing with her mother made that
all but impossible. "I'm not dating right now, Mom."

"I see that, Kaia. So disrespectful."

"What?"

"You're rolling your eyes."

Not yet. "Mom, we're on the phone. You can't see anything."

"I know what I know."

Kaia *did* roll her eyes and sighed loudly. "What did we say
about you staying out of my personal life?"

"Darling, you don't have a personal life."

"Harsh."

"But true."

A loud grumble from the background distracted the conversation, and for once it wasn't any of Kaia's roommates, who had
been working overtime on the same case at MEC, leaving her
alone in the house. She continued to thank her lucky shells that

she'd gotten her dream job at the repository. Dealing with books beat dealing with bad guys any day of the week.

From her mother's end came a low moan, then swearing, something sucking, a gurgling, then more swearing before some rabid barking and snarling.

Kaia had a bad feeling. "What was that?"

Her mother gave a tinkle of a laugh. "Oh, just a few new men in my life. They're divine." That caused her to laugh harder. "I'm kidding. They're not godly at all. Far from it. But I've one in particular who's quite handsome." A pause. "These three are a little long in the tooth. Almost... wolfish, you might say." She giggled.

Sabine Belyaev never giggled unless she had someone splayed out and bound on an altar, typically on the throes of death.

Kaia hadn't planned on visiting her mother for another few weeks at least, as long as she could manage to put off the trip. But now she'd have to make the time. The last time she'd felt uneasy about her mother, Sabine had nearly sacrificed Kaia's ex-boyfriend to Pazuzu, a Babylonian demon.

Fortunately, her mother had seemed more interested in flirting with Pazuzu than slitting Sean's throat. So she hadn't been overly annoyed to find Kaia had "accidentally" sent her ex home in one piece. Just a small misunderstanding. Sure.

Still, the lecture Kaia had received about not visiting unless expressly invited hadn't been pleasant. She'd left in tears, but at least the White Sea Witch had been appeased.

Kaia said nothing about her mother's wolfish playthings, determined to keep the peace. The daughter of divorced parents, Kaia did her best to remain neutral. Her father made it easy. Her mother, not so much. Sabine had no problem getting nasty, so Kaia tried to remain pleasant and funny and not too confrontational.

Unless she could get away with it.

"Hey, Mom, aren't we due for tea this week? I haven't been to the castle in a while." Her mother kept moving it, hiding the pocket dimension somewhere in the Sound ever since Kaia had rescued Sean.

"No, I don't think so. In any case, I'll be out of town until next Friday. Hold on." Her mother muttered to herself. "I leave tomorrow, so... How about next weekend?"

"Oh, Sunday the sixteenth? That would work for me. We're cataloguing for the book sale next Saturday."

"Perfect. I'll jot it down."

Kaia waited. "Where's the conference? I don't remember you mentioning it."

"I didn't? Must have slipped my mind. It's a national potions and elixirs conference."

"Aren't they the same thing?" Kaia knew better and only said that the bug her mom. The newer generations mixed the terms all the time, but old school witches and mages clung to tradition.

"Haven't we had this talk before?" Her mother let out an exasperated sigh, which caused Kaia to chuckle. "Oh, you." She could hear her mother's smile. "You know very well potions are ingredients mixed to perform a function and can be—but aren't always—infused with magic. Whereas elixirs are mixed magical liquids, thus based in magic at their foundation. I know it's a fine line, but it's there for a reason. The conference promises to delve into some rare recipes from a few fae and hell demesnes. I can't wait."

Her mother had a fixation with hells, devils, and demons. Dark magic could give much bang for the magical buck, yet it was too dangerous to handle. Kaia knew that, but her mother remained deliberately obtuse about dabbling in darker arts. Then again, her mother wasn't just any sea witch, but *the* White Sea Witch. As the preeminent sea witch in all of the Pacific Northwest, she had a reputation to uphold.

"Well, I hope it's fun. Where are you going?"

"The conference is in Vancouver, so not too far. I'm excited. It's been a while since I mingled."

You mean since you terrorized more than Seattle and its waters. "I'm sure you'll have a blast."

"Oh, I intend to."

And didn't that sound ominous.

They made small talk for a while longer before Kaia yawned and said good night.

But once disconnected from her mother, she felt less like sleeping and more like panic-calling for advice. She immediately dialed her sister. Technically her stepsister, but they never let genetics define their relationship.

"Hello?" Macy answered, sounding perky.

"Macy, I need some advice."

"Who's that?" a sexy voice in a British accent asked. The new guy Kaia had been hearing about from her parents. A vampire—a revenant, to be precise. His tribe were know for their intelligence gathering and speed and could shift into a raven at will—which all sounded right up her witchy sister's alley. Kaia wanted to be happy for Macy but... a vampire?

"It's my sister, Kaia," Macy answered him.

"Oh. When do I get to meet her?"

"Never, if our dad has anything to say about it."

Kaia warmed. Macy had taken to being her big sister ever since her mother had married Kaia's father. She'd even assumed "Dunwich" as part of her name, officially adopted by Kaia's dad, and never used the term "step" to describe them. They were sisters, period.

Though Kaia would feel bad after thinking it, she often wished Macy had been born her older sister, with Diana, Kaia's stepmom, her biological mother. A witch, Diana Bishop-Dunwich performed strong, clean magic. Nothing like the suffocating malevolence Kaia's mother enjoyed. Plus, Diana had accepted Kaia into the family from the very beginning.

No wonder Macy was so independent and resourceful. She took after Diana and Will Dunwich. Kaia did her best, but she came across as naive and weak. Always worried about everything, like disappointing her father, annoying her mother, or not living up to the Dunwich name, like Macy obviously did.

Heck, sometimes it felt like Kaia lived to make everyone but herself happy. But if she admitted that to her father, he'd worry and cast blame, likely at Sabine, which Kaia didn't want to have to handle.

At least with Macy now coupled up with an honest to goodness vampire, Kaia didn't need to worry about doing anything that might have repercussions on her sister's safety. If Macy could handle death-bringers, she truly had become the "badass witch" she'd always aspired to be. Talk about living on the wild side.

"Kaia?"

"Oh, sorry. Do you think you could get somewhere private? It's about my mom."

Macy muttered under her breath, no doubt something uncomplimentary about Sabine. "Sure. Hold on." Kaia heard a muffled, "No, Duncan, you can't follow me. Shoo." Another pause, and then, "Okay. Speak, freak."

Kaia grinned. "Oh good. You're still you. For a minute there, I thought you'd turned into vampire dinner."

"Ha ha. Dork."

They both laughed.

"Macy, I need a sounding board. I don't want your help. And I don't want any arguments about this."

"Oh man. What did Sabine do now?"

Kaia flushed. "Nothing that I know of, but I don't trust my gut feeling. I'm planning a scrying spell on her place in a few days while she's at a conference." Which actually meant—*I'm telling you, my big sis, that I'm scrying from a safe distance. In reality, I'm swimming over there to check things out in person.* "Am I being nosy? Out of place in my worry? Should I just ignore my feelings?"

"Seriously? You have to ask this after all the crap Sabine's pulled and keeps pulling? And let's not get started on how creepy it is when she casts a spell to look like you to snare men. It's downright incestuous."

"Ew."

"That's what I'm saying. Your mom has issues."

"I know." Kaia sighed.

"But none of that's your fault. You know her better than I do. If you think she's up to something, I say check it out—from a distance. I'm here if you need help, and you know Dad is there for you. Mom too."

"I know that." She blew out a breath. "I just needed to hear it."

"I believe in you."

"I believe in me too." Or at least, Kaia was trying to feel more confident. "Okay, enough about Sabine. Tell me about you and your new kin. That's the right word, isn't it?" Kaia still had a lot to learn about vampires, but she'd been studying. Her job at the Alister Doctrina Repository, better known as the ADR, a magir library located in Lake City, gave her access to all kinds of information. Unfortunately, many of the books on vampires seemed permanently checked out to members of MEC.

She knew little more than what she'd gleaned from a few weeks ago, having spent time with Macy and Cho, her sister's best friend and their pseudo-adopted brother. Cho could always be counted on to rescue her if she got into trouble. And he didn't always tell Macy either.

Macy said, "Yes, Duncan and the others are now my kin—which is vampire for family."

"And the tribe you're in—"

"It's a clan. Vampire clans are small. Ours is the Night Bloode, and it's only six vampires, two dusk elves, me, and Mormo. Oh, and Hecate."

Kaia still couldn't believe her sister talked to the actual goddess herself, but Macy had been pretty complimentary about her patron deity. Hecate, goddess of death, witchcraft, and necromancy, also looked after the crossroads connecting all the planes in existence. A threefold goddess who had three faces, she wore the mantles of maiden, mother, and crone. A most mysterious divinity, she was often associated with all manner of magic.

And Macy had shared drinks with her at an otherworldly bar.

Kaia still had a tough time understanding how much her sister had changed. Macy had always been a strong witch, though one unable to tap into her power. Now she supposedly energized using the bloode of her mate. Bloode with an "e" because a vampire's bloode was made of more than mere blood, but magic as well as bodily fluid. Kaia didn't have the nerve to ask if Macy drank her mate's bloode or he drank hers, or maybe they just had vampire nooky to get strong.

Her cheeks heated. "Right. Hecate."

"Remember, we—the Night Bloode—are a clan." Macy sounded proud to claim them as her own. Not a typical reaction when dealing with creatures known as death-bringers and blood-drinkers, the scourge of the magir world. "We're small. Most vampire clans are like the local upir clan in Seattle, maybe thirty to fifty strong. Several clans make up a tribe, which can be made of thousands of vampires. It's all about units. Clans make up tribes which all add up to the Bloode Empire."

"So what tribe are you? There are ten tribes, right?"

"Yes, but we're made up of vampires from six different tribes. It's unheard of. The only reason these guy haven't gutted each other is because Hecate's using a spell to make them think they're kin."

Kaia blew out a breath. "But doesn't that scare you? That they could turn on one another at any time?" Just one vampire could decimate a *small town*. Dozens of them could conceivably topple a city.

"Nah. Hecate's powerful, and this clan's patriarch, the leader, is very levelheaded. You know how rare that is for vampires. Normally, they just want to kill everything in sight. But Varu's mated. I think his mate calms him. I know I'm a calming influence on Duncan."

Rustling in the background and raised male voices told Kaia she was no longer private on her call. "Thanks, Macy. For explaining and the advice. We'll have to do dinner soon."

"Hold on. Before you escape, catch me up. You dating anyone at the moment?"

Kaia groaned. "Not you too."

"Sorry. Did your mom give you the inquisition already?"

"You don't sound sorry."

"Well, she's got a right to worry about her virgin daughter. Damn, girl, you're nearly twenty-five."

"Shh. Macy," Kaia hissed. She heard more than one male in the background perk up as the voices grew louder all at once.

"Virgin? Yum!" "I can use her in a spell. Hook me up, Macy." "Oh, I bet she tastes sweet. Is she cute? Is she witchy like you?"

"Damn it, Kraft, that's my sister we're talking about," Macy growled.

The vampire said something in German, if Kaia wasn't mistaken, before giving a laugh that sounded like the low growl of a wolf.

"I'm hanging up now," Kaia said, mortified. *Dang it, Macy. You big blabbermouth.*

"Sorry." The noise behind Macy grew quiet again. "I wouldn't hound you about dating if I thought you wanted to be alone. But I know you, and I know how much you want to find that special someone. You've been dreamy about boys forever, and I don't mean that in a negative away."

Because everyone knew sea nymphs were easy. Except for Kaia, a freak among freaky sea people. "I do want a boyfriend, but that doesn't mean I'm going to sleep my way through a pack of lycans or a school of mermen." No matter what most people thought of sea nymphs, they weren't all *nymph*os. And yes, Kaia heard herself saying that and wished she didn't still find the terminology oddly funny.

"I've heard lycans like to share. Yum."

Kaia cracked a laugh. "Stop it. I'll tell Dad."

"Please, don't. He still thinks of you as his baby."

Unlike her mother, who would love nothing better than to use Kaia's loss of virginity in some enchantment to gain power. Her mother had mentioned that once, years ago, and the horror on Kaia's face had been enough to get her to not mention it again. But Sabine never forgot anything she might use to increase her magic.

"No men, human, magir, or otherwise. Alive or dead," she added before Macy could say something corny about vamps doing it better. Kaia couldn't imagine anyone wanting a relationship with a vampire. Sure, they were preternaturally handsome. But that was to lure prey.

Kaia had enough issues with self-esteem that dating someone who wanted to devour her, blood and bones or both, didn't bear thinking about.

"Well, whatever. If you change your mind, let me know. Cho and I know a few guys who might be perfect for you. And they're non-vampire, I swear."

"Ugh. I know what that means. No demons." Cho was half demon.

"That's racist."

"I'm a water person. Demons are all about fire. Do the math."

Macy chuckled. "Fine, fine. Anyway, good luck with Sabine. Let me know if you need help with anything." She paused. "You are keeping your distance, right?"

"I'll be fine. I won't do more than scry from the safety of my own home." She crossed her fingers.

"Good luck. Love you."

"Love you too."

After disconnecting, Kaia made plans. But first, she had a dinner to make and some K-Drama to stream. Danger could wait a bit. Romance and adventure couldn't.

House of the Night Bloode
Mercer Island, Washington

"I'm telling you, something's wrong," Kraft said, irritated. Why did no one fucking listen to him? Sure, he was the youngest of his clan, but that didn't mean he couldn't sense danger.

Mormo frowned. "It's only been his third night away. He's checked in twice already, and we agreed he'd scout around and be back by Friday. Why all the concern for the vryko? You know he's just as comfortable in water as on land."

"I know, it's just..." How to say what he felt without sounding young and anxious? Or like he *missed* the big bastard? Because he didn't.

"Kraft, go help out with the lycan in the basement, would you?"

Kraft had seen the reaper and draugr muscling a raving lycan from the garage into the basement. The lycan didn't look willing to play nice. He snorted. "You mean, before Khent raises him from the dead?"

"He won't if he knows what's good for him," Mormo muttered before turning in a dramatic sweep, his dark robe skirting out from his lean form, and stalked upstairs to a level of the house that shouldn't exist.

Fara, his patriarch's mate, called their home a mansion. Macy called it a lair, which he preferred because it sounded much cooler than "large house owned by a goddess." Situated on Mercer Island, their *lair* had two levels, a main one and a lower level that led out into a spacious lawn that overlooked Lake Washington. They also had a long dock in the shape of an L, where they could sit out at night and watch the moon or fool around with the boat Mormo had purchased. Yet Mormo's *second floor*—above the main level—didn't exist outside the house, and the basement had so many twists and turns that the home took up space on a different plane altogether.

Kraft had only gone up to the magician's floor a few times, only ever with Mormo or Varu, his patriarch, present, and he didn't like it. The area felt too heavy with magic, too much of the goddess's presence lingering over everything, the cloying feel of witchy divinity saturating the furniture and walls. He had a more sensitive nose, mostly due to his ability to shift into a wolf, so perhaps only he sensed it.

The others, with the exception of Rolf, took an avian shape when they took an alternate form. Kraft was partial to fur, not feathers. And his magic wasn't as sophisticated as those of his kin. Like Orion, Kraft relied on physical strength for power, controlling his environment with his body, not his mind.

He had been forced to join this motley group of vampires to pay back a bloode debt his clan had incurred with Hecate some time ago. But he hadn't realized the immense power of those with whom he'd be serving.

Their patriarch wielded legendary Bloode Stones, able to control all manner of vampires. As a strigoi, Varu had speed and savvy, an ability to seduce mortals and magir alike in addition to some weird mojo like teleporting and wielding telekinetic magic. And he could use a fucking *Bloode Stone,* which spoke of his power, since only a Worthy death-bringer could carry such power and not die. Varu was badass, for sure, especially having mated a sweet little dusk elf also with the ability to talk to the red gems. They were a total power couple, Varu the only one who could lead the Night Bloode.

Duncan, a revenant, had speed on his side, the laidback vampire funny and smart as hell—deadly when it came to strategizing and outmaneuvering his opponents. He also worked in tandem with their new Bloode Witch. Kraft knew they were the only clan in existence to have one. He also had a feeling Duncan could do other stuff but kept his abilities hidden, because he could be annoying like that.

Orion was the only one among them who could match Kraft blow for blow and loved to fight as much a born nachzehrer. From the vrykolakas tribe, Orion could move in the water like a merman but was hundred times more deadly. It was weird, especially because the rest of them sank when in water, but not Orion. Plus, the male had a thing for anime and Disney cartoons, which Kraft secretly admired.

That left Khent and Rolf, reaper and draugr, who often seemed to be paired together. Both deadly, both having an odd power over the dead.

Kraft walked downstairs and found them in the interrogation room, a large, padded area warded with Hecate's magic and soundproof to those not Night Bloode.

The most annoying pair of his kin stood over a lycan bound to a wooden chair. The prisoner looked human enough, though his wounds closed rapidly and he seemed much larger than a typical human. He didn't seem bothered by his nudity either, and mages and witches tended to cry about being naked. The lycan smelled good, more like kin than prey, though Kraft would never admit to the others how much pleasure he took in his shifted form.

Khent, tall, dark, and regal, always looked annoyed, as he did now. Able to reanimate the dead, with a mind that never stopped, he deemed everyone below him in importance. Yet he often spoke the truth, was rarely wrong about anything, and frankly, unnerved Kraft with those all-seeing eyes. Kraft could well believe humans had once thought Khent and his clan to be Egyptian gods.

Rolf, the only blond vampire Kraft had ever seen, seemed to laugh at everything, his magic more like that of Mormo's, but with a fae bite. He laughed and teased, a prankster much like the god who dwelled in his homeland somewhere in Scandinavia. The draugr seemed more fae or Viking than blood-drinker, and like Kraft, he too could shift into a wolf.

Kraft had thought that might make them closer than the others, but no. Kraft only felt truly comfortable with Orion.

And now the big bastard was gone, and no one seemed to care.

Rolf grinned at Kraft. "Want in on this? Ten bucks says I can get the lycan to tell us where the artifact is before necro-boy can." He nodded to Khent.

"Fuck off, blood-drinker." The lycan smelled a little of fear but was putting on a good show. He snarled at Kraft, who lifted a corner of his lip to snarl back.

Khent looked physically pained by Rolf's sense of humor. "Necro-boy? I'm—I *was*—one of the Sons of Osiris, you dick." Something he mentioned *every single time* anyone questioned his background. "My people are closer to godliness than yours ever were."

"And that's a compliment?" Kraft didn't understand that, because they all loathed divinity. Even Hecate, and she fed and cared for them.

"Not really, no," Khent admitted. "But I'm better than you all."

"Oh, we know." Rolf agreed. "You've only told us that for the past year we've been kin." He huffed and shifted a braid of blond hair over one ear. Kraft always expected to see it pointed, as if Rolf masked his features with a glamour, because damn if the draugr didn't feel fae. But no, his ear remained rounded.

Unlike the pointed ears of the dusk elves living with them, whom Kraft hadn't seen all night. Fara missing was not a big deal; Varu kept constant watch over his mate. But her brother was a menace.

"Hey, where are Onvyr and Fara?"

Khent answered, "Onvyr's with the others, so he's not killing indiscriminately, thank the night. And more good news—Fara thinks she found another of the items we need her to find."

Another Bloode Stone. With only six in existence, and two in Varu's possession, the other four were a true threat to the worlds.

When Ambrogio, the first of their kind, had fallen to the mortal plane, cursed by the god Apollo to forever drink blood for the offense of falling in love with Apollo's sister, Ambrogio cried. Or maybe he'd been stabbed and bled. In any case, those six drops of bloode that fell upon the earth became the six Bloode Stones.

Only with the stones could the vampires reunite and shake off the curse to forever war with one another. Kraft liked warring. He liked battle. But he knew that were the wrong vampire to get his hands on the stones, the worlds would suffer. Only vampires kept other vampires in check.

Warriors like Orion, who remained in danger. "Orion's gone."

"We know. He called." Rolf shrugged. "I think he's goofing off and playing with our new boat, but Mormo said to leave him alone. So I'm working with this guy again." He thumbed in the direction of Khent.

Khent leaned down to whisper into the lycan's ear, and though the magir growled, he didn't say anything of substance. Just a lot of his wolf mouthing off.

"You will talk, wolf," Khent promised. "Where is the artifact?"

"Suck it, reaper. It's not yours. It belongs to Pack."

Kraft had to hand it to the lycan. It took balls to stand up to vampires. But that bravery wouldn't help him survive if Khent decided to drain him dry.

"My turn." Rolf bounded to the man and drew a few sigils in the air over the lycan's head, which glowed gold.

"Really?" Khent scowled. "That's going to take hours to settle. I was getting somewhere."

"*Hey.*" Kraft growled. "Orion is gone. He's been gone for three nights and hasn't checked in." *Not with me.* "He's in trouble."

"He's fine." Khent waved him away. "And he's not important right now. We all have jobs to do. Even you." The reaper looked down his nose at Kraft, as he'd been doing since Mormo had screwed them all with that spell making them family.

"Look, you undead pharaoh-wannabe, I've had it with your prickly ass."

"*What* did you call me?" Khent drew himself to his full height, still an inch or two shorter than Kraft.

The lycan and Rolf watched with rapt attention.

"You heard me. Sons of Osiris? More like Osiris's little bitches. I mean, who ties themselves to a god?"

Rolf nodded. "You've got a point."

Khent ignored the draugr, his eyes blazing. "I was ruling city-states and gods before you were a calcified curse inside your mother's womb. You will talk to me with respect, fledgling."

"Or what, asshole?" Worry for Orion twisted into a comforting rage Kraft could handle.

"Or I'll eat your heart while you watch." Khent's smile looked icy. *And maybe a little intimidating,* Kraft refused to admit aloud. "Don't worry. I'll make sure to reanimate you along with my other pets. We'll be best of friends then, Kraft. Like you and the ignorant vryko, the one you're missing so much that you're close to crying."

"Oh no he didn't." Rolf sat cross-legged on the ground next to the lycan, a captive audience, and propped his elbows on his knees, his chin in his hands. "Watch this. Kraft's going to go for his throat."

Without missing a beat, the lycan said, "Twenty says the bigger one wins. He smells like victory."

Khent showed sharp fangs and claws and darted for Kraft.

Kraft met him strike for strike, but his anxiety over Orion's absence didn't lessen. It continued to fester, though punching Khent in the face did give him a sense of peace he'd been sorely missing.

Hurry, back, Orion. Or I just might kill these dickheads in your absence.

Thursday, 2:03 a.m.

Kaia loved where she lived. Her contract with the repository paid her well enough to live (with roommates) in a house on the water, so she would have had no problem slipping into Lake Washington from her dock, pleased with the cloud cover masking her movements.

Unfortunately, she had no idea what she might find on her mother's island in Puget Sound, so she made the twenty minute drive from her house to Olympic Beach. Using a borrowed camouflage charm so as not to be seen, she slid into the water—jeans, sweater, and undergarments minus anything on her feet or hands—and let herself be immersed in her home away from home.

As a sea nymph, Kaia's magic bonded her with one of the prime elements, so that her ability to swim and breathe underwater happened naturally, no gills necessary. She took what she needed from the water through her pores, and her eyes turned into bright blue beacons allowing her to see, equipped with nictitating membranes to allow her to mask that light from predators when the need arose.

If she wanted, she could shift her feet into fins and grow the webbing between her fingers. Though tonight, she decided to enjoy the rush of moving fast, undulating through the dark water with her arms by her sides, jetting at speeds greater than most motorboats would handle at full throttle.

Though her mother thought she'd hidden the island from everyone with her magic, Kaia had always been able to see the strands of her mother's power, though she'd kept that knowledge to herself. Sabine was neurotic enough about being stronger and better than everyone. Having her quiet, feeble daughter able to trail her no matter where she went would have thrown Sabine beyond incensed into murderous.

And Kaia refused to consider what her mother might actually do to a young nymph perceived as competition to the White Sea Witch.

So she kept her odd ability to herself while following the lure of her mom's magic. What told others to keep away or influenced their absence had the opposite effect on her.

As she moved, she passed a few mermaids, one a friend she knew from her favorite coffee shop downtown. She waved while avoiding a pair of annoying mermen she always seemed to run into near the island. Most merfolk didn't like clothing, and these particular guys seemed to have a problem that she didn't swim around with her boobs hanging out.

She ignored them and a few shapeshifter seals and bypassed the "keep out" wards, ignoring the aquatic life warning her away as well. Instead, she mimicked her mother's magic, which allowed her easy passage to the island.

Named Belyy Zamok, which in Russian meant "White Castle," the island existed in a pocket dimension. The dark magic left over from the sorcerer who'd created it had faded enough not to be overwhelming. Sabine had supposedly found it a year ago and claimed she'd fallen in love with the white keep, the stone so bright it always looked as if caught in moonlight.

Kaia cautiously approached, alert for more wards and magic traps. Sabine's home in Magnolia had them all over the lawn and in the trees.

The last time Kaia had visited the island, she'd found traps all the way out on the beaches before extending into the tree line. But now, she sensed a vibrating need to go away, and she realized her mother had tuned this particular magic to Kaia, no doubt in response to Kaia freeing her ex-boyfriend from sure death.

Again, she mimicked her mother's magic and passed over the shore and into the trees surrounding the castle.

She forced the water from her clothes as she moved and dried quickly. Fortunately, the snow had stopped early that morning, leaving behind a sheen of ice that had melted that afternoon under cloudy skies. The cold seeped in, especially through her feet and hands, but that couldn't be helped. The connection of bare feet to the ground allowed her to pass as her mother and to feel the magical constructs and beings foreign to Belyy Zamok.

Namely—three lycans.

And *a vampire.*

Kaia stopped in her tracks. Lycans she could understand. Powerful and protective of pack, they could be made to serve her mother with little effort. Sabine might ignore the fact that she had a touch of sea nymph in their shared history, but her sexual appetite couldn't be ignored. Three males to slake her lusts made sense.

But a vampire? Everyone knew not to mess with blood-drinkers. They were the apex predators of the magir world. Heck, of *every* world, rumored to even thumb their noses at gods.

Who did that and *lived?*

The closest Kaia had ever gotten to a vampire had been

spotting one roaming the neighborhood from her protected house, where she'd been cozy with a book and a cup of cocoa. She'd immediately told her roommates, who'd tracked him down and reported him to his patriarch. Apparently, MEC had some sway with the upir clan in Seattle because the upir hadn't returned to Lake City since, and that had been over six months ago.

What the heck did her mother need with a vampire? Did she intend him as a sacrifice to some demon in order to restore her youth? She'd tried and failed to sacrifice Kaia's ex eight weeks ago. Had the woman not learned her lesson? Or was she after something more nefarious, like world domination?

Kaia crossed her eyes, annoyed with her mother all over again. Now she had to pray she could liberate the lycans and somehow get the vampire not to kill her while freeing him as well.

Unless he'd willingly sought a union with her mother.

Whoa. That brought her up short. Why assume her mother had outsmarted a vampire? Weren't they invincible except for sunlight? Maybe he wanted to drink from the White Sea Witch. Stranger things had happened.

Oh boy. That puts a whole new twist on things.

Instinct said she should leave and get Macy and her new vampire mate to handle this. But she couldn't always run to her sister when things got tough. Heck, she was twenty-four already. As Macy often joked, time to cut the cord.

Steeling her resolve and knowing that worst case, she could hide in her mother's magic around the castle or lose the vampire in the water, Kaia trudged on. Before she closed in on the castle's grand front entrance, she pushed more of her mother's power through her, and as she watched, she grew. Her limbs stretched, and hands and feet grew larger, the nails longer and colored a pale pink. She imagined her face had aged as well, her hair no longer a dark black but a long white mane, while her mother's eyes would shine with a preternatural blue.

To her surprise, looking and feeling like her mother felt almost natural. As if she had a similar magic inside her just waiting to be set free.

Focused on finishing this nightmare so she could get home and be done with dark magic, she hurried to the massive front door, made of some foreign wood not found in the mortal plane, surrounded by white stone so smooth it looked like marble.

The gargoyles and house snips, adorable fae air spirits known for zapping people just for fun, guarded the front door. Upon spotting her, they waved and smiled.

"Mistress." One particularly thick gargoyle bowed. "We are glad to see you looking yourself again. Though Kaia's face is lovely, there is none so wonderful as yours."

So she has *been using my face to lure prey. Damn it, Mom!* "Lord Ruin, you're looking good, as always."

He blushed in the way stone creatures do, his cheeks a lighter gray. "The lycans have been restless but tame. The vryko has also been quiet, though that one will most definitely cause trouble."

Tame lycans meant Sabine had definitely whammied them. And a vryko? Hmm. Ruin must have been referring to the vampire. Vryko, short for vrykolakas, a tribe of vampires known for their brute strength and skill in water. What were the odds her mother would involve a vampire with ties to the water?

Great. Just what Kaia didn't need.

But was he a prisoner or complicit in her mother's plans?

Kaia hurried inside, past a white foyer into a white living space. Everything, from the wooden furniture to the stone tables and even the chairs and couches, was in some shade of cream or white. Bright pillows and throw rugs, with a few hand-selected art pieces, provided the only splashes of color in the place. Her mother loved a modern aesthetic.

Fortunately, Kaia felt no one nearby on this level, though the lycans dwelled below.

Descending the stairwell into the basement, she continued down a wide hallway toward her mother's "zoo," a large, walled-in playground filled with chains, beds, and a well appointed lavatory hidden in the back by yet another stone wall. The feel down here was medieval life meets cutesy torture chamber, with a decidedly BDSM kind of feel. She found the lycans imprisoned in silver, two chained to the wall and the other chained on the bed within reach of the bathroom. They were all groggy while snarling every few seconds but made no attempt to escape.

Annoyed with her mother more than she could say, Kaia released her glamour so she could unlock their chains. She only had enough power to use the glamour or free them, but not both.

They paused when they scented her, their expressions turning ugly.

"I'm here to release you, but only if you moon-swear to do me no harm."

Bright moonlight streamed through a barred window high up on the far wall, and as she moved farther into the room, illuminated her presence. Upon seeing her, they did their best to stand up and threaten, but so woozy, they didn't scare her.

The largest one sighed. "We swear not to harm you, By the Moon Our Mother."

"Okay." Kaia hurried to undo their chains that came apart under her mother's magic and ignored their grumbled insults.

"I'm not her," she said, though she knew they wouldn't believe her. Even in their own forms, she and Sabine looked incredibly alike, though her mother had height, a bustier frame, and a head of snow-white hair. "But the White Sea Witch is coming back soon. If you know what's good for you, you three will get out of here while you can."

"Before the demon comes back," the smallest of the three

said. He leaned closer and sniffed her. "She's right. She's not the one who caught us. Different scent, but still a witch."

The others grunted, grabbed him, and left without thanking her.

Part one, complete. Now she just had to execute part two and pray the vryko didn't kill her for sport.

Too easily, she followed the trail of power throbbing inside the walls and took step after miserable step back upstairs and up again, toward her mother's bedroom. Kaia hated stepping foot in the room, grossed out by the oppressive sexual hunger for pain and pleasure her mother—ew, her *mom*—felt deep under the skin.

Her mother might hide her real self from the world under spells, but here, where she dreamed, where she let her unconscious mind go free, Kaia could feel all the ugly covered by superficial beauty. In this one place that should have been her mother's sanctuary.

She immediately felt guilty stepping foot inside.

To her relief, no one lay chained to the bed.

"Witch, get your ass in here," a deep voice rumbled from down the hall.

She flinched. He sounded upset.

Tuned to the foreign energy pulsing in a bedroom down the hall, she entered and found a giant, dark-haired male with red eyes and fangs wearing nothing but a ragged and stained pair of jeans. His chest and arms were corded with muscle, his chest spattered with dried blood despite the healthy skin beneath, covering what looked like a tattoo she couldn't quite make out.

Though not bound, he couldn't be comfortable in those dirty pants, could he?

He snarled, "Where the fuck have you" —he added in a lower voice— "been?"

His gaze raked her, and she studied him as well. Tall, dark, and not so much handsome as fiercely captivating, the vampire attracted with a presence no one could ignore. He was just *there,* so much power in a raging male form. He looked more muscular than the upir she'd once seen. Delicate was not a word she'd ever use to describe him. He was brutish, with so much height and mass.

The word "fast" described him though, because he had her up against the wall, caged in his bare arms, between heartbeats. He didn't seem to feel the cold as he stared into her eyes and smiled.

"Finally, you've returned." He stroked her cheek with a gentle finger, threading his hands in her hair.

Pleased he didn't seem ready to bite her, she relaxed.

She wasn't prepared for the kiss that came next.

O rion had missed the witch more than he'd thought. Having
lost sense of time, he only knew he'd talked to Mormo at
some point after biting the woman. She'd kissed him a few times,
left him to have sex with lycans—which he only knew because
he'd smelled the connection upon her return—then ordered him to
wait for her without causing a problem.

Orion never made problems. He solved them, and he'd do
anything for the beauty he'd promised to protect with his life. For
some reason, that knowledge had troubled him, but then he'd
rationalized the worry away. Who wouldn't want to protect a
woman who looked and smelled like her?

He'd slept a good bit while waiting, not bothered by anything
but her absence.

And here she was, looking sexy yet demure, smaller than he
remembered but even more mesmerizing. So fucking gorgeous
and neat in a navy sweater and skinny jeans, a bit less grand than
the way she'd been dressed before. But he liked it. She looked
more approachable, a woman he wanted to savor, kissing and
touching and fucking until she couldn't walk.

The kiss lit him up from the inside out, not with any bitterness or fire, but with a drugging pleasure better than the finest of bloode wines, so it took him a moment to realize she hadn't responded, stiff in his arms.

He pulled back. "Witch?" He cupped her cheek, bemused by the affection making him feel so tender toward her. He'd promised he'd do nothing to harm her, and he meant it. Even if he had to protect her from himself.

"Y-you kissed me," she said on a breath and seemed so much younger than before.

"You're beautiful, and you stir me." He pressed into her, giving her no question as to what he wanted from her. Pushing her hair from her throat, he leaned close to nuzzle her neck and grew dizzy at the alluring scent pulling him closer. He normally never mixed blood with sex, but the two seemed tied with his sea witch. "Woman, you smell so good."

She put her hands on his shoulders, and he took that as an invitation to lift her for better access, his hands on her ass as he nestled between her legs and nuzzled her neck again.

"Y-you... Oh my God. Did you just *lick* me?"

"I want a bite, sweet. A small sip of that red perfection under your flesh."

She shuddered, and he dragged a fang over her pulse point, breaking the fragile skin there.

"No b-biting," she said, her voice thick.

He could smell her lust and smiled against her neck, deliberately licking up the drop he'd earned.

His entire body locked up, so turned on he feared coming in his pants. "Fuck, woman. Take off your clothes." He paused. "*Please.*"

She kissed him back, and he knew he'd never forget this moment no matter how long he lived. The feel of her was everything. No other female had ever affected him so. She'd been made just for him. His other half.

By the Night. He'd met his mate.

"Mate," he muttered as he pulled back to look into her eyes, her irises no longer dark but a bright blue so light they seemed to glow.

He studied her, taking in the thin face, full lips, and pert nose. Her long, black hair flowed around her shoulders and down her back, waves of sensuality floating around her. Capturing him in a spell only she could sunder.

"Oh wow, I hadn't noticed at first." She surprised him by cupping his cheeks and pulling his face closer. "She put a spell on you, vampire."

"Orion. My name is Orion."

"Orion." She sighed. "I'm Kaia."

He frowned. "Kaia Sabine?"

She just watched him then said, "Let me down, okay?"

He lowered her, as requested. Whatever she wanted, if it was in his power to give, he would.

She rubbed her thumb over his forehead, her eyes narrowing. "Yes, I'm Sabine. Your mistress." She glanced around, taking in the rich appointments he'd been happy enough to use while waiting for her to return. "Are you expecting anyone else?"

He shrugged, not wanting to let go of her but having to when she walked away from him to stand in the center of the room. "I don't care who comes as long as you're here, Sabine." He smiled, and the expression felt odd, as if he didn't smile much. He wished he knew why he thought that, but nothing seemed to matter outside of the great beauty he planned to take to mate.

She wiped a hand over her face. "Did I mention I might be bringing someone home with me, Orion? Tell me, sweetie."

He felt shy under her stare, wondering if he had done enough in his life to merit such a worthy mate. He could smell the sea in her blood, and it tantalized, the rush of desire pulsing through them both.

"I think you said something about a ritual. You were bringing a friend back, the one who lent you that athame for the dickhead your daughter let go."

She tensed.

"You have me now. You don't need anyone else. No demons or lycans." He should have been more upset about his mate sleeping with other creatures, but because she'd wanted it, he'd allowed it. "I'll give you all the pleasure you ever need. And if you want anyone dead, just say so and I'll make it happen."

She looked less than pleased with him.

"What? Sweetheart, I'm happy to help you dispose of anyone or anything. Magir, human, god, demon. Just say the word."

KAIA WANTED to turn and run away and not look back. What her mother had tried to do to her ex, Sean, was monstrous. What she'd done to *a vampire* didn't bear repeating. Ever. Sabine might as well have signed her own death warrant a thousand times over. Vampires hated each other, yes, but kill one of their kind and suffer a death that never ended. Eternal torture until the offenders broke in mind, body, and spirit.

What the hell did Sabine think she was doing bespelling one? And doing so while wearing Kaia's face?

She gave a fake laugh to cover her stress. "This conference has me so frazzled I came back early."

"Did someone bother you there?" Orion growled, looking larger than he had.

Was he *growing?*

She forced herself not to gape at him. "Oh no. I just, ah, missed you."

He smiled, and the pleasure on his face alarmed her more than the menacing look he'd worn before. For some reason, Orion appeared wrong looking so openly joyful.

Gah. What the heck did she know? Her mother was making her batty. "I'm sorry, but which demon gave me the athame? I'm sure he's the one I invited."

"Yeah. Pazuzu, some douche of a demon god. Remember? We laughed about him. But you said he was a real friend and you owed him a debt. And you always pay your debts, which is why I like you so much." His expression flattened after saying that, but he just as quickly smiled.

"I'm *so* glad about that." An enamored vampire? What kind of spell had her mother woven?

"Can I help you pay this debt? The sooner we take care of your friend, the sooner you and I can mate." He looked her over with a carnal grin.

She bit her lip. "Did we already start mating? Um, before?"

"No. You wanted to wait, remember?" He shrugged. "I guess the lycans tired you out. But it's no problem. If we're only waiting to bond because of this debt, I have plenty of money to take care of it. That's what I used to do at home. Investments and trades. It passes the time between battles, although technically the Centaur Slaughter of '74 happened in both Filoti *and* Consolidated Edison." He gave an evil laugh. "It was epic." He rubbed his chin. "I wonder if Mormo will let me take over the house finances. He treats me like common help, but I'm more than brute force." He pounded a hand into his palm.

A vampire offering money to a magir, a being outside his clan, a non-vampire? This was beyond bad. If the Bloode Empire found out, they'd kill Sabine and wipe out her entire family—including Kaia.

She asked, not wanting the answer, "Orion, is your first loyalty to me or your clan?"

"You, sweetheart. You know that." He smiled, showing less fang, but man, he looked scary. "So, anything else you want to know about the Night Bloode?"

"Your *clan?*" she squeaked, knowing that in his right mind, this male kill anyone for daring to steal secrets he'd never willingly give. "Isn't that private information?"

"For anyone but you, yes. I've killed fae for even asking about my patriarch in Thira—that's my home in Greece. My old home, I mean. The Night Bloode's been pretty private since our creation not too long ago. Although Mormo hasn't out and out said I can't tell anyone anything about us. I haven't because no one's ever had the stones to ask. Until you, sweetness."

Kaia felt faint. "Of course. You know, Orion, I sometimes get premonitions. Bad feelings about things. And I have a really bad feeling that we need to leave here. Quietly. Just you and me." She paused. "You're from the vrykolakas tribe, correct? A vampire suited to water?"

"I'm from the only tribe that is." He nodded. "I can swim faster than most merfolk. But I've never raced a sea witch before." He looked her over. "I have to say, I like this version of you best. Your eyes look so blue. Fucking blazing." He stared at her mouth and licked his lips. "We should fuck before we leave." He smiled. "I smell your need, witch, and I like it."

Her cheeks felt hot. Who knew she'd one day be in a position like this? Granted, she wanted her first time over with just so she could get that proverbial virgin sticker off her forehead. But not with a vampire who might tear out her throat in between thrusts. Could vampires even give orgasms? Did they drink blood when they came?

And why am I thinking about saying yes to this clearly bespelled death-bringer? Focus on the "death" part of his name, doofus!

Feeling beyond embarrassed, she shook her head. "Not here. Our first time should be special." *And, you know, safe and consensual!*

"Good point." He gave her a look of such love and trust that she knew she had to make him forget all this at some point or he'd surely bring her a world of pain. Vampires were known to be arrogant, an all-male society that took the patriarchy to new heights. Governed by envy and power, the Bloode Empire was a force no one wanted as an enemy.

And her mother had just snatched a vamp to her side, regardless of the danger and depravity in subjugating another.

Kaia started when a large hand settled on her shoulder.

"Are you okay, Sabine? You look a little lost."

"Not with you here." She gave him her perky best, hating the use of her mother's name.

"You're prettier than Macy and Fara combined. Bella too." He stroked her hair. "I want to swim with you."

She wanted to swim with him too, the call of the water beckoning her return. An alarm went out, and she wondered if the lycans had been found or if someone had noticed her, and not her mother, walking around. Feeling like an idiot for not taking better precautions, she shifted into a glamour of her mother.

"Still pretty, but I like your original appearance best." Orion looked her over. "I do like the white hair though."

Her mother had turned white overnight years ago, and no one knew why. Although at the rate her heart was racing, Kaia might go gray from fear.

"We need to sneak out. Maybe out the back door? We can vault over the back fence." With his strength, that shouldn't be a problem. Alone, she wouldn't have attempted it. The stone wall surrounding the back courtyard had to be a good fifteen feet in height, protecting the garden beds that remained green, despite the weather.

"Come, witch." He took her arm in his and strode through the castle as if he owned it, his footsteps sure on the stone floor. He didn't take the time to look at the lavish decorations or many portraits of Sabine lining the walls, focused on their exit.

Finally at the back door, he glanced through a window and cocked his head. "I hear two gargoyles above. There's an ogre patrolling the garden, and I see a female…" He peered through the window at the moonlit back courtyard. "She has no shadow, and I can see all of her when she turns."

"All of her?"

"Her back has no flesh, just organs and muscle and an occasional bone. There, a rib. See? She's got a garland of flowers on her head, but she's very pale. And smiling." He frowned. "Definitely a threat."

Kaia should have known better. Sabine had secrets buried under secrets. "I thought she'd let that nyavka go."

"What?"

She cleared her throat. "That's one of my nyavkas. She's a Slavic spirit with a particular bias against men. If she tries to lure you into the woods, don't go. Stick close to me."

"No, my beauty, stick close to *me*." He lifted her in his arms as if she weighed nothing and raced outside and over the wall before she could blink.

A roar from the castle told her the guards knew they'd been bested, but their footsteps were lost as Orion plowed through the small swath of forest on swift feet.

Before she knew it, they stood at the edge of the water. He gently set her down.

Wow. Talk about *fast*. He'd bridged the mile from the castle to the shore in seconds.

"The boat's gone." He stared at the empty dock and frowned. "I hope I don't get blamed for that."

"Come on." She grabbed his hand and walked with him right into the water.

"We're swimming back?"

"I'm taking you to my home away from here. Where it's more private."

"Ah, *private.* Now you're talking." He followed her into the water.

Her eyes glowed, able to see in the darkness. "Follow me and don't fall behind."

He saluted, his eyes a bright red that burned. "Gotcha."

She had no idea if he could communicate the way water-magir could, but they needed to leave. Swimming on the surface until she could submerge fully, she sped away, Orion by her side.

Now where to go with a bespelled vampire in her wake?

K aia didn't have much to say to him since he followed close. They moved like sharks through the water, bulleting through Puget Sound in a blur until they made it to the beach where she'd left her car.

She popped her head up while treading water and reactivated the camouflage charm.

"That won't work on me," Orion said right next to her, so silent she hadn't realized he'd joined her on the surface.

She found her breath and forced her nerves to stop jumping. "The charm will cover me. Wait until I'm at my car then join me. If you're fast enough, they won't see you." She knew some vampires could move so fast they could almost teleport.

"No one will see me if you don't want them to."

"I don't."

He nodded, looking at her as if content to stare at her forever.

Kaia had so much to do before her mother learned that her vampire had gone missing. But none of it could be done here in the water before daylight, which brought its own issues. She had to get Orion safe inside somewhere, protected from the sun.

She moved as quickly as possible to her car, still parked alone in the lot, and purged the water from her. Now completely dry, she waved at Orion.

He appeared by the passenger side in seconds.

"Wow." *This guy can end me in so many ways.* "Hold on." She focused on the water all over him, envying the glide of droplets across so much muscle. "Focus, Kaia," she muttered and purged him of the water in his clothes, drying him off. "Let's go."

She drove them not home, but toward the one safe space she knew she could protect. She parked in a common lot away from the Alister Doctrina Repository, her camouflage charm still working. "We're heading inside the basement of that building." She pointed to it. "We need utter si—"

"—lence," she finished, in his arms in front of one of the basement entrances. When he would have smashed open the door, she put a hand to his chest that stilled him without her having to ask. "Wait, please."

She muttered the unlock spell keyed to the entrance and let them inside, allowing herself the comfort of basking in his arms for a few moments before getting down. Kaia immediately missed his strength and slowly beating heart. For all that people referred to those Of the Bloode as the undead, they weren't. Vampires were very much alive, just different from most magir.

"Follow me," she whispered to Orion.

"Yes, mistress." He winked and rubbed her shoulders. "Let's get somewhere private."

Oh God. She refused to answer that and hurried them through several passages dimly lit by fae lamps and down the one passage she sometimes used when she needed a break. No one knew about it, which she appreciated, and she led him into her special room.

"We'll be safe here." She watched him studying the large room filled with empty bookshelves, a large couch, and some old study carols and cabinets pooled in one corner. And there, the couch she'd had teleported into the space last year from one of the open study rooms on the third floor that no one used. It hadn't been a cheap spell, but it was so worth it when she worked late nights.

The couch wasn't large enough to fit Orion comfortably, but he could let his feet fall off the end while he slept.

He yawned. "Sun's coming."

She looked at the phone she'd tucked in her back pocket and frowned. "I can't believe it's that late already." She glanced at him, wondering what to do. He had been bound to her mother, but she couldn't sit in Sabine's magic forever. Her coworkers would notice the change in power signature, as would anyone she happened to run into who knew her.

Kaia needed to sever the link he had with her mother. Easier said than done.

"Orion, I need you to promise me that you'll remember I freed you from her spell."

His eyes narrowed. "Whose spell?" He looked around, seeming once again to grow larger. "I don't sense any danger."

"No, it's something that was done to you. I'm going to fix it."

His tension melted away, and he smiled at her. "Oh, sure, babe."

"Babe?"

"Do whatever you want to me. I trust you." He wiggled his brows and yawned again. "But hurry so we can get a quickie in before I sack out."

"Right. A quickie." A glance at the bulge between his legs showed he was ready for some fun.

She ignored her blush and put one hand on his chest and reached the other toward his forehead. "I need you to sit on the couch."

He sat, and she once again placed her hands on his chest and head. Orion took that as an invitation to snuggle against her, his face pressing lovingly between her breasts.

"Oh yeah. We definitely need some quality private time. You are so soft, Sabine."

Her mother's name on his lips angered her more than it should. Determined to wipe the White Sea Witch away, she closed her eyes and focused on her mother's energy around the vampire. Except it wasn't just her mother but a darker, most foul presence entwined with Sabine's.

Kaia shifted her hand on him and felt a raised patch of skin to the left of the center of chest, over his heart. Scar tissue from a recent injury, she'd bet.

Not sure how the heck to break the spell but determined to try, she pushed her magic through her mother's and twisted it, trying to breaking Sabine's hold. Except the imprint remained, now filled by Kaia. Orion no longer had to suffer the will of Sabine Belyaev but was in the hands of Kaia Dunwich, who planned to set him free.

She let herself feel ownership, wanting the vampire to belong to her so she could then will the possession gone. Kaia breathed him in, taking his essence into her lungs before lowering her mouth to his, giving him back his breath, his willpower, his freedom.

He groaned and turned the kiss from magical to carnal. Before she knew it, Kaia was in his lap and under his control, being kissed to the point of distraction.

He rumbled under his breath and ran his lips down her cheek to her neck. But instead of biting her, he grazed her skin, and the erotic friction nearly undid her. "Yes, sweet. More." Fingers tugged at the snap of her jeans, and the fabric parted as the zipper fell. His rough, warm hand slid under her panties.

"Orion," she gasped.

He kissed her again, his tongue conquering as a thick finger slid between her slick folds and into her. Into a place no man had ever been.

A burst of heat and pleasure tore through her, and she clamped around his finger as she cried out, the drugging desire overpowering. A blast of energy radiated through the room, leaving it bathed in a neon blue glow that slowly faded.

He pumped against her hips before finally stilling and swore under his breath, his finger still buried inside her.

It took her some time to come down off her high, and she blinked up at a satisfied vampire. He withdrew his hand and brought his finger to his lips. Still watching her, he sucked the digit clean and thrust against her bottom once more, caught in a sigh.

"You taste sweet, mate. Like life itself." He looked her over with approval.

Holy crap. She'd had her first orgasm with another person.

Who happened to be a vampire.

She had the worst thought. Did he still think of her as Sabine? "I'm not Sabine."

"Who?"

Thank goodness. She relaxed, watching him button her back up. "I'm Kaia." Wait. He'd called her "mate." Perhaps he meant it in a different way than life mate.

"Kaia." He kissed her, and the sultry gentleness had her squirming once more. The foreign sensation of something inside her had been replaced by extreme pleasure, and she wanted to feel that again.

Orion yawned. "I made a mess. Maybe when I wake, you can clean me with that clever tongue."

It took her a moment to realize he'd climaxed too. In his pants. A flush of heat made her shiver. The sight of him half naked in addition to knowing what it felt like to come in his arms? What she'd been looking for all her life. And she'd found it in a vampire.

I'm in hell, no doubt. But wait. "You know I'm Kaia."

"Yes, mate."

"Mate? Like, friend? Like, 'g'day, mate'?" she added in a bad Australian accent.

He frowned. "Kaia, I'm yours. Just let me sleep and I'll satisfy your need soon enough."

She hurried off him and watched him settle down onto the couch, his legs dangling off an end. "Orion? I need you to wait here until I come back." She pushed her power through him once more, the waves of clean magic rolling through the pathways she'd created. "Stay here until I return, please."

Something snapped between them.

He tensed then utterly relaxed. "Of course. The Night Bloode never back down. I'm yours, love." All life left him, and he didn't move again, lying as if dead.

She leaned close but felt no breath, saw no rise of his chest.

Dawn had come. The torpor brought with the sun's rise was real.

Kaia let out a relieved breath. She'd done it. She'd rescued the vampire from her mother's hideout and had broken the spell. She'd freed him.

Now she had to hurry home, dress, then find a way to get the vampire to forget all about his capture and continue living his life however he saw fit.

With a yawn herself, she left him and hurried back to her car. After getting home and cleaning up, she hurried to change into a cute pair of boots, a heavy skirt, and a warm top. She borrowed a set of clothes from her burly lycan roommate and rushed back to work.

As the hours passed, she grew more giddy.

I did it. I rescued a vampire and lycans from the White Sea Witch without anyone's help. I am awesome!

But as the workday dragged on, she had no luck researching a forget spell that might work on a vampire. And since she'd broken her mother's hold over him, she couldn't use Sabine's magic to make him forget. What to do? She thought about calling Cho for help, but only if he'd swear not to tell Macy.

On her next break, she snuck downstairs to find Orion still asleep, unmoving and in the exact same spot as the one he'd been in when she'd left that morning. She'd brought a bag of clothing and a spare blanket and tucked that around him. Though Orion didn't appear cold, looking at him half dressed made her cold *and* turned her on. Neither of which she needed at the moment.

She turned to leave when what he'd said before came back to her. *"The Night Bloode never back down."*

Night Bloode.

Macy's new clan was the Night Bloode.

What were the odds there was more than one Night Bloode clan in the city? Or that one of them happened to be a vryko in an area populated by upir and one clan of multi-tribal vamps?

Sabine had captured and bespelled one of Hecate's blessed kin while looking like Kaia.

I'm so fucked.

There was no way around it. She had to call Macy.

She dialed her sister with shaky hands.

"Hello, Kaia. How did it go?" Macy asked with a smile in her voice. She yawned. "You're lucky I'm up early today."

"Macy, I'm in trouble. You can't tell anyone. Not Duncan or any of the people you live with."

"What's wrong?" Her sister sounded awake and alert.

"I need you to come to ADR right away. I'm off at five."

"I'm on my way."

"It's only three-thirty. You don't—"

"See you soon." She disconnected.

Kaia stared at her phone. With any luck, Macy could find a way out of this mess. Kaia hurried back to her position at the front desk in time to answer questions from a group of MEC trainees on extinct fire drakes.

More trainees from MEC, in addition to some university students from the nearby magir campus, took her time. So that when she glanced up, she spotted Macy sitting at a table reading a periodical on witchcraft.

Her phone showed she had another few minutes until quitting. But a glance through the large, stained-glass windows at the back of the grand building showed she'd have to race the setting sun.

Scared and tired, she yawned while inwardly panicking, not having gotten any sleep last night.

"Kaia?"

She glanced up at her boss. "Hi, Tom."

The older mage smiled. "Great job today. We had more visitors than we normally do thanks to the new training at MEC."

"No kidding."

"I'm going to work with Ava on closing. Don't worry about staying to the very end." He laughed. "I'm letting you go a few minutes early. Aren't I a great boss?"

She chuckled, so relieved she could have cried. "The best."

"See you tomorrow."

She grabbed her things and walked toward the back exit with a few stragglers. It took everything she had not to run. Once out of view of the main desk, she circled around, caught Macy closing behind her, and darted into a secret passage that led to a downward stairwell.

Macy rushed with her, both of them light on their feet. Once down in the tunnels, Kaia hurried to the archives room.

"What the hell, Kaia? What's going on?"

Breathless, Kaia waved her on. "Tell you once we're inside. Hurry."

They came to a stop a minute or two later, and Kaia prayed she'd beaten the sunset. But when she pushed the door open and stepped through, a force knocked her into the wall and held her off the floor, hands on her shoulders fixing her in place.

Orion breathed her in. "Ah, my apologies. I'm not quite myself yet." He gently set her down before wrapping her in a hug.

To her shock, that hug felt so darn good. Warm and safe, like home.

"What the fuck?" Macy growled. "Orion? What are you doing here?"

He growled low before turning and shielding Kaia with his body. Upon spying Macy, he relaxed. "Bloode Witch. How's Smoky? Did you feed him while I was gone? Is Kraft still alive?"

"Smoky?" Macy blinked. "Kraft? What about...?" At his look, she let out an exasperated sigh. "Yes, yes, your kitten is just fine. No doubt curled up with that handsome battle cat that keeps terrorizing everyone but Onvyr. And Kraft was alive just last night, though I haven't seen him since waking up." She looked from him to Kaia. "What's going on here?"

"Orion, let me go," Kaia muttered, surprised he did so without a fight.

He put his arm around her shoulders, pulling her close. "I found a witch, obviously."

"No, I rescued you last night," Kaia corrected. "Don't you remember?"

His expression terrified her. "I remember everything. Don't worry, I have plans to kill the sea witch. That she took your form to enslave one Of the Bloode is an abomination." He kissed the top of her head. "But have no fear, she won't harm you, ever. I'm going to drink her dry and feast on her marrow. Consider it a mating gift."

Macy's eyes couldn't get any wider. She choked. "Did you say *mating gift?*"

"No," Kaia said at the same time Orion smiled, showing a fang, and said, "Yes."

Then Macy acted completely out of character. Instead of defending her little sister or doing her best to gut Orion from stem to sternum, she laughed so hard she cried.

O rion didn't know what he'd said to amuse Macy, but his little mate didn't look pleased. By the Waters of Nu, Kaia was lovelier every time he saw her. He felt a stirring between his legs, lusting after the beauty. He hadn't felt such an attraction in decades.

His sleep had revived him, allowing his bloode to replenish the magic that had been missing during his stay at the White Sea Witch's abode. That bitch had stolen his will with a spell. He also recalled a few stolen kisses he hadn't much minded, and an attempt to drink his bloode he'd quashed by nearly taking her head off.

But she'd blown some dust in his face, which had confused him, allowing her to stab him with an athame. That stupid dagger had smelled of cinnamon and ash—brimstone. Having not long ago battled a demon in an alternate pocket of one of the hells, he knew the scent well. Unfortunately, the spell had stolen his rage, made him quiescent, and messed with his memories.

Until Kaia rescued him. Kaia, his mate, a gift from the fates he didn't believe in for having done something worthy.

"Tell him not to move," Macy said. The pretty redhead

looked typically aggressive, dressed in dark clothes and powered up with bloode from her mate, the revenant. Though a human, she'd surprised them all by fitting into their clan, always wanting to kill something that offended her mate or her kin.

That still didn't mean he considered her his equal.

Orion quirked a brow.

She narrowed her eyes. "Don't move."

He deliberately took a step in her direction. "Or what?"

"Orion, please don't move," Kaia said.

He froze, but he didn't mind, because his mate had asked. Macy didn't look pleased. Was she jealous that a new, prettier female would soon be living with them? Fara hadn't minded when Macy had moved in, but the fae weren't as vain as humans. She'd been welcoming. Would Macy mind that Kaia was like a shining star that made everything brighter and better?

"Orion, come here, would you?" Macy asked.

He didn't move.

Macy nodded to Kaia, who groaned and said, "Orion, could you join Macy for a minute?"

"Sure." He walked to the Bloode Witch. "What do you want, female?"

Macy looked him over. "What happened to your clothes?"

"I brought him new ones." Kaia hurried to a bag he'd missed on the floor. But when she brought it closer, he recoiled.

"It smells like dog."

"It's lycan." Kaia frowned at him. "Borrowed from a friend."

"Lycans aren't friends," he said with a sneer but hurried to smile at his dark-haired beauty. "But if he's your friend, he must be a step above his pack."

"We need to get out of here, and you need clothes." Macy glared at him. "I don't care if the clothes belong to a wet poodle. Put them on. My sister's doing you a favor."

"Your sister?" Orion looked from Macy to Kaia. "No. She's gorgeous. You're—"

"Hey, be nice," Kaia growled.

He loved her aggression. So small and soft, yet she had claws. "I was going to say she's beautiful the way an asp is beautiful, sleek and deadly. But you're like a rainbow and spring, a fountain of life from which only the worthy may drink."

Macy gaped.

"What?"

"You never talk like this."

"How?"

"Poetic. Nice. Complimentary. In complete sentences. Take your pick."

"Woman," he growled, "you're lucky I respect the revenant or I'd make you pay for that remark." In truth, he thought her both amusing and courageous to talk to a member Of the Bloode with so little thought to her own well-being. But he wouldn't let her know that.

Kaia seemed to be ignoring them. She continued to glare at the bag of clothing he'd insulted.

He sighed. "Would you like me to wear what's in the bag, sweet?"

"Yes, please." She didn't sound *pleased* with him.

"I'm sorry." He drew her into his arms and kissed her forehead. Then he dropped his jeans.

The women stared at him, Kaia's eyes so big she looked comical.

"Holy crap! Thanks for the warning," Macy said, took a long look, then turned around. "Wait 'til Duncan hears about this." She snickered. "Kaia, you have a problem."

"There is no problem," Orion said, pleased his mate had yet to blink. She'd also focused past his chest and abdomen to the part rising to greet her. "Take off, Macy. Kaia and I need to fuck."

Kaia clapped her hands over her face

He took his time dressing in sweat pants a little too tight for his taste and a tee-shirt that fit, sculpting his torso.

Macy snorted with laughter. "Oh my God. I know I wanted you to fix your V-card, but with a vampire? Kaia, I'm totally impressed, and a little scared if you want the truth."

"I didn't do this on purpose, Macy," Kaia snapped, still hiding behind her hands. "I imposed my magic over Sabine's to free him. But I think in the process I somehow convinced him we're mates."

He frowned. "I knew we were mates before last night."

Kaia shot him a panicked look then turned back to her sister. "Help me, Macy. He's a vampire!"

"Not just *a* vampire," Orion helpfully pointed out. "I'm *your* vampire." He smiled. "Just think, I'm vrykolakas. You're a sea witch. Our element is the same."

Macy glanced from him to Kaia. "He has a point."

Kaia turned to her. "Are you kidding? He'll kill me."

"I am quite large, but I'll be gentle."

"I don't mean with your penis! I mean you'll probably rip my throat out with your fangs. Your *fangs*."

Macy snickered.

Orion frowned. "Wait. Your V-card?" His eyes widened. "Kaia, are you a virgin?"

"She is," Macy answered for her. "And she's not a sea witch, exactly, she's a sea nymph."

"And a *virgin?*" Orion goggled. Sea nymphs were known to be lusty creatures. They rarely had enemies, so soft and loving that he'd had several of their kind as friendly outlets when living with his old clan.

Macy nodded. "Weird, right? She's repressed."

Kaia moaned. "This is so embarrassing." She pointed at her sister—and that relationship he still had a tough time believing.

They didn't look much alike. Macy was tough. Hell, she'd battled demons and mated Duncan just a few months ago. Kaia was like Smoky, soft and cuddly with little claws. "Stop telling everyone about my love life."

"Technically it would be a lack of a love life," he tried to help.

"And you, stop talking," Kaia barked.

He shut up and watched them.

"Oh man, he's quiet." Macy snapped a picture of him. "I'm keeping that on file." She moved closer, studying him. "I need his bloode and don't want him to kill me for taking it."

Kaia moved to his side. "Can she have your bloode?"

He waited for her to allow him to talk, the silly creature. But he'd obey whatever she wanted, because that's what a vampire did for his mate. A sharp pain burned deep inside, rejecting the idea of blind obeisance, but that spark of rage-like hostility didn't belong anywhere near Kaia, so he shoved it back down.

She flushed. "I'm sorry, Orion. Please, say whatever you want. Can Macy have a drop or two of your bloode? I want her to help you get better, and she needs it."

"If that's what you want. Sure." He lengthened a nail and punctured his left forearm. A punch of power released as it trickled over his arm. "Hurry. I heal fast."

Macy wiped her finger through the cut then licked her finger.

"Macy!" Kaia looked shocked.

"She's our clan's Bloode Witch. It's okay," he hastened to reassure her as Macy wiped a bit more and smeared it on a tissue she tucked into a pocket. His arm healed, and he wiped the small bit of bloode away. "See? All better."

Kaia studied his arm and patted his tiny wound. "It doesn't hurt?" She watched his claw retract back into a human-looking nail. "Does it hurt when the claws come out?"

"No, my arm is fine. It's a small sting when vryko claws come out to play, but so worth it." He smiled at her, wanting to sigh at the perfect female he'd been blessed to join. And a virgin? Orion had never lain with a virgin. He'd have to make sure to be extra gentle so as not to harm her.

He laughed and drew her into a hug, not even bothered that he smelled like a pack animal, the scent of sea nymph filling his soul... well, if had a soul. Macy was right in one respect. He didn't normally feel so giddy or poetic over a female. But he liked it.

"Oh boy. This is going to take some work," Macy said, watching him.

He reluctantly let Kaia go, aware she hadn't protested his touch. Not now, and not before. She very much liked the look of him. He'd seen her reaction when witnessing his massive erection. He wanted to tell her he only got that way for her. He didn't remember ever getting so aroused in the past. But she smelled hungry, needy. Wanting.

She smelled perfect.

"We're fine," Orion said in hopes of taking that frown off his mate's face.

"Orion, I want you to be free. Not bound to anyone, but living with your own free will."

He shrugged. "Whether I'm with you or not, I'm still bound to Hecate until my clan's bloode debt is repaid. And now I'm bound to my Night Bloode brothers. And sisters," he added with a glance at Macy. "We have to gather the rest of the Bloode Stones to protect us from some kind of ancient evil that's coming back to destroy life as we know it." He shrugged. "Eh. I'd much rather be with you. What do you think I should do?"

Macy paled. "Oh, Kaia. This is bad. Orion's a gruff bastard who's not one for sharing secrets. I bet you could tell him to cut off his own hand and he'd do it for you."

He immediately extended his claws. "Right or left?"

Kaia grabbed his non-clawed hand. "Neither. Never cut off anything. You stay whole, you hear me?"

He released his claws and patted her gently on the shoulder. The poor creature looked distraught—over *him*. So pleased, he had a tough time holding back his joy. "Of course, my lovely mate. I'll always protect you, and I can't do that if I'm less than whole. Don't worry. Nothing will ever hurt us."

"Do you see what you've done?" Macy asked his mate.

He didn't care for her tone and scowled.

"Me? I tried to save him."

"You stole him from the witch who stole him from Hecate. She's not going to be pleased. You have to give him back."

"I would if I could." Kaia shot him a sad glance, and he didn't like Macy making her feel badly.

"Alright, witch. You should go now. My mate's been most generous with you. But she's tired and needs to feed." He stroked Kaia's hair. "You're making her sad."

"Jesus. I'm not trying to hurt her feelings, jackass. I'm trying to save her life." Macy turned to Kaia. "He can't go back. Not until this is fixed. I know Duncan would try to help, and Rolf might find this amusing as heck, but Khent and Kraft will try to end you for bespelling a vampire. Varu, our patriarch..." She swallowed. "Kaia, he'll kill you and make it hurt. He doesn't believe in second chances for those who hurt his kin."

"He'll try." Orion huffed. He might have been more upset about the idea of his kin trying to hurt Kaia if he thought they could do it. But he knew he could end them. The secret fountain of rage deep inside him registered on a level none of them understood, including the goddess who owned his debt. They all thought him no more than an average vryko, and he was content to let that lie. "No one touches my mate and lives."

Macy glared. "He'll kill you too, Orion. If you're a threat to the Night Bloode, he might feel bad about it, but Varu will end you. I heard all about how he killed a master strigoi—his own sire."

He snorted. "Duh. I know. I was there."

She continued, "Dude is a nasty killer, and the only one safe from him is his mate."

"That I respect." Varu was a Worthy patriarch and vampire. He had his priorities right.

Macy blew out a tired breath. "Look, I'm trying to help. You two need to hold up somewhere until I find out how to break this spell. I'm still not sure how Sabine had the power to bewitch you though."

"She used a dagger coated in brimstone."

Macy's eyes widened. "Whoa. A demon blade. That makes sense. Nothing affects you guys, normally. Not from this plane or the fae realm. But it figures the hell planes have sway over death-bringers. We just don't know much about them."

Kaia asked in a quiet voice, "Could he be possessed?"

He liked that she continued to hold onto his arm. "I'm not possessed, Kaia. I don't think." He felt inside himself but sensed only his powerful bloode and a tie to the female next to him. He heard her heart racing and urged her heartbeat to match the rhythm of his.

She calmed, and he smiled.

Macy looked more disturbed. "Orion, step me through whatever you remember."

He sighed. "Is this necessary? I'm happy with Kaia."

"Please." Kaia looked up at him, worry on her face. "It would be great if you told Macy what happened. I want to know too."

"Fine. It was Sunday night. All the others scattered so I got the shit job of investigating the mystery island. Neptune didn't like that someone was squatting in his territory, I'm guessing."

"Sounds about right," Macy muttered.

"I took the new boat. It's a sweet little thirty-five foot yacht, all decked out. Really nice."

"Orion, focus."

He flipped her the bird, but Macy only grinned. "Anyhow," he continued, "I docked just south of Whidbey. I thought it odd to see the mystery island, and I could tell it's a magir construct. It's in a pocket dimension." At Kaia's nod, he continued. "So I walked off the boat, through the snow, and heard a woman cry out. Lycans were fighting and ripping at her. I killed a few, let some go in hopes they'd try harder to kill me. It's so disappointing when no one puts up a good fight anymore."

"Wait," Kaia said. "You walked onto the island? Into the woods?"

"Yeah."

"Nothing stopped you? No wards or traps?"

"No. I think that's the point, that island opens up its doors, so to speak, so it can trap whatever lands. The woman was hot." He settled his gaze on her. "You, I mean, the sea witch, but I didn't know she was the sea witch when I bit her. She told me to bite, and I drank her down." He frowned and rubbed his chest, memories of the sea witch's blood not quite right. "She was sweet at first. I think." He stared at Kaia, seeing her face imposed on another woman, one slightly taller with a fuller build.

"Orion?"

"It's a little fuzzy. I think I blacked out after I drank from her. I was inside a fancy bedroom. We talked, her and me. I do know she had that brimstone dagger. I think..." He rubbed his chest again, feeling the burn of more than just a blade. Darkness, a presence pushing through his veins. "Then Kaia showed up and we got the hell out of there."

Kaia patted his hand. "Thank you."

"Sure, sweetness." He leaned down to kiss her again, needing to touch her constantly. To mark her with his scent. She was his.

He really needed to finish their bonding, and leaving a magical bit of himself inside her would do just the trick.

He saw her flush and knew she'd received the message he'd sent. The way vryko mates often did, the passing of messages like water gliding through the pores of thought. A psychic bond that lasted until the female bore fruit. Then she'd leave, and strong vryko fathers would raise strong sons.

Orion glanced at Kaia's belly and thought wistfully of putting his own son there. Just one of course, because vampires could have only one child with one mate. But wouldn't it be fantastic if his son turned out to be a twin? Rare but not unheard of. Oh man, he couldn't wait to get started.

Kaia turned to her sister. "What do we do, Macy?"

Orion had an easy answer. "Nothing. Let's head back to the house. We're mated. There's nothing to do except find a bed to share." He had no issue whatsoever with letting his mate lead him. He trusted her. He didn't know her all that well yet. But that was okay. They had nothing but time. The Bloode Stones, his clan, Hecate, all of that paled next to his beautiful mate.

Now he just needed to show her.

KAIA SHOT Orion the fakest smile she'd ever used. "Hey, Orion. I need to talk to Macy about some girl stuff. Can you wait here for us? And don't listen."

The hulking vryko grinned. "Girl stuff, eh? Well, sure. I'll be right here. Waiting."

She swore she saw a vision of herself in his lap, his hand down her pants. A memory from earlier that had her face hot enough to melt clean off. "Um, right. We'll be back."

Once outside the archives room, she pulled Macy close but kept her voice down. Sound traveled underground.

"What the hell did Sabine do to him? He's forgetting details and was stabbed with a brimstone dagger. I wonder if it was the same one she used on Sean."

"Your mom's a real piece of work," Macy growled. "She put not only *her* life in danger but *yours* too. All those magir dead, and the ones that escaped are going to blame you."

"I hadn't thought of that when I released their chains." Kaia bit her lip. "Where do we go from here?"

"Tell me everything that happened from leaving the house to now. Your side of the story."

Kaia recounted her timeline, ending with Macy and her stepping outside to talk.

"Sabine is powerful, but not this powerful. Obviously she used Orion's bloode to bind him, but in conjunction with brimstone and a ceremonial dagger, I'd say she's planning to offer him to Pazuzu. Unless she moved onto a better demon?" Macy shook her head. "Let me research this. In the meantime, do your best to stay close to the vryko. He's not acting right, and I'm afraid something bad might happen to him if he's anywhere around his own kind."

"You don't trust your clan?" Weren't they Macy's new family?

"I do, but I don't. I know it sounds confusing. Look, I'm going to get help. We'll keep this quiet though. Duncan would be torn if I asked him to keep this to himself, so I'll only tell him if I absolutely have to. The less vampires who know about this, the better."

Kaia swallowed. "You really think Orion's patriarch will kill him?"

Macy lowered her voice. "I do. The Bloode Stones are a secret, Kaia. He never should have told you about them. Which makes me fear that he maybe told your mom about them. And who the hell knows what she'd do with that kind of information? But her trying to bespell one of the Night Bloode? She had to know who he was. Your mom knows all the big players in town, and Orion's a big one."

"Crap." Kaia ran her hands through her hair, wanting to pull it out. No, wanting to pull *her mom's* hair out. "I ruined her spell, Macy. She wasn't happy when I ruined her plans to kill Sean. What if she's trying to kill Orion in the same way?"

"But vampires don't have souls." Macy frowned. "Or do they? In any case, I'm on this. I want you to take Orion and go somewhere far away from here while I work on finding a way to separate you. I'll take a little more bloode before I go though. And Kaia, be very careful about how much intimacy you allow between you. He's not himself at the moment."

"Oh my gosh, Macy. He's clearly bewitched. I would never take advantage of anyone not in their right mind."

"You misunderstand. Your mother used your face to entice him. You were already his type before her magic zapped him. I'm just worried about all his mate talk."

"Me too." Though it was nice to be so adored, none of Orion's feelings were real. "I'll take care of him."

"I know you will. Just make sure to take care of yourself too." She pulled a wad of cash and a prepaid credit card out of her bag. "Take this emergency money and disappear. I don't want to hear from or see you until *I* call *you.*" She also handed Kaia an older flip phone. "Don't judge. It works, and I'm the only number on it."

Kaia hugged her. "What about Dad?"

"Who do you think I'm going to for help? He sure as heck won't tell anyone. Between him, Mom, and maybe Cho, we can work on the magic and demon angle of your boy's condition." She paused. "No one can know this happened. Ever."

Kaia nodded. "I swear."

"Hopefully not on your life."

CHAPTER EIGHT

Sabine felt a rush of nerves as her lover rose from bed. She was sweaty yet energized by her tumble with Pazuzu. In his natural form, he looked monstrous. But then, in her natural form, so did she. The cartoon about a certain sea witch and some pasty little mermaid wanting legs was more spot-on than most would think.

She watched Paz strut around the room. He made a handsome human, she had to give him that. In this form, he had a blood-red mane of long hair framing a hard face that was model perfect, even his straight, sharp, white teeth. His pitch-black skin looked more like a dark elf's than a man's, but the dual set of leather wings on his back in addition to the talons at the base of his legs and scorpion tail were nearly as impressive as his long, serpentine dick. Talk about magical.

Smoke escaped his mouth when he spoke, his voice a blend of sinister and tonal perfection. "I cannot give you what you want without more of this one's bloode." He swallowed a goblet of Orion's essence and sighed. "His power is exceptional, though the flavor of his bloode feels like yours."

"It should. I cast that spell you gave me using the athame. A sea witch possession, of sorts." She grinned. "You're rubbing off on me in all the best ways."

Paz chuckled, and the room buckled. She loved that about him, that he destroyed so casually. She flicked a finger and reset the wards his amusement had torn through. Though she wouldn't have minded if half the assholes at the magic convention died, she didn't want to think of how poorly she'd be treated if the blame fell on her.

Sabine made a living off trading favors and making illicit deals. She'd come to the conference more to network than learn anything she didn't already know. Hell, she'd forgotten more about magic in the past three hundred years than most of these pathetic magir might learn in decades.

"Are you certain you will meet your end of the bargain this time?" Paz asked as he settled back on the bed and brought her to sit on his lap.

"I am." She had just mentally checked in to Belyy Zamok and found her wards in place, her spells still set. No problems to speak of.

"I can't give you any more leeway or Hanbi might ask questions."

Hanbi, king of the underworld demons in the Babylonian pantheon and god of all evil, didn't mess around. The stories Paz had shared about his father still gave her nightmares. But the power such evil wielded... Yes, she'd been tempted. And she'd already failed once thanks to her clueless daughter.

Sean, Kaia's weak ex, had of course been too nice for her. As a child born of a human and an angel, the nephilim's soul would have been a real coup for Paz, something to brag about. But Kaia had to go and ruin things.

Annoyed yet understanding she'd failed as a mother, Sabine

had no one to blame but herself for Kaia's deficiencies. She loved the girl, so pretty and smart. Kaia was an honest reflection of Sabine's potential, minus the power that made Sabine the White Sea Witch. Just as well, or Sabine would be forced to kill the kind little bitch. Kindness. Ugh. So cloying, that condition. No matter how hard she'd tried, Sabine hadn't instilled in Kaia the lessons she herself had learned at a young age.

That power was all that truly mattered.

But Belyy Zamok had finally paid off. The honey-trap of an island filled with magic and sexual temptation had scored her dozens of mermen and lycans, powering her through blood sacrifice.

The vampire had been a true prize, though. Unexpected yet incredibly fortunate. Necessary not for his soul—which many still argued did not exist—but for his bloode, for which Paz and his family had great use. With Orion's bloode, they could return to the mundane plane. Just as Hecate and her annoying family walked among the humans, so too could the king of all evil. Pazuzu's line would become a plague for everyone, mortals and gods alike. Only those who pledged their loyalty, like Sabine and her friends, would see real benefit.

Sabine did have real friendships, mostly with warlocks and sorceri, beings who felt as she did, that darkness and chaos were to be celebrated, not feared.

Warlocks weren't witches turned bad, and neither were sorceri mages who turned to evil. They were powerful magic users who didn't like using celestial or terrestrial magic when they could power spells through blood and sacrifice and gain status in the blink of an eye.

She hissed when Paz's serpentine cock nipped at her hip, leaving a bloody bite.

"Pay attention, Sabine. You chose well with the vrykolakas blood-drinker. The water in your veins and in his stirs dark appetites. Elemental destruction, elemental preservation. My father is intrigued enough that he's in talks with those who mourn Abaddon's death. Hanbi pledges to return to show the world who truly rules this plane and welcome the Darkness that comes."

She'd been hearing about some big bad evil coming for decades, and though the demons put great stock in a chaotic apocalypse, she didn't buy it but would never say so. "Those petty gods and humans have no idea what's in store for them. Your kind will soon rule this world."

"Yes, we will. But Sabine, we had an agreement, and you are overdue in your payment." He bit her several more times before showing the pleasure he could also wield like a weapon and had her panting like a bitch in heat. "We will have the death-bringer or we will have *you.* And you look tastier the more I see into your bleak vessel, your soul dark though your power is rich with pain." His wings fluttered. "I'm excited to have you either way, sea witch." He moaned and began to feast.

She knew real fear as Paz ate her energy, snapping up her reserves in payment for her failed attempt with Sean. Pazuzu could only come into this world through her dreams, manifesting using her power, hence her need to refuel with so many dead bodies on the island.

Granted, Paz had given her more energy than she could hold, but he'd also showed her how to tap into the demonic line to bring him forth, and thus made herself that much more powerful. Something she'd always wanted, to rule over everyone who'd ever looked down on her.

And everyone did. Sea witches, in particular, were more disdained than their cousin sea nymphs. And she had both heritages inside her.

She felt each agonizing pull as Paz ate her magic and filled her with his acidic essence, the sex still good though incredibly painful.

Sabine took her deserved punishment and repaid the demon god who would make her into so much more, perhaps even a queen to rule at his side. As soon as this blasted conference finished, she would return home and finish draining the vampire dry, a true offering made to Hanbi through Pazuzu at the next blood moon.

And gods and demons help her daughter if the little shit interfered again.

ORION INSISTED on driving them in the car he'd stolen, since her car could be traced. Kaia knew where she'd like to go but didn't think it would fit Macy's idea of keeping a low profile. So no spas for them. Instead, they traveled to a tiny vacation hamlet on a lake a half hour outside her boss's hometown just outside the city.

She hadn't realized she'd dozed off until he tapped her shoulder.

"Kaia? We're here I think."

She blinked her eyes open and stared at a fairytale house that looked more like something built for hobbits than people.

Orion shook his head. "Are you an LOTR fan?"

She blushed. "Kind of. My boss told me about this place. It's weird but private, and we have it to ourselves for the next week, so there's that."

"As long as it's not too small." He eyed the sloped roof. "But if you like it, I like it."

She swallowed a sigh. He'd been saying things like that, subtle reminders that he right now had no will of his own. If she remained quiet, some of his personality would come back, opinions about human food or places to visit in the city he thought she'd like. But if she commented, he'd revert to anything to please her.

Fortunately, exhaustion had allowed her to avoid the Kaia-pleasing aspect of the trip while asleep.

She got out of the car and followed the directions she'd been given, punching in the keycode to remove the key affixed to the doorframe.

Inside, the small home was delightful.

Plush furniture, a colorful but not too vibrant palette of decor, and a large kitchen dominated the first level. The one bedroom suite above had a large hot tub on the outside deck overlooking a small lake. Only one home sat across from them, far enough away not to be a bother.

They'd passed the closest town ten minutes ago, so it would be an easy trip to swing back and pick up something to eat.

But the best part of it all was the root cellar where the owner kept a "magical" space for wine tasting. Cold and damp but protected from the sun, the spot where Orion could rest without worrying he might burn up and die looked ideal.

Kaia yawned and glanced at the time. Just after nine at night. "I need a nap."

"Go ahead. I'm going to scout around after I bring in our bags."

She didn't ask, but he'd managed to grab clothing for both of them from a retail store on their way. A thieving vampire, her hero. Eh. She was too tired to care.

Kaia flopped onto the bed, closed her eyes, and woke to a dark sky, the moon a sliver when thin clouds parted. She wondered if her mom had found out about her missing lycans and vampire yet. She checked the flip phone and saw no missed calls from Macy, so probably not.

Macy had taken care of excusing her from work, pretending MEC needed her help researching a classified case. Something her father would also support. Orion, however, would be a true test of Macy's ability to hide them. Before Kaia had fallen asleep, she'd overheard him call Mormo to say he needed more time. Then he'd cussed out Kraft, a friend, she thought, and demanded they watch over his kitten.

She still had a tough time envisioning Orion taking care of something so small and cute. Yet another contradiction concerning the large vryko. Was he kind because of the spell, or because he truly cared for a feline and a woman he thought he'd mated? Vampires were known to be cruel, calculating, and evil. But the more time she spent with Orion, the easier that was to forget.

She sat up and looked around, spotting him in a plush chair in the corner watching a small television mounted to the wall, the volume so low she couldn't hear it.

Seeing her awake, he turned it off and joined her on the bed.

He leaned close to stroke her face, and once again, she wished at least a part of this facade were true. Such caring actions made her long for a relationship. Sadly, the only man she'd grown close to that hadn't wanted to sex her up within five seconds of meeting her had been Sean, and her mother had ruined any hope of rekindling that.

Male magir and human men responded too readily to her pheromones, the gift (curse) of a sea nymph, so she remained shutdown when in public, to the point that most fellow magir had no idea she was anything more than a low level nymph or witch.

Not a witch, a *sea witch*, she thought, wondering how her mother and father could both be so powerful yet she only had a small portion of their power. Her mother was the White Sea Witch, the big bad water witch in the northwest. Her father, a grand mage, controlled several elements and had a lot of clout in MEC, working with a demon for a partner.

Kaia got scared when confronting house snips, able to avoid trouble only by pretending to be her mom.

She sighed.

"Are you okay?" Orion reached for her hand.

At that moment, her stomach rumbled. "I'm hungry." Which meant he was probably hungry too. "A-are you?"

His sly smile had her blood pumping. Then he flashed a long white fang and laughed.

"I ate earlier." Orion winked. "Don't worry. I left them alive. A few coeds on their way out to party on a Saturday night."

"Where? Here?" There was that house across the lake.

"Nah, in the town we passed. I made sure you were safe and the area deserted before I hurried to town and grabbed some food for us."

"Oh?"

He lifted her off the bed so fast her head spun. Then he carried her down the stairs and sat her at the kitchen counter. "What would you like?"

For this to be real popped into Kaia's head before she could stop it. Fortunately, he was studying the contents of the refrigerator and didn't see her blush. "What do you have?"

"We have a lot of stuff. I didn't know what you like, so I got plenty of protein and some sweet and salty snacks." He removed a carton of eggs, bacon, ham, a roasted chicken, and a carrot cake and set them all before her.

"Why carrot cake?"

"It looked tasty, and the woman frosting it said it was the freshest thing they had."

"Oh, nice. I'll have a piece of that."

"No meat?" He cocked his head. "What do sea nymphs eat?" He studied her. "You know, I've known a lot of sea nymphs, and I've always noticed their joy with life, especially in living below the sea. But you seem different." He paused. "Not as happy. Do I make you upset?"

"What? No." *Well, kind of.* "I'm unhappy that a sea witch messed with you and used my face to do it. But most of my issues have nothing to do with you."

"Oh?" He grabbed a plate and cut her a large piece of cake. Then he cut one for himself.

She watched, curious. "I don't know a lot about vampires. Do you eat regular food?"

"We can. Most of us don't since blood is all we need to replenish. But eating human food won't kill us. We process it and flush it out of our systems in the normal way."

"Oh." How interesting. She hadn't realized they could eat regular food. "So you eat cake?"

"I will this night. I want to know why you like it." He took a bite, watching her.

Then his expression changed. He looked ill.

She couldn't help laughing as he spat his mouthful into the sink and washed his mouth out with several glasses of water.

"That's disgusting."

"It's actually delicious. Pretty sweet though." She blazed through her slice and still felt hungry. Considering all the energy she'd used worrying and magicking him earlier, it made sense she'd need to power herself up again. She stood.

"What are you doing?"

"I'm going to make some bacon and eggs. You're right. I do need the protein."

"Sit, sweetheart. I'll make your food."

He called me "sweetheart." Oh stop, he's bespelled. "You

know how to cook?" She sat and watched him move around the kitchen, surprised to see him so capable. "Orion, tell me about yourself."

"What do you want to know?"

She shouldn't ask such an intrusive question, especially when he had no choice but to answer. But when would she ever get a chance to question a vampire again? Never.

"Well, what was it like living in Greece?"

He paused for a moment before cracking some eggs and laying bacon down in a pan. He half-turned to watch her while he cooked. "Santorini is where I was born, in the caves below the islands, connected to the sea." He sighed. "It was so nice there, well, except for the sun. That was a huge downer." He chuckled.

She laughed with him. "I'll bet. The pictures I've seen are incredible. The sky is so blue, the water almost turquois. And I think it's the city of Thira where the buildings are white stone with sandy tiled roofs and narrow walkways. It's like paradise... except for the sun."

"Truly."

"Do you miss it?"

He flipped the bacon. "I don't know. I did when I first got here."

"Would it be okay to know why you're here?" Before he could answer, she added, "Would your patriarch be upset if you told me?"

"Varu? Nah. And if he was, he can kiss my ass."

She blinked. "Aren't you supposed to be respectful to your leader?"

He chuckled. "Maybe in other clans. In the Aegean, I was part of the Water Cleave Clan, and we obeyed the letter of the law. My father is still the lieutenant there, and our patriarch is still a bit of a dick. Which is to say he's pretty typical among patriarchs. They command, snarl a lot, and bite you every now and then, but basically they build strong vrykos."

"So you always have to be tough?"

"The strong survive." He sounded so matter of fact about his life.

"Do you have a father or mother? Any siblings?"

"My father, Tassos, is a pretty tough guy. He kicked my tail all over the place until I hit my second century. Then we evened out." Orion grinned, but the expression didn't seem a happy one. "I fucked him up." He blinked at her, and she'd swear he would have blushed if vampires could feel embarrassment. "I mean, we fought and I won. But I didn't want to be our clan's lieutenant, so they let me become our clan's enforcer instead."

"How big was your clan?"

"We had about fifty vampires in all. Sometimes our master would shift members around to even out clan numbers. It's not easy to do though, because we don't like those who aren't kin."

"You mean those vampires who are from a different clan aren't kin, right?"

"Yeah. Kin, family, clan. All the same. Just because a vampire is a vryko doesn't mean he's kin. Only our master, the vampire in charge of the entire tribe, has the power to shift vryko loyalty. It's not fun." He rubbed his scar again, and she wanted to hug him. "When I came here to pay back our clan's bloode debt, I tried to kill the others on a daily basis." He seemed happy about that fact as he scrambled her eggs. "It was fun. Still is, but now we just fight to keep up training, not to kill." He frowned. "But I know I could have ended Varu if Mormo hadn't put that spell on us."

She tried to steer the conversation away from Mormo and anything that might be secretive about the Night Bloode. "Tassos is your father. Are you close?" He set her food on a plate before her, and she dug in, surprised at how good it tasted. "This is awesome."

He smiled. "Good. Eat, mate. You'll need your strength." Her flush caused him to chuckle. "So me and my father. Close? What is close? He never tried to kill me himself." Orion scowled. "He taught me to be strong, to lead by example. And he's not a bad guy even if he drinks more than he should. But he's too black and white, and I like living in the gray. I also don't like commands. Rules are meant to be broken, you know?"

Did she. "So, ah, your mom? Is she still around?"

"No. You don't know much about vampires, do you?"

"No." She took a bite of bacon and gobbled it up in seconds. "Do you want some?"

He took the strip of bacon she handed him and ate it. "Not bad. I do like meat."

"I'm not surprised."

He leaned back against the counter and watched her. "Anyway, to answer your question, when vampires mate, it's permanent. There is no other female for them."

"Oh."

"We find a female to bear our young, enjoy the getting of that young" —he smiled and licked his lips— "and care for the female. Once she's pregnant, a vryko will go through hell to keep her safe."

"That's nice."

He shook his head. "It's nature's way of ensuring we survive. Our birth numbers are low, and we need more warriors to stay strong. My kin wasn't so happy when they realized Hecate meant to enslave me here. I was meant to be returned when this is over, but I have a feeling the Night Bloode will stick." He made a curious face, one she couldn't read. "I'm not sure if that's good or bad."

His talk of enslavement made her feel so guilty.

"Yeah, so the female gives birth, sticks around for another few months until baby vamp is weaned, then disappears."

Kaia stared. "As in, the baby's father kills her?"

"What? No. That's crazy. We respect the mate, but she has no place in the clan. Vampires are bitchy by nature. We're cruel and possessive. We don't like to share." He frowned. "Didn't you fuck a bunch of lycans a few days ago?"

"What?" She choked on a piece of egg and had to drink down the water he handed her not to choke. "I'm, ah, no. I'm not experienced like that. Macy mentioned my, um, status earlier."

His expression cleared. "Oh right. Sorry. My mind isn't right lately. I keep remembering bits and pieces then forgetting them."

She had the feeling he never would have admitted to a weakness if in his right frame of mind. "Right. So you never knew your mother?"

"Nope. My father and kin raised me. All vampires come together to protect their fledglings. I did have a few good friends though." He smiled. "Crazy fuckers. They liked to screw with this kraken we had living close. And the monster was so pissy about it. We screwed with mage scholars on a vacation in Turkey. Then there was that school of possessed mermen who thought they ruled our sea. Fun times."

"If you say so." She grimaced. "That's a lot of fighting."

"Yes, but that's what we've been bred to do." He crossed his arms over his chest. "Do you know how vampires came to be as a species?"

"Mostly." She pushed aside her empty plate, feeling full. "Do we have any coffee?"

He smiled. "We do. Fara and Bella seem to really like the stuff, so I tried making it. It's okay, but not great. Have you ever had elven farewell tea, which is made from the leaves of a plant that devours fae whole? It's delicious."

"Ugh."

He laughed. "I told you we were bred to fight. Ambrogio is Primus, the very first of our kind. He was a regular human and a warrior who fell in love with Selene, one of Apollo's priestesses. Except she was actually Apollo's sister, not just a human. Apollo found out about their love, didn't approve, and cast Ambrogio away, dooming him to forever drink the blood of others, a monster, killed by sunlight."

"That's terrible."

"Gods are dicks." He nodded. "But Selene wasn't having it. She fell with Ambrogio, gave him her blood, and they turned into the first vampires. Apparently, and I just learned this, they had a ton of kids, scattering them over the human world. But those kids were powerful, so the gods got together to curse them. Now we can only coexist peacefully in small groups. And we can only bear one child with one mate. No others."

"Do you only have boys, since there are only male vampires?"

He frowned. "No. We don't talk about it much, but female children leave with the mother. They aren't allowed to live with us. Not that they'd fit in if they did. Female children don't possess vampiric traits."

"Isn't that a biological impossibility?"

"We're Of the Bloode. Regular rules don't apply to us."

"You have a point. So all the girls or women leave. Do your kind have any women around when you're growing up?"

"No. A few magir accepted by the patriarch are allowed to visit. Some like to see if they're compatible as breeders. It's good money."

She gaped. "Your clan pays for females to have children?"

"So what? Humans do it all the time with surrogacy. It's legal here."

"Well, I guess." Actually, a friend of Diana and her dad had hired a surrogate, so she knew people did pay for babies. But the way he talked about it seemed so mercenary, not to bring new love and life into the world. "Do you ever adopt vampires from other clans?"

"It's rare, but it has happened. But you'll almost never find a vampire raised by a clan outside his own tribe."

"Wow. That explains so much."

He joined her at the counter. "How so?"

"It explains why vampires are so mean. You don't have any softness in your lives." She flushed. "Although I don't mean to be sexist. Men can be soft too, I suppose."

"Not vampires."

Fascinated, she had so much more to ask. "What about relationships with people not vampire?"

"Lesser beings?" At her frown, he gave a chagrined apology. "Sorry. But that's what we've always called non-vamps."

"What about the mates living in the Night Bloode? I'm pretty sure they're not lesser."

"Kind of. Well, not to their mates. Varu would kill anyone who hurt his mate. But she's fae, and she's not offended by much. Not like your sister." He huffed. "Our Bloode Witch takes compliments as insults. I told her she was crazy mad, and she zapped me. I mean, crazy mad is great where I'm from."

She bit her lip not to laugh.

"She's fierce. She would have given her life to save Duncan. Non-kin never do that." He pushed a lock of her hair behind her ear. "They'd rather look for weaknesses to obliterate my kind."

He wasn't wrong. She'd heard her roommates talk about what a problem vampires were. That the many worlds would be better off if vampires ceased to exist. She wondered if he knew that, and if he did, if that ever hurt his feelings. It would surely hurt hers. Bad enough people thought sea nymphs were nothing but empty-headed skanks too stupid to realize when they were being insulted.

"Can I ask another question?"

"Sure." He watched her.

"Well, if mates aren't supposed to live with clans, how is it Macy and Fara live with you guys?"

He paused. "Well, neither's given birth yet. Though both Varu and Duncan seem enamored enough I don't think babies will matter. It's odd. But then, we're a clan of six different tribes, and that's unheard of. Plus, we have a dusk elf living with us who's not mated. Not Fara, but her brother."

"Really? I've never seen an elf before."

"You're not missing much. Onvyr's an asshole. He's fine one minute, trying to lop your head off the next. I guess he's got issues from his time spent in a master vampire's torture chamber. But I mean, get over it already. Pain is fleeting, right?"

"Have you ever been tortured?" It seemed like vampires thrived on battle and bloodshed.

"A few times. You battle with an enemy vryko or stray upir clan, mages who refuse to tithe. It happens. You get captured, tortured, then you break out and kill as many as you can. You go home and the clan plans revenge, and the cycle continues. Eh. Been there done that." His expression darkened. "Or you piss off your kin and they throw you and your best friend to the enemy, daring you to escape and get back on your own or die trying."

She put her hand on his knee. "That's terrible."

He covered her hand with his. "You know what's the worst though?"

"No, what?"

"Having a mate so close yet you can't even get her to kiss you."

"Orion." She tried to tug her hand away, but he wouldn't let her. She knew she could tell him to let her go, but she'd been trying not to order him around.

"Just one kiss, Kaia. Being near you makes everything right. What can one kiss hurt?"

"The last time you one-kissed me, you put your hand down my pants."

His slow smile heated her right up. "And you came so sweetly over my fingers." He lifted her hand to kiss it. "Have you ever come before?"

She couldn't talk about *this.* "Orion."

"Come on. Tell me."

"It's embarrassing."

"So that's a no, then."

"Yes, I have." She wasn't that pathetic.

"With someone else or just by yourself?"

"By myself," she mumbled, looking at her feet. "It's not easy being a sea nymph. Men always expect more, and they don't like it when I tell them no. Or that I have a brain in my head and am useful for things other than sex." She glanced up at him. "Do you have any idea what it's like to be considered inferior unless you're naked and on your back?"

O rion didn't like the pain in her eyes. "Who hurt you?"

"Not one person specifically. There have been a few."
Kaia sighed but let him pull her in for a hug. "My last boyfriend
was special. He didn't push the issue of sex, and he was a
genuinely sweet man."

Orion contained a growl.

"Too sweet. I was kind of ready for more than a few kisses
after our seventh date. But I don't think I was what he needed. We
broke up. Mutually. Then my mom invited him to her house on
some pretext of trying to get us back together. She tried to kill
him."

"*Whoa.* That's harsh."

"No kidding." She growled. "Sometimes—a lot of the time—I
don't like my mom. And then she'll try to help me or be nice, and
I feel bad for being a bad daughter."

He rubbed her back and rested his chin on her head, smelling
the fresh innocence, the allure of someone who wanted good
things in life for others. "I think dislike and hate can be good.
Hate and the drive for revenge can power you to great feats. But
then, I deal in violence on a daily basis."

She nuzzled his chest, and he felt a warmth he wasn't used to, one he hadn't realized he was missing. "Do you ever deal in affection, Orion? Is there anyone you do like? People you would want to protect?"

"Besides you?"

She nodded.

"Well, I'm pretty fond of Smoky. He's the cutest little gray cat we rescued from the house of a dead sorceress. He's an animage, actually. Your sister once tried to steal him." He scowled. "But I stopped that. Now she uses his brother to aid in her magic."

"You have a kitten."

He couldn't explain why the little gray cat meant so much to him. "I do. Maybe it's as you've pointed out. I don't have much softness in my life. Smoky makes up for that."

"That's nice." She remained tucked against him and patted his chest, making him feel as if she cared. "What about Kraft? You mentioned him a few times. Is he your friend?"

"I suppose. Vampires, we're not like you magir. Trust is hard to come by, and bloode ties that should mean everything sometimes bite you in the ass. Spiro and Nikkos are the two kin I left behind that I miss." He paused. "Spiro was the one who got kicked out with me when we annoyed my patriarch one too many times. He didn't make it back." Annoyed that his kin's passing still made him grieve, he shrugged off the sentiment. "But such is life for death-bringers. We don't always bring death for others. Sometimes we bring it for ourselves. Spiro could make me laugh. I think maybe Kraft reminds me of him."

"What's Kraft like?" She pulled back to watch him, not content to just hear his words, apparently.

Orion liked this. A lot. Sitting and talking with his female, basking in her attention. He would have told her anything she wanted to know, great secrets of the Water Cleave and Night Bloode clans. Yet she asked about *him.* "Kraft is an asshole. I mean it." He chuckled. "He's a nachzehrer, and they're a lot like my tribe, the vrykolakas. We're both larger than our other kin and try to solve problems with our fists instead of magic. He's also the youngest of us. His wolf is a fierce thing."

"Wolf?" She looked at him with curiosity. "Are you a wolf?"

"I shift into a raven."

"Really?" She blinked. "Can I see?"

"You want to see me shift?"

"After you're done talking."

He couldn't resist the shine in her eyes. They were dark brown, almost black, until she powered up or came, he recalled with fondness, when her eyes turned a neon blue and glowed. "I'm done talking now."

"No, tell me about Kraft. You like him because he's like you? Does he make you feel not so alone? Or do vampires not feel emotional pain?"

"You ask a lot of questions."

She blushed. "I work at ADR, the Alister Doctrina Repository. We're the biggest magir library in the Pacific Northwest. I like knowledge."

"A female as smart as she is beautiful. I like that." He liked her pink cheeks even better. "Vampires do float through life on the wings of affection, like so many of the lesser magir and humans."

"Orion."

He grinned. "We possess. We hate. We anger. We also laugh and enjoy life, but our way of enjoying isn't the same as most magir. We're not a soft society, Kaia. So it's not easy for us to find friends. Or mates."

"Do you want a mate?"

Was it weak to admit the truth? "I've wanted a mate since I was forty years old. I can't explain why. I'm not dying to procreate or anything. I guess I just want someone who wants me.

For sex, for a respite from constant battle. It's probably stupid, but I can't be upset I found you. No matter the circumstance."

She bit her lip.

"Kaia, don't do that." He leaned close and kissed the bite away. Nothing too deep, because he didn't want to scare her off. He wanted to give pleasure and comfort, and if answering her questions made her feel better, then he would keep talking until he grew hoarse.

"Sorry. I just... Orion, I have to be honest with you. The sea witch damaged you. She had you under her control."'

"I know. And I'll make sure she doesn't do that ever again." An oath. He'd kill the sea witch. Period.

"Yes, but in controlling you, she tampered with your will. I tried to undo her magic, except now my will has replaced hers, and that wasn't my intent. I want you free. But I can't figure out how to undo the spell. That's why Macy is helping us. We can't take you back to your kin yet, because they might find you a danger."

"Ah, Kaia? I know all this. I heard Macy and you explaining it all back at your library."

"I know you did, it's just... I'm afraid you think we're mated because of the magic tampering. Right now, I can get you to do whatever I want. I won't, but I can." She twisted her hands together, obviously nervous but brave enough to admit the truth to him, and began pacing. "I'm so sorry. I've done my best to try to free you, but until Macy comes back with help, we're stuck together."

"So you think we're mating because of a spell, and not because we're compatible mates? Is that why you don't want to fuck?"

She turned red, as she did when he spoke frankly. He found it adorable. "I'm allowed to say no."

"Sure, but your body says differently. You get wet for me."

She blew out a breath. "Fine. You're attractive in a rough kind of way. But that doesn't matter. I won't take advantage of you. It would be wrong. I'd hate for you to regret being with me later."

He couldn't believe she would say such a thing. "Really?"

"My blabbermouth sister told you I'm a virgin. I am. Not that I don't have needs, I just want to trust my partner, to feel affection for him. And I don't know. None of my past boyfriends felt right." She swallowed hard and lifted her gaze to meet his. "You feel right, but I'm scared. I don't either of us to be hurt."

"And you think by giving me multiple orgasms, you'd be hurting me?" He laughed so hard he lost his breath. "Woman, you're as nutty as your sister if you think I'd forego sex with you for *any* reason."

"I think you're complimenting me, but I can't be sure."

He laughed again. "Oh, I am. I've never been so hard in my life. And I rarely come in my pants after fingering a woman."

"That's crude."

"It's honest." He walked to her and put his hands on her shoulders. "I know what I want. Look, we have time together, alone. You say you want to help me. I believe you. I'm happiest making you happy. I'll leave the matter of fucking your brains out to you."

"*What?*"

"I'm yours, sweetheart. We have days to spend together staying safe while we wait for Macy to figure things out. Whatever we do is up to you."

"But your opinion matters just as much as mine." She looked so sweet with her concern. Worried she might be hurting a vampire's feelings. She really was too naive for her own good. Kaia needed a strong mate to protect her.

Someone like Orion.

She did have a point though. He didn't normally care what others thought so long as he was happy. He did the killing or fighting then relaxed however he wanted. Right now, he cared for nothing but making the pretty sea nymph happy. The way a vampire might see to his mate.

What harm could sex do but give him—and her—plenty of hours of mindless pleasure?

"I'm happy just being with you," he said plainly. "Focus on what *you* want and I'll make it happen. Now, are we going to fuck or would you rather watch TV?"

Sadly, she opted for the television. But she sat in his lap upstairs. The large, upholstered chair fit him perfectly, and feeling her breasts against his chest, her heart beating in time with his, made the world right.

She fell asleep against him while they watched a murder mystery. It ended, and he turned the channel to a rerun of one of his favorite animes while he stroked her hair, the long, black stuff like silk. He remembered the sight of it floating in the water, a dark halo framing such beauty. She sighed in her sleep and curled closer.

Definitely a snuggler. He smiled and realized he'd never had more peace with a female he hadn't even bedded properly. Such an odd happenstance that he wondered what it would be like *when* —not *if*—they had sex. Would he feel more for her or less? Was all this fascination for the nymph a need to conquer? Or because he had in fact found his mate?

He noted the time and realized Kaia would be a mess when she next woke, her sleep cycle off kilter. But no matter. He'd wait up here with her until the sun forced him to seek alternate accommodations.

Orion didn't believe in gods, destiny, or demons in charge of his choices. But Kaia could order him about however she wanted. She meant something to him. How to show her how he felt? And so what if a spell had brought them together?

He paused as something inside him struggled, a feeling of anger that didn't belong near Kaia, so he forced it back down.

He felt good with Kaia in his life. Like he felt when he'd met Kraft, when he'd rescued Smoky, when Varu had finally become his patriarch. The pieces of the grand puzzle were coming together. Kaia belonged to him. He'd just have to find a way to make her see that.

KAIA WOKE PLASTERED over the vryko. She yawned, relieved to see it still dark outside. How terrible would it be for Orion to burn to death because he didn't want to disturb Kaia's beauty sleep?

She lifted her head to see him watching her. "Hi." She felt shy.

"Hi." He was so much bigger than her, but in his arms she felt nothing but cared for and safe. In the arms of a vampire.

It seemed only natural that when he lowered his head, she lift hers to meet his kiss. Nothing overwhelming, a soft press of lips, yet the the feel of him sent her heartbeat into overdrive and her entire body on alert.

Need, pure and true, sizzled in her veins, and she moaned into his mouth, wanting to feel him everywhere.

He pulled back, his eyes bright red, a fang peeking out when he smiled. "Girl, you know how to kiss."

She blushed. "So do you." She looked at him, seeing a handsome predator, one many women would be hard-pressed to deny. "I bet you've had a lot of practice kissing."

He stroked her cheeks. "Some. But none of those kisses ever got me as hot as you make me."

"That's nice."

He groaned when she shifted in his lap. "It's not nice. It's painful."

"Really?" Kaia knew a lot about sex. She read books, watched movies, and studied articles about the biology behind carnal desire. But nothing matched feeling it for someone who mattered. "What does it feel like for you?"

"My balls ache. My skin is sensitive everywhere, and when you touch me, you make my dick spike. I see you and imagine doing a whole hell of a lot to you that would make you blush an even prettier pink than what you're wearing now." He sighed. "I can't stop remembering what it felt like when I had my finger inside you, or how good you taste."

His words fanned the flames of desire. "You're good at all the sex talk."

His intensity faded a little, and he chuckled. "I'm better at the sex act." He shifted under her. "But I'm not trying to force you into anything. You asked the question; I gave the answer."

"Yes, thank you." Even to her own ears she sounded prim. "What time is it?"

"A quarter to seven in the morning, I think."

"I slept too long." She sighed. "It's almost time for you to turn in, and I'm awake."

"Hmm. What should we do?"

She had several answers, but her sister's warning to steer clear of anything that might complicate the spell already over Orion had her shying from sex. To her surprise, she wanted to experience it. With him.

"Can we talk?"

"Sure." He didn't complain or try to change her mind, which she found refreshing.

"Do you think it's bad that I'm a virgin?" She hadn't meant to ask that, but she needed a man's perspective on her status, and no way did she want to talk to her dad or Cho about it. And her male roommates, while sweet, were too much like brothers to contemplate such an intimate conversation.

He blinked. "Really?"

"It's been off-putting for some of my dates. Sorry. I probably shouldn't have asked."

"I can tell you what I think, and that's that you've been dating the wrong guys." He studied her. "What kind of men have you dated? Humans? Magir?" He smirked. "Vampires?"

"Ha. Vampires. No, just you." He looked way too satisfied by that. "I dated a few guys in high school, but they were gropey and immature. I dated a nice mage a few years ago, but I felt weird about how proud he was to be dating a sea nymph. He had to let everyone know when we went out, and I felt more like a trophy than a person."

"He was an ass."

"I came to that conclusion when we broke up. There were a few other guys, though not many. Human or magir, it always ends the same. With both of us being disappointed in a lack of chemistry."

"Hmm. Now, don't take this the wrong way, but sea nymphs are known for liking sex. They indulge, a lot. But you don't. Why is that?"

"I guess it's because I don't want to be like my mom." She frowned. "She's never been too discriminating with lovers, which is why she and my dad didn't last. And she's never been shy about sharing her exploits with me. Ever since I was little. I found it embarrassing, then weird and kind of gross. I mean, she's my mom."

"True, but sex isn't a bad thing."

"I know that."

"Except you equate sex with your mom, and that's turned you off to being intimate with anyone."

"I—yes." She blinked up at him. "That was very insightful of you."

"Told you. I'm more than a pretty face."

They grinned at each other.

"It's easy to talk to you," she said. "I feel like I can tell you anything and you won't judge me for it."

"I won't. I'm not perfect, so who am I to judge? And Kaia, I've known a lot of sea nymphs. Even slept with a few." He didn't seem embarrassed or bragging about it, just stating a fact. "I know what sea nymphs are like, and they're lovely ladies, inside and out. But not like you. You're... more. I can't explain it." He shook his head. "I'm not embarrassed about my past. And you shouldn't be embarrassed about yours, either. Besides, your sexual history is no one's business but ours."

"Ours?" She raised a brow.

He nodded. "Yep. Since I'm going to be the guy you end up giving your V-card to, I have a say in your history. I'm going to *be* your history." He chuckled at the piqued look she shot him. "Have I told you I get a kick out of you when you're feisty? I love a chick with smarts and sass."

She gave him a large grin. "I'm not a chick, you big goof. I'm a nymph."

"A sexy one who owes me a kiss." He turned his head and pointed at his cheek. "Come on. I've been a good boy, haven't I?"

She leaned up to give him a peck on the cheek.

He sighed and looked down at her. "Why does that feel so good, Kaia? Holding you in my arms, seeing you smile, it's everything."

She didn't know. But she put her head back down on his chest and breathed him in, the clean scent of affection and vampire stealing into her heart.

The next evening, after Orion had patrolled the grounds and learned no one was actually staying in the cabin across the lake, they decided on a swim.

"It feels lovely in here," Kaia said, sighing as she stepped into the cold water. Though the outside temperature gave her chills, once she surrounded herself in water, she felt nothing but comfort. Even had she gone native sea nymph, wearing nothing at all, the water would have felt like bathwater. Hmm. Naked swimming with the vampire?

The truth was she'd thought about it, but teasing the big vryko wouldn't be safe or fair. She knew he wanted her. But she meant it about being good to him, afraid if they did have sex, that physical tie might further cement the magical tie between them. Her goal was to give him his freedom, not make things between them worse.

He smiled at her as he walked in the water, clad in only his jeans. Likely because he knew how much she liked looking at his body. Such a broad chest with muscular arms, a body long and strong and colored a light tan, an odd shade for a creature doomed from ever seeing the sun.

"How are you so tan? I thought all vampires were pale."

"That's another piece of fiction right there." Orion dunked his head and swam around with the grace of the merfolk. When he surfaced, he said, "We come in all colors and sizes. The melanin is a trick, a way to better blend with our prey. Pretty tough to surprise humans if we're all pale as death with fangs."

"I guess, but your eyes surely give you away."

"What?"

"They're red."

"Huh. That's weird." He swam closer to her, and they remained in place with no effort, comfortable in the lake's icy water.

"What color are they usually?"

"Black, but we get away with pretending our eyes are dark brown. That's something all of us have in common. That we're all male too. Our eyes turn red when we experience great hunger, distress, or..." He grinned.

She sighed. "Or?"

"Lust." He smacked his lips.

Kaia had the sense to avoid that comment and dove deep. She shot through the water and swam deeper, threading through strands of vegetation and fish. There was nothing magical in the water except for them, and she appreciated the empty space to just be.

Orion followed her, the two of them laughing as they raced through the water.

"You're so graceful," he said in the way of water-magir, his words easy to hear, carried by their element.

"So are you, for a land-dweller." She winked.

He guffawed. "Ha. I'm of the vrykolakas tribe. I was birthed in the water."

She hadn't realized that. "Really?"

"Yep. I slid out of my mother right into the Aegean's warm embrace."

"That's wonderful. I did too! Well, not in the Aegean, but in the Pacific Ocean. I love being underwater so much. I have a great life on land, don't get me wrong. Working with ancient texts and history I help to reimagine, so it won't be forgotten, is my dream job. But sometimes I feel like I'm in a foreign place in the city. The air isn't always warm or comforting, not like the hug of the sea. Or a lake or river."

"Yeah. I totally understand that. I've been pretty busy rounding up rogues and looking for Bloode Stones since coming to the Night Bloode. A lot of the time, I don't get a chance to enjoy the nearby lake. But Hecate added a fresh-water pool that connects to Lake Washington. I wish I could use it more." He swam behind her and tugged on her hair. "When we go back, you should check it out. Fara and Onvyr have been planting fae trees and flowers around, so it feels like a grotto more than a manmade pool."

"That sounds nice. I live on the water so I can slip into Lake Washington after work each night and sometimes early in the morning. I don't think I could ever live away from the water."

"I know. I almost disobeyed my patriarch when he ordered me to come to Seattle to pay back our bloode debt. Leaving felt wrong, as if I was being disloyal to my homeland. But then I came out here, and the house we live in is on Mercer Island, surrounded by water. That made all the difference."

She understood how tough that must have been. "Do you plan to go back after the bloode debt is repaid?"

"I don't know. It's different here."

She ignored the searching look he shot her. "Aside from the obvious, how so?"

"I'm more included here than I was at home. Being an enforcer made sense for me, and it allowed me to fight an awful lot, but the same old clan wars get old fast. The other magir aren't much of a challenge."

"So you were bored?"

"I guess. I'm not bored here though." His smile had her heart racing. "I'm swimming with a hot sea nymph, under her spell. I know you want the spell gone, but I'm enjoying my time off. The guys are okay and all, but you're so much more."

He kept complimenting her, keeping her off balance. "You like them. They're your family aren't they?"

"Yes, but they're not my mate." He darted away before she could chastise him for calling her his mate again. They'd discussed his attraction at length, and she made sure to let it be known she had no desire to hamper him with a bond of any kind. But he kept telling her how pretty she was, how much he liked being with her. And aside from the occasional request for a kiss or a heated look at her body, he hadn't come on to her at all.

Kaia liked him so much more. When he opened up and shared with her, it was like she could believe she'd found her other half. Orion had deep hurts he didn't know how to acknowledge, a strange family he wanted to like but didn't quite fit him. Though he hadn't said it, she sensed in him a dissatisfaction with his role in his Night Bloode clan.

He swam in circles then straight up, breaching the surface like a dolphin before diving back to join her once more. "Dare you to do that."

"Please. That's a game for children. See if you can keep up with this." She repeated his moves but added a series of flips and twirls both below and above the surface that had him clapping and demanding an encore.

Laughing themselves silly, they swam for hours, neither tiring until Orion mentioned he was hungry.

Once outside the water, she rid herself of the water soaking her clothes then did the same for him.

"That's pretty handy."

She smiled and shivered but didn't have time to be cold. Orion took her in his arms and sped into the living room, where he built a fire.

"Are you hungry?" He grabbed a blood bag and filled a mug with it.

She didn't want to know where he'd gotten it, but she liked that it wasn't fresh. The thought of him feeding off a stranger didn't feel right. The more she thought about it, the more she grew... jealous.

Yep. There it was. Kaia once again falling for a man that wouldn't suit. And not a man this time, but a *vampire*. Yet, he and she had so much in common. It wasn't fair.

"What's with the sad face?"

She shrugged. "I'm having fun, but this is a dangerous time for us both. It feels wrong to be enjoying myself."

"Fuck that." He leaned back against the kitchen counter. "I work my ass off for a goddess who isn't mine, am ordered around by a magician and a stubborn strigoi. I rarely have time to enjoy myself. I know you're a hard worker, so I doubt you take time off for yourself. Do you?"

"Well, no."

"And being here doesn't exactly count. You got roped into this because you saved me."

"I *tried* to save you. I don't know that you're saved yet."

"Well, here I am. Not at the Night Bloode mansion."

"I thought it was a house." She was interested to see the place but knew that would never happen. Once Orion got his independence back, if he didn't eat her, he'd never want to see her again.

"House, mansion, same thing. My point is that I'm not anyone's bitch-boy running errands. I'm here with the hottest chick I know and swimming." His red eyes sparkled. "Tell me this isn't great."

"That's my point. It is great." She frowned. "I want cake."

"That's my girl." He set his mug down and cut her a slice.

She ate while he downed his mug then made them both some cocoa.

"You like hot chocolate but can't take the sweetness from my dessert?" she asked, amused.

"I've got my reasons." He finished off one mug and got himself another.

"You forgot my marshmallows."

He rolled his eyes but fetched them for her, and it made her want to giggle, being attended to like a princess by a savage vryko.

"You're so nice to me."

He smiled into her eyes. "I won't say why, but we both know it's true, and it's not the fault of some spell." He waited for her to drink some hot chocolate, then he made her put the mug down and pulled her toward him.

To her surprise, he lifted her to the counter and pushed her knees apart to stand between her legs. He still towered over her, but at least this way, they were closer in height.

"Orion?"

He studied her face. "I don't think I can wait any more. I know you want to protect me, and I am so grateful for that, but I don't want protecting. I want you, Kaia. Whatever you want to give me. A hug would work." He grimaced. "I know I said you could set the pace, but I'm impatient. We won't have much time before the real world intrudes, and I'll have to break a few necks when they get a look at you. You're mine," he growled low.

How the heck could she say no to that when she wanted to kiss him with every word he uttered?

He just waited, her protector, with his heart in his eyes. And though she'd probably regret it later, she couldn't hold back.

Kaia put her hands on his shoulders and tugged. He leaned in, and she reached for his neck, dragging him closer. He went willingly, so careful, his gaze glued to her eyes, his filled with emotion.

She focused on his lips, parting hers to share that breath of want. His groan made her tingle, all of her wrapped up in his essence, in the touch and taste of him. Orion surprised her by being so gentle, so that it was Kaia's aggression that pulled them both into a spiral of need.

Gasping and hungry but not sure what to do with all her feelings, she pulled back, staring at him wide-eyed. "I, I want..."

"You want to feel good, sweet?"

She nodded, but that wasn't true, exactly. She wanted *him* to feel good, to feel what she felt, a melting need that consumed.

"Let me lead you," he murmured as he kissed his way down her neck to suck at her throat.

She arched up in a gasp.

"That's it. Give yourself to me."

As much as she wanted him, she couldn't use him to his detriment, afraid she'd do something that might take away more of his freedom. "Orion, I—"

"Nothing more than a little pleasure, I swear."

She nodded, bemused by the red spark of his gaze, mesmerized by his raw beauty.

"Lift your arms."

She did and watched her shirt fly away. Then her bra. Orion's eyes heated. He lifted her off the counter to strip away the rest of her clothes, then he set her back down on it, naked before him.

"Fuck me," he rasped, looking her over.

She blushed, not used to being so open in front of anyone. But the way he watched her made her feel special. Beautiful.

Wanted.

"Spread your legs for me."

She did, not sure what came next. Orion didn't give her time to think. He leaned down to take a nipple in his mouth, sucking while he kneaded her other breast.

A burst of heat took her by surprise, and she cried out, gripping his hair to hold him tight without realizing she'd grabbed him.

He moaned and sucked harder, and a jolt of electric desire shot straight between her legs, making her wet.

He had to know because his other hand sought the slick heat there. He moved his mouth to her other nipple and teased while a thick finger slid inside her, just as he'd done the other day.

She couldn't help rocking as he sawed that finger in and out of her, and then he stopped the motion while rubbing the nub between her legs.

"Orion, please," she begged, needing more.

He pulled away from her chest to stare at her while his finger moved. "You're so beautiful." He kissed her, his finger moving faster, rubbing harder.

She moaned into his mouth, so close to the edge that she keened when he pulled away.

"See what you do to me?" He unzipped his pants and took himself out, his cock huge and wet at the tip.

She had never seen a naked male up close, and the scent of wild ocean and wild vampire made her shiver, wanting him in the worst way.

"Lean back a little," he said as he pumped himself, the erotic act startling yet titillating. "More," he murmured, then moved down and put his face between her legs.

She cried out when he licked her, lost to everything but the sensation of him kissing her most intimate spot. He licked her, sucked her clit, and continued to drive her mindless with so much pleasure.

A glance down at him showed his arm moving fast, and she wondered if he was really masturbating while going down on her.

The notion had her coming before she was ready, the orgasm rushing through her in a crashing wave.

She cried out, so amazed at the sensations coursing thorough her she had little appreciation for his skill before she was coming again, and he was moaning as he licked her up.

Breathing hard, she stared in shock when he stood and continued pumping his cock, the organ thick and flushed. "I'm coming, sweet. So fucking hard," he said on a moan and jetted all over her belly and thighs in thick ropes of seed. "Yeah, marking you," he muttered and left a huge mess, finally pulling the last of it out before his shaft flagged, semi-hard.

"Orion." She had never experienced ecstasy like that before in her life. "Come here," she ordered.

He let her kiss him in thanks, the taste of her on his lips erotic as hell. He kissed her back, and the thankful embrace turned carnal all over again. She felt energized yet still missing something.

"When I come in you, then you'll know," he murmured.

She nodded, wishing he could come in her right now but afraid to further bind him without his explicit—non-enchanted —consent.

"I know, Kaia. You can't stop thinking that. It's okay, I won't blame you." He sighed, and something about his words bothered her. "I know you won't believe that I'd welcome you in my life, but it's true." He paused. "Want to try something else?"

"I want to try everything." She couldn't believe she'd been missing out on this for so long. No wonder sea nymphs had so much sex. It was fantastic!

But only with the right partner, she'd swore she heard in a deep growl. Before she could ask if he'd indeed said that, he kissed her so thoroughly she would have done anything he wanted if he'd caress between her legs again.

"Want to taste me?" he asked, his voice like gravel.

"I do." She wanted to hear him moan, see him shake. To drive him out of his mind, as he'd done her.

"Oh fuck." He licked his lips, focused on her breasts. "Your tits are so perfect. So tight." He closed his mouth around her left nipple. Then bit with a gentle scrape.

She nearly shot into his arms while he sucked, and she knew he'd taken a small bit of blood. "Again," she ordered, staring at him in awe.

He grinned. "Yes, mistress." He did the same to her right nipple and swirled his tongue over her.

She nearly came again before he pulled back and reached for her. He set her on her feet then took off his clothes, letting her see all of him, including his huge erection.

"There we go. Now, on your knees and open your mouth." He loomed over her as she knelt before him, feeling shivery, sexy, and supplicant. And loving every second of it. "Lick me." He held himself, so thick and hard.

She licked with a delicate swipe of her tongue, not putting her lips around him yet. His hiss of satisfaction pleased her to no end. She licked him again, tasting the saltiness of fluid beaded at his tip.

"Fuck, Kaia. Are you sure you never did this before?"

She smiled up at him and took the head of his shaft between her lips. His look of concentration as he watched her swallow him was worth nearly twenty-five years of waiting for the right male.

He was so thick it took some effort, but she managed to get her mouth around him and took about half of him before she gagged. He held himself so stiffly she wondered if she'd done something wrong and pulled back.

"Orion?"

"Don't stop," he begged. "Again, suck me harder."

His desperation excited her, and she took him deeper, experimenting, rocking back and forth, aware he held still while she swallowed as much of him as she could. Her jaw ached, but the experience gave her a sense of empowerment she never would have expected.

Curious about his maleness, she ran her hands up his strong thighs, surprised to find them hairless yet not surprised at so much muscle. He had the frame of a bodybuilder, all brute strength with little softness. Except for the smooth sac between his legs.

She cupped him, curious when he tightened, his testicles like knots, drawing up tight. He gripped her shoulders before deliberately relaxing his hands and apologizing.

Worried, she asked, "Did I hurt you?"

"You'll hurt me if you stop," he growled. "Please, don't stop. Do it again. Now, right now."

She smiled, relieved, and took him in her mouth while fondling him once more.

He jolted, pushing deeper into her mouth before stilling himself, and she wondered if he felt the same exhilarating joy she had experienced earlier. His excitement spurred her own, and she thought about touching herself while using her mouth on him, the way he'd masturbated while licking her.

A large hand palmed her head, and he moaned. "Yeah, do it. Get yourself off while you blow me." Then he started speaking in Greek, muttering words she couldn't understand.

Spurts of saltiness filled her mouth, and he began to jut into her mouth, not enough to make her gag, but to show his excitement.

She drew closer to orgasm, rubbing in time with her bobbing head.

"I'm close. So close," he moaned and started to pull back.

She didn't let him. She grabbed his ass, keeping him in place while she sucked. As she came in a burst of color, she drew down on him, taking him deep, and was rewarded with a shout and his release.

Spent, she gripped his hips and swallowed, not put off by the salty wash of him down her throat. Once he seemed to soften, she slowly pulled her mouth away, licking him clean while he shivered and stared down at her with wide eyes.

Then he drew her into his arms and hugged her so hard she squeaked.

He gentled the hug. "Sorry, sweet." Kissing her all over, he gave her words of praise and love that startled her, not because a vampire was loving her, but because she felt the same.

It's only sex, she kept reminding herself as they moved upstairs to the bedroom. They caressed and talked in quiet tones, watching the moon from the comfort of the lush bed. When dawn approached, she joined him in the basement in his makeshift bed and held him while he slept like the dead.

And let herself feel giddy with the blossom of love.

S unday night, Sabine entered Belyy Zamok, more than ready
for some fun with her lycans and a bit of attention from her
vampire. The lycans were a lovely diversion. She could pull quite
a bit of animal energy from not only their blood but their bones,
where most animal magic resided.

The vryko would be more of a challenge. Before she'd left,
he'd resisted her urge to draw his bloode until she'd used the
demon-coated blade. She expected more of the same attitude upon
her return, so she'd stocked up on some elixirs from the conference that might help. The divine sellers had made a big profit, and
she wished she had easier access to godly bits and bobbles instead
of having to spend a fortune. But to get what she ultimately
wanted, she'd pay the price.

Besides, she had no intention of letting Paz feed on her
again. That damn well *hurt*. She put a hand over her heart,
feeling the burn from where he'd pulled on the seat of her
power. She wouldn't be surprised to find her hair turning dark
again. What few knew was that the white in her hair was a
symbol of her power. She wasn't just *any* sea witch—Sabine was
the White Sea Witch. All caps, and emphasis on the *White*—the

sea witch equivalent of a supreme witch, master vampire, or top-tier mage.

She left the boat she now claimed as her own, a small luxury yacht courtesy of Orion of the Night Bloode, and trudged past the shore toward the castle. Trees, vegetation, and roots shifted to clear a path for their beloved witch, the island keenly tuned in to its master.

She spotted a hexed centaur on her way. "Grab my bags, would you, dear?"

He nodded and passed by her, and she wondered how he'd get aboard the ship with that equine form. "Not easily," she murmured with a grin, in a fine mood.

All in all, the conference had been a success. She'd made a few soul-binding deals, had found purchases she'd had her eyes on for quite some time, and had paid off a part of her debt to Paz, which had been weighing on her for months, ever since Sean had escaped.

Demons, like sea witches, made binding agreements. Just because circumstances changed didn't mean the deal was off. She knew and understood Paz's situation, and she'd been glad to get at least that burden off her chest.

So to speak.

She rubbed the area between her breasts, still sore despite it being a soul-base pull and not a physical one, and walked past Lord Ruin into the keep.

"So glad you're finally back," the gargoyle rumbled. "We have a bit of bad news."

Not at all what she wanted to hear. She turned to study him. "Oh?"

"The lycans are gone."

Her pulse rocketed. "Excuse me?"

"They left. I thought you'd let them go until we realized the vampire had also fled. The nyavka said she spotted the two of you running for the beach. She thought you were going somewhere to play until we found the lycans rowing away in that tiny boat off the northern entrance."

In a calm voice, she asked, "And you didn't think to call me?"

Ruin looked abashed. "We didn't think anything of them leaving until you called yesterday, and by then they'd all been gone for three days. We thought you'd allowed them to leave. We did see you, after all."

Her voice rose with each word. "I was in *Vancouver*."

He stared dumbly back at her, and she lost it. Sabine spat at the beast and let her venomous feelings take root. Her saliva turned to acid and ate through his face.

Though he screamed himself hoarse, it wasn't enough.

After ridding her castle of all her house snips, two more useless gargoyles, and the centaur with her bags who had unfortunate timing, she sat on her favorite couch and stared out the windows at the fog swallowing her view.

The vampire was gone. The lycans didn't much matter. She could get more or force them to return. But one Of the Bloode? Too much time had passed. By now, he'd have reported what she'd done.

She paused. Or would he?

The spell she'd cast had been guaranteed to make him lower his guard and gradually obey. She hadn't figured out how to get him to abide by just any command. If she made a command that interfered with his safety, his instincts for self-preservation would kick in, as they had when she'd tried to take his bloode. But with what she'd gathered from the conference, he would have been hers for the taking. And she'd *so* been looking forward to riding that large specimen.

So who the hell had impersonated her and absconded with her treasures?

She had many enemies, all with varying degrees of power, but only one name came to mind that could fool her guards. Yet Sabine had a difficult time believing it.

Could *Kaia* have impersonated her? Though a feeble sea nymph, the girl did have the blood of a great sea witch in her veins. Not to mention that of a grand mage. As much as Will annoyed her, he was a powerful magir all his own. But Kaia knew better than to come to the island without an invitation.

The mousy little bitch had no backbone. She couldn't even get up the gumption to ask a man out on a date. She never argued with Sabine, and she'd do anything not to upset her father. So fond of conciliatory behavior, Kaia did little to rock any boat, content to live in the placid waters of the dreary mundane.

Since Sabine had killed everyone who might have been able to shed light on the theft of her slaves—*ah well, I'll do better next time*—she did the next best thing and cleaned up this shitty mess.

The lycans would be no problem. She'd worn Kaia's face while dallying with them. *Ha. There you go, girl, deal with that.* But the vryko might remember. She'd been both herself and her daughter during his captivity, and he'd retained too much of his own wits while imprisoned.

To break her hold over him, Kaia would have to understand how to insinuate her power into his, replace Sabine, and work with the demon influence of the spell. That was was above her paygrade.

Since Sabine hadn't heard from Will, it was doubtful Kaia had confided in her father.

So, if none of her enemies was responsible for this theft, Sabine had to look at her daughter.

Best case, Kaia had an angry yet subdued vampire on her hands, one still bound to Sabine. Worst case, Kaia had usurped the power over the vryko and now had her own vampire slave, bound to her every whim. The vampire would be helpless, caving to whatever his new master wanted. Kaia would *hate* that, the self-righteous little prig.

Sabine needed to find her daughter right way. She could force Kaia to give him back. That wouldn't be a problem.

But why? Why would her ungrateful, weak-willed daughter steal from her own mother? What had Sabine ever done to make Kaia act so horribly?

Allowing herself to shed a tear and revel in the drama, she snickered, wiped her eye of its one tear, and made a few phone calls. Covering her ass and sure she could use something the vampire had been good for, she magically called out to Paz.

"Darling, I forgot to mention something I think you'll want to hear," she said when he answered.

"Oh?"

Sabine twirled a strand of white hair around her finger and smiled. "Have you ever heard of Ambrogio and the lost Bloode Stones? Because I've got a lead on something you're going to find very interesting."

ORION AND KAIA spent the next few days in a perfect state of happiness. With no one to interfere or distract them from each other, they were able to walk and talk, swim to their hearts' content, and best of all, explore each other's bodies.

Orion didn't understand why he'd been avoidant of relation-ships for so long. He'd always wanted a mate, yes, but he couldn't imagine ever wanting Kaia to leave, the way his father had forced his mother to go. Everything about his sea nymph pleased him. Her laugh, her sense of humor, her looks, and by all the demons in hell, *her body.*

If she hadn't been so adamant about no sex, he'd have consid-ered this time absolutely perfect. Hell, they'd been communicating telepathically for days and she hadn't realized, so in tune with him that their communication seemed natural. But he'd been sending her thoughts and receiving hers, like true mates did, ever since Saturday.

If only she'd worry less about his state of mind and more about her own desire. He knew she wanted all of him, and he wanted nothing more than to be the one to show her every pleasure of the flesh. But she got so agitated at thoughts of harming him without meaning to that the sexual desire turned into a fearful thing, and that he didn't like.

They'd been pretty creative, and he'd been having the best time getting her naked in all manner of places. Though they hadn't yet played in the water. He'd been saving that one, as it meant something more to share affection and bodies within their element, a more binding process than Kaia would be comfortable with. Water gave life, and he and she might very well *make* life if they fucked in the water.

The thought made him hard, and he worked to will away his erection since they were supposed to be playing cards together. Not naked, but hey, he wouldn't bet against the idea that at some point before dawn, she'd be on her back, her fists tangled in his hair while he ate her out until she screamed.

My nymph is a screamer.

He grinned, loving the flush on her cheeks, especially because she hadn't caught on to his one-sided telepathy yet.

"So why cat pajamas?" she asked as she picked up a card, stared at her hand, and discarded a different card. "I doubt your Smoky is going to like them. Cats are finicky."

They'd spent part of the previous evening watching a shopping network on television.

He chuckled. "I know, but it's payback for him waking me up before sunset. Especially when he has a full bowl of food."

"I guess that makes a kind of vampire sense. Revenge on a

kitten." She chuckled. "I really want to meet him and his brother, Nightmare. First of all, great names. Secondly, how the heck is your kitty's brother finding venomous centipedes and scorpions? And thirdly, how is he not dead after dumping said toxic creatures in your shoes?"

He grimaced and drew his own card, pleased at what he'd picked. "I wish I knew. He's fast too. I can never catch the little sucker." He put a card down.

"Are you sure it's not your kin messing with you?" She took her turn. "From what you've described, that sounds like it could be Rolf tricking you."

"Well, he's immature enough, yeah." He grunted, recalling the last prank the blond vampire—who had a few hundred years on Orion—had committed. The draugr had replaced Orion's toilet paper with a roll of duct tape covered with one sheet of paper, making for an awkward stay in the bathroom. Because yes, vampires *did* use the facilities. He picked up another card and discarded one he'd been saving for a run.

"Or maybe Kraft?" She smiled and called "gin."

They both put their cards down, and he wasn't surprised to see she'd won again. "Damn, girl. You're a real card *shark*. Ha, see what I did there? Not card sharp. Card shark."

She rolled her eyes. Since becoming intimate, she'd let down her guard and now gave back as good as she got. He loved her wit, always loving and funny, but sometimes with an unexpected bite that never failed to make him laugh.

He sensed that she was thirsty and called a time out. After making them both mugs of cocoa, he sat down again. Then immediately got up to bring her marshmallows. *No wonder she's so sweet. It's all that damn sugar she ingests.*

She laughed. "Okay, that was funny."

Once again, sharing a brain. He saw that as a positive, that she was truly his mate, spell or no spell. He had never heard of a witch interfering in a vampire's mating, and he didn't think it possible. Maybe when Macy returned, he might persuade her to convince Kaia they were okay. Then they could get started making a baby.

And after Kaia gave birth, she'd have to stay with him. Together, they'd find a place in the Night Bloode. If that didn't work, they'd go rogue and find a place to live together by the water somewhere.

"You are so sweet to me," she said with a chocolate mustache.

He grinned. "Aw, such a cutie, even though you look like you just ate sh—"

"Orion of the Night Bloode, watch your moth."

"I was going to say *sheeeeer* sugar."

"Sure you were." She swallowed a melting mini marshmallow and tried not to grin.

"I saw that."

I think love you.

He choked on his next sip, thrilled to hear what she'd finally admitted to herself. Because she should absolutely love him. He was the strongest, most admirable vampire he knew, and the only male who could satisfy all of her. He understood her, wanted her, and appreciated everything about her. Hell, he thought he might even love her, and vampires didn't love.

She frowned in concern. "Are you okay?"

"Yeah, sorry. I was just wondering what your father might think about us. I know you love your mom but you don't always like her." She refused to talk about the sea witch and shielded subconsciously when he mentioned her. But her father she loved without reserve. "You haven't said much about your father."

"Dad? Grand Mage Will Dunwich?"

Memories of Kaia's father, a mage he'd fought next to while battling a demon, came back to him. The male looked just on the lesser side of middle age for a human, so Orion had no idea how old he might really be. Mages aged much more slowly than their human cousins, the witches. And they weren't human but magir, able to use the magic within them to great effect, whereas witches had to borrow power from an outside source to make use of it.

"I met your father."

"Oh, right, when you fought Abaddon with Macy." She watched him with admiration. "I can't believe you went up against demons."

"To be fair, it was goblins. A whole horde of them," he muttered. "And their champion, who was a total dickhead. I just happened to be in the same hell plane when we fought."

"I'd be too scared to deal with demons. Uh-uh. No way."

"You stick with me and you'll never have to. But in any case, I doubt your dad would let you."

"No, he wouldn't." She smiled. "He divorced my mom when I was just a baby. My mother needed to get away and didn't want a child, not when I came out a lot less powerful than she'd hoped. But it turned out to be a blessing. My dad is kind and loving, and he married a wonderful witch in Macy's mom. She's the mom I dream of, and he's my perfect dad." She sighed. "But sometimes I feel like I'm not enough."

"Bullshit."

"No, I mean it."

He reached across the table to clutch her hand. "You're plenty enough for me."

"Aw." She stroked his fingers, and he felt that affection all the way to his toes. "I'm kind of wimpy, I hate to say. I play the peacemaker. My dad gets freaked when my mom acts all mighty, and she does some nasty things."

"Like what?"

"She cursed a group of high school kids messing around, turned them into trashcans for a day. That was fun for them."

"Ew."

"Yep. And she's always making deals with the desperate and unloved, promising potions for true love and money and success, and in the process, she steals their power, sometimes even pieces of their soul."

"That's tough." He kind of liked the sound of her mom, but maybe if she hadn't been such a bitch to Kaia. Only the strong survived, and it sounded like Kaia's mom was a survivor.

"But for all that she can be so nasty, she's also loving. She'll be supportive when I get a raise, and she tells me that of course I'm smart and pretty and wonderful. But I think she says that because I'm *her* daughter. I just want her to love me."

"And your father?"

"My dad is awesome. He loves me unconditionally. He's always there to help. Heck, he got me into my house, pulling some strings so that my roommates and I could have a spot on the water. I share the house with three guys, and two are water-magir. We all get along so well."

"Three guys?" he repeated, not liking the sound of that.

"Don't be jealous." Kaia bit her lip. "I mean, I kind of like that you are, but my friends are just friends. I'm not really into dating anyone from MEC anyway."

"Why not?"

She blinked at him. "Because what they do is way too dangerous." She paused. "Not like being a vampire or anything." A species everyone wanted to kill.

They both had a laugh at the kookiness of that thought.

"Anyway, I know I sound super dramatic and whiny for not taking more pleasure from my great life. And now I have you."

He wanted to get back to her father, because he had a feeling she'd left out a few details. But the way she was looking at him woke him up in a hurry.

O rion always seemed to know what she felt or thought. As if they shared the same brain.

Kaia wanted to smack herself for falling so hard for a vampire, but she couldn't. She'd done her best to let Orion do what he wanted, but he kept making their time together all about her. She would have felt bad about that except he seemed to take great enjoyment in their play.

Whether it be board games or swimming, watching television or buying weird stuff on the late night shopping network, they had fun. She hadn't *ever* experienced such enjoyment with a man by her side. She missed him when they weren't together during the short periods where he'd head out to scout around or to grab food for them.

He'd been subsisting on real food since his blood had run dry yesterday. But she'd swear she felt his craving. She wanted him to drink from her. To take her, to finally make love to her.

The temptation was too great. She knew she'd have given in if he asked.

But he didn't.

With Orion, she felt like a better version of herself.

She only hoped he wasn't going to eventually feel like a worst version of *himself* when the spell wore off. If it wore off. She'd heard precious little from Macy except for one brief text to check-in.

Orion pushed his chair back from the table and stood, a familiar gleam in his eyes. The sight had her readying to receive him. One thing she could finally say—Orion had brought her sex drive to life in a big way. She truly felt like a sea nymph for the first time in her life, always wanting sex. But only with him. Thoughts of intimacy with any other man did nothing for her.

He picked her up in his arms and kissed her, the soft peck on the lips turning carnal in a heartbeat. "I think you deserve a prize for winning again tonight."

She wound her arms around his neck and licked his throat, knowing how much he loved it. She nibbled, and he groaned. "What's my prize, vryko?"

"Something more to show you. Something I've been holding back."

"Oh. Show me."

He whisked them up the stairs. They'd started their love nest in the chair where they watched TV, but after fooling around in the grand bed with the lake visible just beyond the windows, he'd decided the bed made a better place to "roost."

She agreed.

He set her down and stripped naked. But he left her clothed. "First, a treat for you." He motioned to his erection.

She snorted. "Sausage, it's what's for dessert."

His cock bounced, smacking his taut belly. Her vryko had a beautiful cock, more than average in length and girth, and she still hadn't had him inside her.

"This is good practice for you. But if you don't want it, I—"

She knelt and grabbed him, pleased with his gasp of pleasure. "You're so easy."

"With you, I appear to be." He guided her head toward his groin, his fingers spread over her scalp, emphasizing how much bigger than her he was. But the fact she had all the power as she sucked on the head of his dick before taking him in her mouth was always a treat.

He moaned her name. "Kaia, yes, sweet. That's it. Take me."

She bobbed over him, slowly, learning more of him and taking a bit more each time she blew him.

He loved her mouth on him, watching with narrowed eyes, and the bloode-red of his pupils and irises had become her favorite color. She imagined she could hear him egging her on and closed her eyes, lost in his taste.

Yeah, suck me between those luscious lips, Kaia. Oh fuck, I could come just thinking about that mouth. So good, yeah, eat me up.

She grazed his inner thighs with her nails, and he jerked in her mouth, a spurt of salty fluid down her throat. Then she rubbed his balls, loving whenever she could touch him. His differences from the female form never failed to enthrall her. She could play with him all night long, watching him come for her a particular treat. She also realized her libido wasn't normal, but Orion didn't seem to care.

She sensed him nearing his end and sucked harder.

"Not yet," he rasped and pulled her back. He quickly took off her clothing then placed her on the bed.

"Spread your legs, nymph," he ordered, and she did with a sigh. "Show me where you want my mouth."

He seemed to love watching her. Especially when she touched herself.

"Oh yeah, get yourself nice and wet. Look at that puffy clit." He watched her spread her slick arousal over herself. But it didn't take him long to take over. He pushed her finger aside and used his own, watching with intent.

His thick digit felt so good inside her, but she wanted something bigger. They both did.

He kept his finger inside her and sucked her clit between his lips. The thrilling sensation made her lose her focus on anything but pleasure. When she neared her end, he pulled back, the big tease.

"Orion," she whined, "don't stop."

"Tonight we're doing to play with danger." He smiled, and she saw fangs. "I won't enter you, but you'll feel it. And I'll feel it. Okay? Trust me."

"I do." Two simple words, and she mean them wholeheartedly.

His expression softened, and he mounted her, leaning over her on his elbows, his cock thick and heavy between her legs, not positioned to thrust inside her, but to thrust against her.

Orion watched as he began to move, gliding that shaft over her clit, sliding in her wet desire.

"*Oh.*" They hadn't done this before, both of them aware how easy it would be to have penetrative sex.

"Yeah, so good." He moved faster, still watching her while he pumped, and she imagined him inside her, filling her with his cock.

"More," she said, wanting to kiss him. But he remained above her, so she caressed his chest, toying with his nipples.

He groaned and thrust harder, grinding against her clit. The friction felt impossibly good. She knew she wouldn't last.

"Watch us," he said and looked down between them.

She did the same, seeing that large cock between her legs, so close to her sex. He pushed back and forth, making her squirm, until he notched between her legs, his cockhead at the mouth of her pussy.

He froze when she would have taken him gladly inside, arching up to receive him.

Then he shoved her back down, and his strength undid her. The next time he slid over her clit, she seized and cried out, coming so hard. *Bite me, oh please.*

He swore and rocked faster. To her great satisfaction, he bit her neck. A spatter of hot seed hit her belly as he sucked and moaned, riding her as he swallowed.

The sensation made her climax surge once more, until they were sliding against each other, a mess of frustrated desire and ecstasy waiting to be mixed.

When Orion finally withdrew his fangs and licked her to heal her bites, she was done.

"I can't move."

"You're okay." He kissed her neck and nuzzled her breast, then settled part of his weight on her. "There you go, follow my heart."

She felt herself calm, a strange lethargy making it difficult to stay awake. "You bit me, and I came again. Is that what happens to people you bite?"

He grinned against her breast and kissed her nipple. "No, sweet. That's what happens to you when I kiss you, because I want you to feel nothing but pleasure from my fangs. Did you like my dick against your clit? Didn't it feel good?"

"Yeah." She sighed. "I really want to make love with you."

"Me too." He hugged her and felt as if he'd finally found home.

Wait. She'd just sensed *his* happiness. Or maybe she imagined it, because she sure as heck had found her home—with a vampire. Crazy, but there it was.

"I wish we could hold the world at bay," she admitted and petted his soft hair. "No sea witches casting spells. No battles for you to fight. Just you and me making love."

"Yeah."

But that sense of contentment had faded. She didn't know why. Instead, she yawned and fell asleep.

ORION FROWNED. No more fighting? That's what he wanted? That didn't sound right. Neither did making love when he loved fucking or having sex. But then he slid his hand through the mess he'd made on his sea nymph, covering her with his scent, and forgot about his confusion.

Yeah, she'd probably think it gross, but he liked marking her, saturating her with his possession. They were so close to mating. He could almost taste the union, could almost feel himself coming inside her, flooding her with his seed.

He groaned softly and patted her belly, wishing he could get over this odd, gnawing feeling that something was missing.

But it wasn't, and he should be thankful to have such a wonderful female by his side.

He watched the stars twinkle in the sky and let himself bask in peace. A few hours later, hungry for her again, he woke her to indulge in some sinful sixty-nine.

His face, her place, where everything made sense.

Her chuckle had him laughing as well.

"'My place?' Really?"

Ah, his mate was reading his thoughts. Perhaps they didn't need to have actual sex to cement the bond, because he couldn't imagine being any closer to perfection than he was now.

KRAFT YANKED Duncan to face him, finally away from the others on a mission to scout a den of ghouls away from the city up north.

"I don't know why you're touching me, mate, but you're close to getting that limb nipped," Duncan drawled, his accent annoying. Like his designer suit, flashy shoes, and expensive haircut were annoying. His witchy mate, *she* was annoying too. They waited for her to finish scoping out the empty ghoul den with some bloode magic, waiting by the car as they'd been *ordered.*

Ordered by a witch—a lesser being. Meh. He liked Macy, but if she hadn't been a Bloode Witch and under Varu's protection, Duncan bedamned, he'd have taken a bite of her already. Kraft couldn't seduce or mesmerize like the others, but his ability to instill fear was bar none.

"If your mate doesn't stop avoiding the issue of Orion being gone, I'm going to bite her."

Duncan hissed. "Fuck off. You lay one fang on her and die."

Kraft didn't often get angry. Well, really angry. He raged all the time for fun, but the powerful beast that lived deep inside him, when let loose, could not be stopped or contained until it tired itself out. Worry over Orion the past ten days had taken its toll.

Though the others couldn't seem to care less.

Mormo didn't seem bothered; Varu was apparently too busy with his mate and "talking" to the third new Bloode Stone they'd found; Hecate had conveniently disappeared due to some catastrophe in fae lands. But Kraft *knew* that Orion was in trouble.

Hell, even Smoky acknowledged the loss, meowing in sorrow until Kraft had taken the tiny meal to his own bed to stop all the howling, telling the kitten he'd wait to eat him until the vryko returned.

But that didn't stop his grief or his suspicion that their Bloode Witch knew a hell of a lot more than she'd admitted. She'd come back smelling of Orion the past Friday but said Kraft had been mistaken when he'd called her on it.

Enough of that shit. "I don't need your permission to talk to her though, do I?" Kraft flashed his fangs at the cocky bastard. Duncan might be faster than all of them, but he wasn't stronger. Kraft attacked without warning and shoved the revenant into the

SUV, crushing the vehicle to pin him inside. While Duncan swore and struggled to go free, Kraft yanked a tree out of the ground and shoved it through the front windshield, making it that much harder for Duncan to escape.

It wouldn't take the revenant long, so Kraft raced to the ghoul den and rushed Macy.

She glanced up from the sigil she'd been carving into the cave wall with bloode magic. "Hey, Kraft, what—*oomph.*"

He put her over his shoulder and moved deeper into the cave, jumping into the nearby pit a good thirty feet down. They landed, surrounded by the strong smell of ghoul. He withdrew a small, sharpened, wooden stick from his back pocket and held it to her throat, all before she could move.

Though Macy shared Duncan's bloode to power her magic, she had to be alert to the threat to act. And Kraft, her kin, shouldn't have posed a threat.

She blinked at him but didn't move.

"Smart. You try one thing with your magic and I'll stab you. You'll heal, sure, but before the poison has taken effect? I wonder how Rathenow ghoul toxin will mix with your bloode. Because in my old clan, we used it as a form of torture to get enemy vampires to talk." He smiled, showing his fangs.

"Oh boy, ah, please don't stick me."

Duncan's roar was closing in.

"If I stick you, you will no longer be mated to your revenant," he whispered, nose to nose with the pretty human. "Because you'll be too interested in consuming his flesh. And should you reverse the toxin, you will be rendered infertile." He smiled wide. "Effective, no?"

She swallowed. "Very."

Duncan appeared above.

"Tell him not to move or your future dies."

"Stay there," Macy yelled. "Please, Duncan. Don't move."

"I'll fuckin' *kill you,*" Duncan threatened. "True death, nachzehrer. You bloody rotter."

"*Sehr gut.*" Kraft nodded, ignoring Duncan. "Now, where is the vryko, and why are you hiding him from me?"

"Seriously?" Duncan yelled. "*That's* what this is about?"

Macy swallowed, her eyes glued to Kraft's.

"You will tell me." He pushed the stick no bigger than a pencil into her throat. "It takes little to break the skin, *ja?*"

"He's been bespelled," she said in a rush, her heart pounding. "He's safe with a friend of mine."

"Who?"

She blinked. "Kaia."

"He's with your sister?" Duncan shouted. Though Kraft could hear the revenant speaking in a normal volume from such a distance, Macy was still human.

"Loose lips, asshole," Macy shouted back while remaining very still. "Look, Kraft, Orion's in a precarious situation. He's not himself, and I didn't know if Varu or any of you might hurt him."

He lifted a brow. "Right. So you kept him from us to save him from us."

"Exactly."

"My, my, I have the wrong end at your neck." He flipped it. "This side is much more pointy." He put pressure on it.

The muffled grunts of ghouls approaching grew louder. Apparently, they were hiding out in this cave after all.

"Shit." Macy's heart raced, and Kraft smelled her fear. "Jesus. I'll take you to him. I swear. I was going to leave after we got back tonight anyway. I found the cure."

Duncan landed several feet from them, his eyes red, his claws out. The sophisticated vampire in all his glory.

Kraft snorted.

Duncan roared, "Here and now, I vow I'm going to—"

"Oh stuff it, honey. He's worried for Orion."

Duncan narrowed his eyes on his mate. "So it's okay for him to turn into an even bigger arsehole than usual and *threaten my mate?*"

"That's right. The death of her and her womb if I don't get my answers."

Duncan grew deadly still.

Macy stared beyond Kraft. "Seriously, I promise. Bloode swear, pinky swear. Whatever. I'll explain everything after we deal with the ghouls." She said to Duncan, "Duncan, please. He's got poison on the end of that stick. Rathenow ghoul toxin."

"Rathenow?" Duncan paused and raised a brow at Kraft.

Kraft gave a subtle shrug, and Duncan turned, likely so his mate wouldn't see him smile. "You swore, Bloode Witch. This is no simple thing you have agreed to do."

"I know. I'm sorry. I know how close you two are."

Duncan coughed, but Kraft heard the snicker he didn't quite hide.

Pulling back the stick, he tossed it to the ground.

Macy rubbed her throat. "Should you leave something like that around for anyone to find it?"

Duncan picked it up.

"Duncan, no." Macy rushed him, but he held her back. "It's toxic! Who knows what it will do to you."

"What? This broken number two pencil?"

"But..." She studied it then scowled at Kraft. "What about the ghoul toxin?"

"From Rathenow? A lovely little town in the district of Havelland? Really, what mischief in your brain." Kraft huffed. Then he shifted into his wolf to get away from the angry witch.

Duncan tried to placate her while Kraft tore into the ghouls, warning them to go back where they'd come from, far away. But a few didn't want to listen. While he convinced them to leave, he let Duncan tend to his snippy mate.

No longer in a foul mood since he'd finally gotten what he wanted, Kraft chased ghouls for fun until it was time to leave. Running up the sides of the walls, he bounded much farther than any normal nachzehrer might move in wolf form and awaited the pair at the top of the cave.

When they returned to vehicle he'd demolished, he realized he might actually deserve the angry looks turned his way and gave a sorry yip.

Macy glared. "Don't talk to me."

He cocked his head and gave her the puppy dog eyes domestic canines had mastered. Ha, there. A subtle softening in her expression.

Until her mate snorted.

"And you, stop laughing," she snapped at Duncan.

"I'll make him pay for scaring you, luv, I swear."

"You'd better." She gave Kraft the evil eye. "Because if you don't, I will."

That gave Kraft pause. She was, after all, their Bloode Witch. None of them had any idea of what she might be capable.

But none of that mattered, because in just a few hours, they'd be on their way to saving Orion from some horrible fate.

He could feel it.

CHAPTER FOURTEEN

K aia woke up to the smell of chicken and waffles downstairs.

The time had passed eight in the evening, and she yawned as she dragged her feet to the bathroom and showered. After dressing, she made her way downstairs and sighed inwardly at her man.

I have a man. Well, a vampire, but he's male, so that counts. She smiled at him.

He smiled at her.

Then she did what she'd been doing each day since they'd arrived. She went and gave him a big kiss.

"I like waking to that," he said.

"Me too." She took a deep breath. "Ah, breakfast." At eight at night, but who cared? "Thank you, Orion."

"It's my pleasure."

She paused. "You really don't have to do things for me if you don't want to. I appreciate it, but please don't feel like it's your job to take care of me."

"But it is, mate." He rubbed her nose with his, and the darling expression made her heart swell.

So this is love. She sighed. "You're pretty great."

"For a vampire?"

"For a man. Male. A romantic partner, how's that?"

"Romance? I don't know if I'm all that romantic. That might actually be part of the spell."

"I don't care. I like you as you are." Her smile faded. *But is that who you are? How much of this is really you and how much is the spell?*

He took her chin in his hand and stared into her eyes. "No spell could make me feel this way. Stop worrying."

"You always know what I'm thinking."

He winked. "I'm that good."

She laughed, feeling amazing.

He opened his mouth and froze.

"What's wrong?"

"Stay here." He vanished, out the door so fast the curtains swayed in his wake.

She'd given Macy directions to the place but no one else, and Macy hadn't texted that she'd be arriving. Nervous, Kaia grabbed a rolling pin from the kitchen and moved to the front, peering through the curtains in the sidelite to the left of the door.

Moments later, Orion breezed through with a relaxed expression. "My kin and your sister have come to visit."

"Oh good."

Their shared relief faded as they realized what that meant.

Kaia shrugged and tried to pretend she wasn't bothered. "Well, our happy vacation had to come to an end sometime. And hey, at least you can get back to normal."

"With you by my side, yes." He seemed adamant about that, so she had some hope that they might continue this relationship. Orion was so sweet and kind, loving and thoughtful. Could his non-spelled self be that different from the male she'd fallen in love with?

Macy walked through the door with two vampires. Not quite as large and imposing as Orion, the handsome one in the suit had a proprietary hand at the small of her back. Kaia had heard about Macy's fancy mate, so she figured he had to be Duncan.

The other one looked as if he wanted to eat her, and she took a step closer to Orion.

Tall, dark, and fierce with shaggy hair and muscles to rival Orion's, the snarl of danger was there and gone when he glanced to Orion. "About fucking time." He dragged Orion into a bear hug then quickly put his snarly face back on. "Who the fuck is this?"

"Watch your fucking tone," Macy growled in a voice Kaia had never heard her use, shocked at all the F-bombs dropping all over the place.

The angry one rolled his eyes. "Let it go already, Macy. You got pranked. Hell, Rolf gets me all the time. I let it go.'"

"After you try to feed his head to his arse," Duncan murmured.

Macy turned to Kaia and pulled her in for a hug. "I'm so glad to see you. I'm sorry I hadn't texted or called much. We were working overtime to find something to break the spell, and I'm happy to say we found it." She shot the crabby vampire a look. "I mean, it's not a *ghoul toxin* or anything, but it should work."

He sighed loudly and started complaining in German. Kaia didn't know the language, but she clearly understood his tone.

"Who is he?" she asked Orion in a low voice.

"That's Kraft."

"That's your friend?" Huh. Kraft seemed like a jerk, but then, perhaps he'd been worried.

"*Bester Freund, ja.*"

Orion grinned. "He's the only one of them who can almost kick my ass."

"Almost? I do it on a daily basis. It's the only way to keep that bloode-gut in check." Kraft looked him up and down and shook his head. "What have you been doing since you've been gone?"

The sudden silence had all attention shifting to her. "What?"

Macy blinked. "I think I see something."

"I smell it. He marked her good." Duncan winked. "Nice job, mate."

Kraft glared. "What's this? I thought you said he was under a spell."

"He is," Kaia said. "Macy, help him, please."

Orion shrugged. "It won't change the fact we're mates."

"Fuck me," Duncan said as he studied her. "Oh boy. Another Dunwich in the house?"

"I think already one is too many," Kraft muttered, his accent thick.

"Watch it, wolf breath." Macy scowled. "You're already on my short list."

Kraft grinned, showing sharp teeth.

Kaia didn't know what to think of him. He seemed angry and jokey in equal parts, though he didn't seem to like her much and she didn't even know him.

Macy nodded for them to follow her outside.

Kaia and Orion joined her by the lake, with Kraft and Duncan behind them.

"You two, in the water."

"The water? Why?" Kraft shut up when Macy shot him a look.

She explained to Kaia and Orion, "The witch who cast the spell was a sea witch. The one who took over for the sea witch is a sea nymph, her daughter. And Orion is bound by water and by bloode, by lust and by heart, of two shall he become one again."

Power swirled in the air.

"Daughter?" Orion looked at her.

She blinked. "Didn't I tell you that?"

"No," he said slowly as he walked into the water.

"I told you she was a sea witch."

"Yes, but not the White Sea Witch."

Kaia hadn't intentionally kept that information from him. At first maybe, but in the days they'd been together, she hadn't intended to keep that from him. She'd never lied about it, she just hadn't told him point blank, "Hey, my mom bamboozled you."

She moved into the water with him, but Macy remained back on land. She drew sigils into the air and had her mate hold a paper and read off the spell, which she repeated in a language Kaia couldn't place.

"Now, Kaia, put one hand on his head, the other over his heart. Like before."

"Okay." She had to reach but she managed it, staring into Orion's eyes.

"Still mates," he promised in a low voice.

She wanted to reassure him, but the magic swelled, burning through her. Around them, water swirled and turned a bright blue, the power in Kaia flowing through Orion, lighting him from the inside out as it traced through his veins and heart to his head. His eyes flashed blue then faded to black, no longer red.

A subtle difference in the vampire before her startled Kaia, and she lowered her hands, unsure.

Orion wobbled for a moment but quickly righted himself. He blinked and stared at his hands, at Kaia, and all around. "What the ever living fuck?"

Kraft laughed. "Oh yes, he's back."

Macy blew out a breath. "That wasn't as hard to undo as it must have been to set. The tough part was getting the right spell to sunder your love lines."

"Love lines?" Duncan asked.

"Well, under Kaia it was molded to a love line. But Sabine had it more like a collar and leash, spelled for obedience."

Kaia half-heard, studying Orion as he studied her. "Do you remember this week?"

"I remember everything," he snarled and hauled her off her feet, staring at her eye to eye. "Your bitch of a mother stole bloode from me. I intend to get it all back," he promised, his eyes glowing red before fading to black.

"I-I rescued you." She feared him as she had upon their first meeting.

"Did you? Or was this some power play to steal from the mother you resent as much as you love?"

It hurt that he'd use what she'd shared in confidence.

He dropped her and turned to growl at Kraft, no one safe from his vitriol, apparently. "And what the fuck are you laughing at? I was under some ass-nasty sea witch's power for days and not one of you shitheads came for me?"

"Hey," Kraft barked. "I was the only one who wanted to come after you. Mormo acted like you being gone was no big deal. If you remember, old man, you called in several times telling us everything was fine."

"What the hell good is working for a goddess if she has no idea when her clan is in danger?" Orion stomped out of the water, swearing and glaring, his gaze unerringly finding Kaia each time and casting nothing but blame.

She tried to hold back her tears, but they came anyway. Falling in love had been a stupid thing to do, and she knew it. Because she'd fallen in love with a fantasy.

Everyone knew vampires were nothing but monsters.

ORION WATCHED the pretty sea witch, no sea *nymph,* Macy was explaining, walk into the water and disappear. She needed a minute.

Oh really? Because I need a minute. I'm a walking hardon for a beauty who cast a spell on me. No, wait, it was her mother. And fuck it all, I think I told her about the Bloode Stones and the Night Bloode. Oh yeah, we're all royally fucked now. Terrific.

He brooded while Duncan brought him up to speed on what he'd missed. A whole lot of not much.

"She's still in there," he said to no one, bemused that he even cared.

He'd lied about remembering everything. He clearly recalled his time with Sabine, the White Sea Witch. Of her casting a spell, trying to take his bloode then doing so successfully with some magic dust and a dagger coated in brimstone. And of course, stealing not only his bloode but information she shouldn't have, *especially* if she was working with demons. But his memories of sweet little Kaia were murky.

He remembered wanting her, walking around with a painful erection half the time. He also thought he might have mentioned his father and kin from Santorini, about being alone or wanting a mate. Damn it. What had he told her? He felt a foreign sense of shame that he might have acted like less than the top-tier predator he was.

Done in by not just one witch, but two?

"Are we leaving or what?" He walked into the water. "I'll just go grab her."

He found the sea nymph floating listlessly across the lake underwater in her clothes, her eyes a bright blue and so sad he hurt deep inside. Which made no sense.

"Yo, nymph, it's time to go."

She looked at him with longing, which confused him. There was no sense of shame for her actions or hostility that he'd been freed from her spell. Just a well of grief atypically found in a sea nymph, who were known for their free lifestyles filled with sex, fun, and joy.

He studied her, having no problem whatsoever with her looks.

She was gorgeous, much prettier than the sea witch who'd nabbed him. Then again, the sea witch had used her face to trap him, though it had been artificial. Nothing like the true beauty before him.

"Hey, Kaia, right?"

"Yes."

"Did we, ah, did we have sex? Is that what we did all week while we were here?"

"No." Hell, she looked even sadder. "I didn't want to bind you to me against your will, and I worried that intimacy would make us mates in truth."

"Huh. Okay."

He'd swear she was crying, though in the water it was hard to tell. That she might be upset bothered him more than it should. He rubbed his heart. "Well, it's time to go."

"Okay." She drifted by him, and he stopped himself from reaching out. He supposed he shouldn't blame her for what her mother had done. The young nymph had saved him. Well, she'd gotten him out of there before he'd had a chance to rip her mother's throat out. He didn't think he'd been mistreated with her. But not having his memories or control over what he'd done the past week enraged him.

He forced himself to wait until she left the lake before following, needing some distance so he didn't harm her.

But when he left, he saw her wiping her eyes and wondered why it felt like he already had.

CHAPTER
FIFTEEN

"I've been taking care of your kid's meal," Kraft was telling him, and it took Orion a moment to realize the vampire was referring to his kitten. "Smoky's been crying a lot, and he started sucking up to me. I think he misses you, and since I'm the only one close to your size, he's tolerating me. Even sleeps on my bed."

Orion grunted. He sat in the back, letting Kraft take the front passenger seat while Duncan drove with a smooth confidence. Then again, the revenant did everything smoothly, Mr. Sophisticated with fangs.

Kraft continued, "Varu and Fara have been working hard with the third stone. It's different than the first one. The second one has been pretty quiet. But this third one talks to Varu all the same."

He had nothing to say to that and out of the corner of his eye watched Duncan and Kraft exchange a look.

Duncan said, "Every now and then, it talks to me too. It's weird. It actually has a decent accent."

"He means it sounds like a Londoner." Kraft snorted. "Not like a red-blooded Bavarian." He mouthed off in German.

The two vampires exchanged quips before devolving into a

discussion about pantheons and who had more strength during battle.

They drove in the SUV he'd stolen while Kaia rode with Macy in one of the Night Bloode's vehicles. He didn't like the separation from the sad sea nymph. Though pleased to be free of witchy influence, no longer bewitched, now he felt empty, as if a part of himself had gone missing.

Perhaps Macy had screwed up and taken a piece of his non-existent soul, giving it to Kaia. Wouldn't that suck goblin balls.

"Why so quiet, Orion?" Kraft asked.

"Leave him be, Kraft. He's been under the spell of a witch for days. Trust me, I know how that feels. It's not pleasant, even if you do end up mating her." Duncan chuckled. "Though I have to admit it was fun making Macy pay."

Kraft asked him about bloode magic—in particular, what it felt like to be Macy's bitch since Duncan had to provide her bloode.

"I'll give you a bitch, you bloody wanker," Duncan shot back.

"I do like to be bloody, lightweight."

Orion didn't listen, focused on his own befuddled discomfort.

Of course he had every right to be angry. Yet when he directed that anger at the dark-haired nymph, he felt echoes of hurt and bewilderment, disappointment with himself.

Why should he be disappointed with himself? Because he'd been bespelled? Vampires could withstand a hell of a lot from their kind and most magir. But demons were a whole other level of fuckery. *Of course* he hadn't been able to protect himself against demon magic.

Kaia might not have put the spell on him to steal his will, but she'd been there to take advantage of it. Hadn't she?

The past six nights with her seemed a dream, snippets coming to him of her smile, of him doing all manner of things from making her food to protecting her while she slept, and even once or twice of swimming with her. But laughing? Orion wasn't a big laugher unless it was at someone else's expense.

Then he'd recall how she kissed, how she tasted. He shifted in his seat, bemused to find himself growing hard. *Did we have sex despite her denial? Is that why I'm still fixated on the female? Or is there something more? Why do I care that she doesn't like her mother and worries about disappointing her father? Or that I have a sudden hankering for hot chocolate and carrot cake?*

The flashes faded, the swirl of memory washing down the drain in his mind and disappearing.

An hour passed.

"You're pretty quiet," Duncan said as they turned toward Mercer Island.

That woke him up, and he looked behind him but didn't see the SUV. "Where'd they go?"

Duncan answered, "We thought it would be a good idea for Macy to take her sister to their father's, so they can check her out there. He's a grand mage, his wife a strong witch. His home is protected from the White Sea Witch better than Kaia's place on the water."

"She should be with us." Irritated at the separation and not sure why, Orion floundered for an excuse that sounded believable. "She might still be holding onto me with her magic. What if I told her something?"

"Mormo will figure it out," Kraft said. "We're all meeting together, Hecate too, to see what we need to be on the lookout to handle." He swore. "I hate witches." He shot a look at Duncan. "Except for Macy. But she doesn't count. She's our witch."

"*My* witch, but okay." Duncan smirked.

Sure, Duncan could be a smartass. His mate had committed herself to him and the clan. But Kaia hadn't exactly— *She's not my mate. Stop thinking she is.*

Yet the more he told himself to forget about her, the more he missed her.

"She's going to be watched, right? I don't want to find out later that she and her mother planned this from the start."

Duncan frowned. "We've got a handle on it, Orion. Relax. Just sit back and shut up."

He grunted, swearing at them under his breath, but on the drive home, he felt nothing but an ache under his breastbone, where his heart beat a forlorn rhythm, Orion surrounded by kin yet once again all alone.

"OH MY GOD. I knew this was going to happen." Macy handed Kaia another tissue without looking, her eyes on the road.

Kaia took it, wiped her eyes, then blew like a foghorn. "Sorry," she said, muffled by the tissue. "I can't help it."

"You miss *Orion?*"

Kaia frowned at her sister. "You can stop asking that. Yes, I miss Orion. I'm telling you, he was different than he is now. He was sweet and kind." She sniffed, doing her best to stop crying. "I knew it was a mistake, but it's hard not to like someone when all they think about is you. He was so helpful and sweet."

"You said sweet already. Ugh. The vryko I know is a big pain in the ass. He's funny but also once threw me across the room. He's all for equality, even when beating people up, so I guess that's a plus."

Macy didn't understand. Kaia had met the *real* Orion, the vampire with doubts and hurts buried deep. Of course he wouldn't show that to anyone else. He had to protect himself, living in a house filled with killers. No softness, no mercy. It was a wonder any of his kind survived.

"How do you live with them?" she asked her sister.

Macy shrugged. "I love Duncan. Vampires aren't what everyone thinks they are. Oh, they kill. They're natural predators. But they don't all go out murdering people just because they can. They have a drive to dominate, and they go by the old code of might makes right. It can be annoying, sure, but to keep vampires in check, you need strength.

"Revenants are different than the vrykolakas. Duncan's all about being smooth and sneaky. His smile is the last thing you'll see before he slits your throat." She smiled, as if that was something to be proud of. "But Orion is in your face. He's big and mean, and you know not to mess with him because he can and will end you." She glanced at Kaia before returning her eyes to the road. "I just have a tough time seeing the big guy making you breakfast or rubbing your feet. That spell Sabine laid on him must have really burned out the core of who he is."

"I can see that now." Kaia wiped her eyes. "It's not his fault. But it's not mine either." She allowed herself to feel more than hurt, to tap into the anger at what she'd lost and embraced it. "I didn't cast that spell. My mother did. I tried to free him."

"Exactly. Get mad, not sad."

"I can be both."

"Right. And speaking of your mother... How are you going to handle her? She's got to know it was you who broke her prisoners free since you did it before. What do you think she'll do?"

Kaia sighed. "I don't know. We're supposed to meet for tea this Sunday. If she doesn't know it was me that freed Orion and the lycans, and I don't show up, I'll look guilty. If she does know and I show up, she'll be pretty mad."

Macy turned wide eyes to her. "She could kill you, Kaia."

"No way. My mom is brutal, but I'm her daughter." Yet doubt lingered. "You don't think she'd hurt me, do you?"

"I want to say no, but I've seen your mom in action. Maybe if you hadn't caused her to lose a vampire, she'd be okay. But Kaia, she trapped one Of the Bloode. Then she *lost* him. She has to know Orion will bring the wrath of the Bloode Empire down on her head. Sabine is no fool. Unless Orion can't talk, and you say nothing about what you saw."

"Who would I tell?" She paused. "She might have used my face to deal with the lycans. So they might be after me too."

"Too?"

"Well, Orion can't be happy with me. I know it's probably better to give him time to cool off and have Dad check me over, but Orion could decide he wants revenge on Mom *and* me."

"I'll deal with that."

"You shouldn't have to."

Macy frowned. "I'm your big sister. I'm also the clan's Bloode Witch. It's my job to deal with witchy stuff. I doubt Mormo will want him going off half-cocked anyway."

"Mormo is the magician. Hecate's servant."

"Yeah. He's a powerful guy. None of us really knows what he is, though my bet is some kind of demi-god. He shares her power, and he can be scary as heck. No one has *ever* attempted to gather a group of vampires from different tribes to form them into a cohesive unit. Yet he, with Hecate of course, has done it. And Sabine messed with his people. There will be repercussions."

"I just hope those aren't aimed at me. If Hecate decides to do something, she needs to realize my mom had a dagger coated in brimstone. We're talking demonic influence. That worries me."

"Me too." Macy was quiet for the rest of the drive, leaving Kaia to her thoughts.

She tried to stop missing the vampire and was only half successful. She did manage to contact her roomies to let them know to reinforce the house protections in case her mother stopped by, that was if they ever got done with their mission away from home.

Drake texted back, *On it. Don't worry. We got you.*

Her eyes welled. Her three roommates had been nothing but friendly and supportive for the past two years that she'd been living with them. She knew some of that had been because her dad had a lot of status at MEC. But over time, they'd become good friends, giving her advice and helping out when she asked but never acting overbearing.

Unfortunately, due to their time-demanding jobs, they weren't home often. But they trusted her to keep the house in one piece. She liked taking charge of the utility bills and cleaning up the common areas as well as enjoying the protection a lycan, a shapeshifter, and a water mage provided. Since they were rarely home anymore, they hardly made a mess. And even when they were home, the most she had to do was clean up a sink full of dishes when it was her turn.

Macy pulled into the family driveway. Will and Diana stood on the front porch, waiting, a beacon of safety and strength bound in love. Kaia did her best to hold in her misery, but when her dad opened his arms, she couldn't help racing into them and pouring her heart out in tears on his shoulder.

"She's okay. Just a little emotional," Macy said. "The spell took a lot out of us."

Diana didn't say anything. She never spoke ill of Sabine in front of Kaia, but she didn't have to. Her father normally did his best to hold back, but not this time.

"I swear, that woman doesn't have a lick of sense. I'm getting MEC on this. It's one thing to steal magir and sacrifice them for whoever the hell knows what reason. That's a criminal offense in its own right. But getting the vampires involved? She's going to start a war we can't possibly win!" He patted Kaia's back. "Come on, honey. Let's take a look at your power base." He guided her inside. "Heck of a way to go into your twenty-fifth year."

She blinked. "Gosh, I'd forgotten about that." In just another week, she'd have a birthday.

Another year, still single, no one to look at her with his heart in his dark-red eyes. She sniffed and let Diana fold her into a hug.

"Oh, Kaia. You were so brave to help like you did. Not smart going in without help though," she chastised in a gentle but firm voice. "But we're so proud of you for getting those magir to safety."

"Yeah, don't overlook that, Kaia." Macy agreed. "Without you, who knows what those four would be? Sea chum, most likely."

"For the White Sea Witch who's outlived her purpose, yeah," their dad muttered.

Once inside, Kaia took a brief break to use the bathroom and wash her face. She stared into the mirror. "You can do this. Time to get back to normal, woman."

She sat across from her dad at the kitchen table, a place where they shared meals, where she'd grown up doing her homework and gossiping with Macy and Diana. Where her father had helped her with algebra and led her through some basic water-casting magic.

Home. Safety.

She took a deep breath and let it out, appreciating a sense of much-needed calm.

Her father cast a spell using golden light, warm energy that poured around her and through her, settling the raw bands where her magic had tangled with Orion's. Her dad stared into her eyes. "Relax, Kaia, keep breathing, in and out, nice and slow. Stare into my eyes. It's okay."

She listened and allowed herself to trust, something that knucklehead of a vampire would never do.

Her dad frowned. "Let me in."

She pushed out every thought but love and tranquility, allowing herself to float in the sea of her mind. Her consciousness provided a raft, and she lay upon it, drifting in happier times, memories of Orion she'd keep to herself, but the image of his smiling face and deep-red eyes didn't make her sad this time, but happy.

After some time, her father pulled away, and she blinked at him, still smiling. "Am I okay?"

He exchanged a look with Diana, then with Macy.

"What?"

"Your spellwork is good, Kaia. Really good. You broke Orion from your mother wholly. There's no residual of Sabine in you either."

"But?"

He blew out a breath.

"What Dad is trying to say," Macy cut in. "Is that your tie to Orion and Sabine is clean. But your magic has changed."

"Changed?"

Grand Mage Will Dunwich stared at his daughter with pride and worry. "Kaia, you're in the process of Becoming. Your magic is larger than it was."

"Wait. Becoming? Becoming what?"

"That's the bazillion dollar question," Macy said then glanced down at her cell phone. "Shoot. I have to go. House meeting." She kissed her mom and dad on the cheek. "I'll talk to you soon."

Will glared. "Yes, you will."

Kaia had missed the interplay, but she saw the speed with which Macy darted from the house, heard the vehicle start and race away, and knew Macy was in trouble for something.

Her father turned to her. "Bad enough Macy's mated to one death-bringer. Now how about you tell me about the one one you saved, and don't leave anything out."

Kaia wasn't ready. "Dad, I'm so tired. Can we do this tomorrow? It's been a stressful week."

Diana cut in. "Sure we can, honey. Let's get you settled into your room." She led Kaia to the guest room she used when she visited. Her old room upstairs, down the hall from her parents'. "Get some rest." Diana paused. "And try to come up with a better excuse for the vampire marker that's a heartbeat from declaring a bonding. I'll try to talk your father down from the ledge I'm sure he's ready to leap off of." She kissed Kaia on the forehead then left the room, shutting the door behind her.

Marker? Bonding? Too tired to deal with anything anymore, Kaia slid out of her clothes and under the covers.

And slept like the dead, her heart seeking the beat of the vampire who no longer slept by her side.

O rion wasn't surprised that they waited until Macy returned to start the meeting. He'd been able to shower and change into clean clothes, which did nothing to appease him.

A frothing rage continued to boil, and he'd need to get it out lest it fester and turn into an anger that wouldn't stop.

Ignoring Rolf, Kraft, and Khent, he paced in the living room of the main floor, only relenting in his anger when Smoky—no, *Shadow,* he sensed the kitten now wanted to be called—bounded over to him and rubbed his tiny head over every part of Orion he could reach. Adoring the tiny creature, Orion would call him whatever he wanted.

"At least *someone* missed me," he directed to the draugr who shrugged and stood on his hands, upside-down, his blond hair kissing the floor, while Fara entered the room and stared in awe at Rolf's command over his own body.

The gray-skinned dusk elf, Varu's mate, didn't use a glamour at home. Fara looked every inch a fae. She had long black hair streaked with white, delicately pointed ears, and lavender eyes a little too large to be human—all contributing to her unearthly beauty. She wore a pair of jeans and a cashmere sweater, but nothing about her looked mortal.

"We thought you were on a mission for Mormo," Rolf said to him. "Who knew you were playing around with a sea nymph? If I'd known how much fun you were having, I'd have bolted out to meet you and left the lycan in the basement to his own end."

"He's still alive, but for how much longer I can't say," Khent said from the couch, watching Rolf perform acrobatics. "Mormo keeps interfering in my business, and I don't like it." He turned to Orion. "Nice to have you back. But perhaps next time you can hold off your vacation until business is taken care of? The lycans have been a royal pain. I have better things to do with my time." He sneered at Shadow, who hissed back. "And keep your feline in order, or the next time he sneaks into my laboratory, I'll stuff him and raise him from the dead."

"Oh, smackdown is *on,*" Rolf exclaimed and rolled to his feet. "I really did miss you, Orion."

Kraft snorted. "Meh. That didn't sound all that believable."

Rolf's face fell. "Seriously? I've been working on my delivery for days."

Orion wanted to be angry, but he found Rolf amusing. "You're still a dickhead."

"But your favorite dickhead."

Fara cleared her throat, the delicate dusk elf lovely as always, and smiling. "I didn't have to practice. I did miss you, Orion. Unfortunately, Varu has been so busy with the new Bloode Stone that he didn't pay as much attention to my warning as he should have," she said as her mate walked in.

Varujan, their patriarch, exuded menace as he surveyed the room. Until he spotted Fara, then he smiled. And that smile continued to Orion. "Yes, fine, you were right. I should have paid better attention." He walked over to Orion and grabbed him by the forearm. A wash of power settled over Orion, a reconnection to his clan that made him feel welcomed and appreciated.

"Wow."

"Right?" Rolf grinned. "He and Fara have been working with the power gems to feel the rest of us. When you went missing, it was the impetus to fine-tune the stones."

Orion blinked. "To each of us?"

"Yes." Varu nodded. "The Bloode Stones want to know you better. I think they sensed when you were taken and enslaved, but the new stone we retrieved muddied their awareness. It's still adjusting."

Orion concentrated. "I feel them now. Or do I?"

Varu sighed. "They're inside me."

"Oh, kinky."

"Shut up, Rolf," Khent and Kraft said at the same time.

The familiar banter eased some of Orion's tension. Holding Shadow, who purred with contentment, while being near Fara and the others soothed that part of him that had been trapped, forced to hide behind a veneer of kindness and peace. Orion was a vampire, a vrykolakas and member of the Night Bloode. Death and killing were a part of him, but so too were kinship, bonds of friendship, and a female he couldn't stop thinking about.

Varu frowned. "Who are we missing?"

Duncan and Macy arrived. "We're here," Duncan announced unnecessarily. "Where's the white wizard?"

Macy snickered. "And Hecate. Is she coming?"

Bella entered, the lone human servant in the house who did whatever Mormo needed. "Mr. Mormo's coming," she announced. A pretty, young woman with long, sandy hair caught back in a ponytail, she exuded cheer and efficiency. "Oh, Orion. Welcome back." She clapped. "I'm so happy to see you. So are Shadow and Nightmare." So she knew the kitten's new name as well.

"When did he start calling himself Shadow?"

"Oh, a while ago. I think it's good he chose his own name, don't you?"

Personally, Orion had liked Smoky, but whatever. He looked around but didn't see *Shadow's* brother. "Where's the little bastard?

"Probably shitting in your shoes," Rolf answered.

Fara choked on laughter. "Rolf."

Orion saw Varu hide a grin as well while Macy sputtered about her loveable feline.

Khent chuckled. "You know, for a thief constantly stealing my scorpions and death beetles, I can't stay mad at him. He is pretty clever. Macy, you have a remarkable familiar."

She cocked her head. "He's sleeping off a bender. Apparently, he got into some cream that was supposed to go in a dessert."

Bella's eyes widened. "Not my custard pie!" She raced to the kitchen. "Oh, Nightmare! You are in so much trouble when I catch you, buddy."

Orion turned and nearly walked over Mormo, who had suddenly appeared. The magician wore a smoking, ripped black robe over black tactical wear and a holstered weapon at his side, which was shocking in itself since he typically used magic, not a gun. His long white hair had smears of blood and ash in it, and when he moved, Orion saw the pointed tip of an ear, which was super weird, because Mormo had rounded ears.

Unless the bastard had always been wearing a glamour. Hmm...

"A new look for you, Mormo," Kraft said. "It's like black ops meets the *Legend of Zelda*. I like it."

Mormo's ears turned round once more. "I hate the Norse," he muttered, glared at Rolf, who ignored him, and stalked through the main living room to the kitchen, yelling for Bella.

The main living room was a large, spacious area filled with a sectional sofa and many bookcases, holding all manner of magical knickknacks and books. Done in creams and browns, the room was inviting and connected the main entrance to the rest of the house. On the wall facing the sectional sat a brand new large-screen television, to replace the one that had broken not long ago thanks to some in-house fighting. Across from the living space was a large dining area that overlooked the backyard through floor-to-ceiling windows.

Only Hecate's magic protected them from the sun's rays during the day, should any of them be moving during daylight hours. Though Varu didn't get so foggy when the sun was up, most of them felt the exhaustion that forced a sleep until sunset. Off of the dining area sat the kitchen, a glorious expanse of counters, a large kitchen island, and top-of-the-line appliances, including a magical refrigerator that seemed to hold all kinds of food items.

So why Bella would be upset over missing cream was anyone's guess.

"Where's Hecate?" Varu asked as everyone started moving toward the kitchen.

"She's on her way," Mormo answered and grabbed a beer from the refrigerator. He downed it in one swallow.

Everyone watched, but only Fara asked, "Are you okay, Mormo?"

"No, I'm not okay." He looked around the room. "My mistress should have been back by now." His gaze landed on Orion, and he frowned. "What happened to you?"

"Are you fucking kidding me?" Orion could only stare back.

"I sent you to find an island. Then we suddenly hear you're in trouble? You need to communicate better."

Orion opened his mouth and closed it, wondering if he should just rip the guy's arms off or start and end with a decapitation.

Mormo kept talking. "One slip of a sea witch and you're no

good to me. Do you have any idea how difficult it is to keep things running with just five vampires, two fae, and a witch?"

"Technically, mate, it's *Bloode* Witch," Duncan murmured.

"Bloode Witch, yes, thanks." Mormo grabbed another beer and drank while Orion planned which body part to tear off first. Ripping Mormo's head off would be too easy. "So while the lycans out of western Washington are getting ready to attack the local pack in Seattle—and we're talking a major blood bath coming—we're also dealing with some lycans who've gotten their paws on a fourth bloode stone"

"Maybe," Kraft interrupted. "The lycan in the basement hasn't confirmed anything, and we're still not sure who he belongs to."

"Because you keep babying him," Khent directed to Mormo. "He can live with three limbs. Let me cut off his leg and I can use it to get to the truth."

"So can I," Kraft said. "I can beat him to death with it."

Orion tried not to laugh, because he was fucking pissed, but he'd missed Kraft's attitude. "Or you could beat him to death with both his arms."

"Yeah, that." Kraft nodded. "Orion gets it. Because he's smart like that." A pause. "So when I tell you our vryko is missing, *you... should... listen,*" he roared.

Fara and Macy winced. Varu sighed.

"Not so loud," Khent said drily. "The magician has poor decision making skills, yes. But he's not hard of hearing."

Rolf patted Kraft on the back, egging him on. "Preach, bro."

Hecate and Onvyr arrived in a flash of light, the battle cat that often appeared in the house not far behind and still the size of a Siberian tiger. The three-faced goddess arrived with only one face, fortunately. Tonight she looked older and wiser, dressed in ceremonial robes of black and gold, a wreath of some kind on her head, encircling her temples. Her long hair had been braided down her back, a dark-red threaded with white.

She glanced around, her gaze lighting on Orion. "Oh, good, you're back."

Onvyr, the other fae in the house, had clearly returned from battle. He had night-dark skin and white hair, the dark elf part of his dusk elf heritage prominent during the night—unlike Fara who remained gray all the time. Onvyr's lavender eyes looked battle-hardened. He had bloody wounds and dirt all over him, a bruise under his left eye, and wore the clothes of an elven warrior —black trousers, boots, and a sleeveless black leather tunic with a tactical belt holding a few potions. He wore a bow over his shoulder, a quiver of arrows at his back. In his hand he held a bloodied blade that smelled of wounded divinity.

"We kicked ass." Onvyr grinned and said something in his native tongue to the feline.

The giant cat with black and white stripes and a mouthful of very sharp teeth chuffed and made some odd sounds.

"Catherine will have your cream downstairs, dear," Hecate said.

The cat gave what sounded like a laugh before trotting away and disappeared down a stairwell that appeared then vanished in a flash.

Hecate gave Onvyr a look. "We really need to work on your aggressive tendencies, Onvyr."

"Whoops. My bad."

She narrowed her eyes on him then explained, "A small group of elves were in talks with a few Norse gods about coming to peace over shared territory. Then Hel showed up with some dead warriors to change the terms, which had Danu's Children up in arms."

Fara looked worried. "Onvyr? Are you okay?"

"I'm great. I saw Dad. He said hi."

"Really?" She smiled.

Orion didn't want to ruin the elf family moment, but he had a problem that needed to be addressed. "I'm really glad you're all back in one piece."

Rolf raised a brow and looked at the elven warrior.

Meh. So Orion could have done without Onvyr. But hey, at least the elf was killing other fae and gods and not trying to kill vampires, his crazy for once directed *away* from the Night Bloode.

"But I want to discuss a certain sea witch having the gall to capture me, put a spell on me, steal my bloode, and possibly share information about the Bloode Stones."

The room grew silent, all attention on him.

His anger rose at the memory, and he growled at Hecate, which had both Mormo and Onvyr getting tense. "How the hell could you not know I was trapped?"

"I knew, Orion. But you were where you needed to be, and you seem just fine now." Hecate flicked a finger at him, and a wash of power coated him from head to toe. She nodded. "No lingering effects that I can tell."

"Oh my *fucking* gods."

"Hey. Don't blaspheme," Macy said, her worship of the witch-goddess evident.

Mormo nodded. "Thank you, Macy. Well said."

Orion swore. "The sea witch nearly *sacrificed* me. She took my bloode."

Varu stirred. "Hecate, this is serious. No one has leave to steal bloode from our kind. Especially not a witch."

"Luv, I *willingly* give you my bloode," Duncan said to Macy. "It's not the same."

Bella motioned to Onvyr. "This is a lot of vampire stuff I don't want to know about. Let's patch you up."

He nodded, and the pair left.

"You're damn right." Orion seethed, careful not to smush the kitten snoozing in his arms despite all the noise. "I was at the

White Sea Witch's mercy for days. It took her daughter to come to my aid." And didn't that stick in his craw, that he'd been rescued.

Macy cringed. "Sabine Belyaev is bad news. She's my sister's —technically my *stepsister's*—mom. Kaia's the one who helped Orion. She also rescued a few lycans as well. We think the island acts as a trap to catch the unwary and lets Sabine sacrifice them to increase in power and for use in dark spells. I talked with my dad, and he said MEC has been looking into a lot of magir going missing in the waters south of Whidbey Island."

"So your mission was a success," Mormo said. "It just took a while to get you back to us."

"I was under a spell," Orion bit out.

Hecate looked interested. "She took your bloode, you say?"

"Not with the first spell, but with a dagger that smelled of brimstone." He thought back, and a name came to him. "I think she talked to a guy named Pazuzu."

Hecate and Mormo exchanged a glance.

Varu frowned. "Hecate, if the sea witch is using magic, can't you talk to her? You're the goddess of witchcraft, after all."

"Yes, but not every witch prays to me." She looked thoughtful. "Sabine prays to the dark gods. Pazuzu is one such being. His sire is another."

Mormo swore. "Do you think she's talking to Hanbi too?"

"I hope not."

"Who's Hanbi?" Varu asked.

"The king of all evil. Someone we really don't want involved with Bloode Stones and the human plane. I—" Her energy scattered. Orion could feel it. "Well, hell. I need to go talk to Artemis again. Loki is annoying her." She shot Rolf a look.

He raised his hands. "Hey, don't blame me. I know the guy, but we're not tight."

"We'll talk later," she warned him. "Orion, let Varu have a

look at you." She stared into his eyes then laughed. "Ah, so it comes to be. Finally." Then she vanished.

Mormo shot him a considering glance then vanished as well.

What the hell?

Kraft frowned. "What did that mean?"

"Nothing good, I'm sure." Just once, Orion would like the goddess to be clear about things.

Varu shocked him by apologizing. "Orion, I'm sorry I didn't look for you sooner. It took Kraft to bring attention to you being missing for so long. The Bloode Stones have been very vocal lately, and we know trouble is coming. We're getting spread too thin, and we need to protect our own. From now on, when we go out, we go out in pairs."

Orion nodded, bemused to have his patriarch admitting to a wrong and trying to correct it. Patriarchs didn't do that. They commanded, made mistakes or not, and moved on. Vampires died. Vampires lived. It was what it was. But Varu had apologized to him in front of the others.

Fara looked pleased, which in turn pleased her mate.

But the others looked taken aback, Rolf thoughtful.

Varu assigned likely partners, since they normally teamed up as such. "From now on, Kraft and Orion, Rolf and Khent, and Duncan and I will go out on missions. If the Bloode Witch is needed, she'll be with us, Duncan."

Duncan nodded.

"But in the meantime," Varu continued, "we need to do some research. Macy what can you tell us about Sabine Belyaev and her daughter? How is it a sea witch can control an entire pocket dimension herself? That implies a lot of power."

"And a dagger connected to demons or Pazuzu is bad news," Khent said.

"What do you mean 'or' Pazuzu? He's a demon, right?" Kraft asked.

Khent replied, "Yes and no. He's a demon in the Babylonian pantheon, but he's also known to represent the wind, as the bearer of storms and drought, and as a protector of pregnant women. He's had many different names and purposes. But it's his role as a demon that's most concerning."

Varu scowled. "The only reason demons might want bloode or a Bloode Stone is to cause chaos."

Orion frowned, doing his best to remember details. "She took my bloode. She asked questions about us, about the Bloode Stones." That part was a little vague. He swore. "I think I told her you have one, Varu. And she had questions about our clan and Hecate's purpose in gathering us." To fight a great Darkness coming to obliterate all life.

Varu's eyes blazed red. Back in Santorini, Orion's patriarch would have cut out his tongue, though falling under a spell had not been his fault. Still, Orion should have known better than to get caught by a pretty woman on an enchanted island. But Varu didn't attack or castigate him.

He shook his head. "We'll learn what we can about the sea witch."

"She's the *White* Sea Witch," Macy said. "Very powerful, very dark. Her daughter, who freed Orion, is my sister."

Varu stared at Macy, and Orion saw her flinch.

Duncan stepped closer but didn't interfere.

Varu's voice was soft when he said, "You knew Orion was missing, that the witch had bespelled him. You said nothing of this."

The tension grew thick. Duncan put himself in front of his mate. Which reminded Orion, for some odd reason, of Kaia and how upset she'd be if Macy took harm.

Damn nymph.

He cleared his throat. "Varu, I can answer that." He planted himself next to Duncan, putting two vampires between her and his patriarch. "She thought I might be compromised and worried you might stake me because of it."

Varu rubbed his chin. "Still might."

Fara elbowed him. "Stop it." She turned to Orion. "Of course he won't stake you. You're family."

"I was kidding." The stare he shot Orion told him that no, Varu had not been playing around. "The truth is, we are Night Bloode, our own kin. We are made up of six different tribes, but that only means we bring diverse talents to the table, making us greater than other clans. I'm not my father. I do not believe in killing for the sake of bloode sport," he directed to Macy. "I believe in protecting assets and fortifying our strengths. Destroying Orion makes no sense. Destroying you..." He looked Duncan in the eye and said, "also serves no purpose. But you will not keep secrets from me in the future, Macy."

"No, Varu," she said and bowed her head.

Duncan sighed. "It was my fault too. I knew something was going on but said nothing."

Varu nodded. "Your job is to keep us aware of our enemies. And our Bloode Witch." Varu gave a small grin then turned to Orion. "Did you deliberately betray our clan?"

"Hell no. I would have escaped the sea witch myself but had no chance to prove it. Kaia rescued me."

"I need to talk to this Kaia."

Hearing her name on Varu's lips bothered him. "I'll get her."

"She's at my dad's." Macy shot Orion a look. "I'll bring her by tomorrow night, okay? In the meantime, I'll talk to MEC about Pazuzu."

"Good." Varu opened his mouth to say something and paused, looking at Orion. "Tonight, we're on a break. I think we've earned it."

Khent scowled. "But the lycan—"

"He can keep."

"Waste of my fucking time," Khent said under his breath, continued to mumble, turned on his heel, and left.

Kraft whooped. "I'll set up the games in the basement." Rolf left with him.

Duncan and Macy shared a kiss before trailing the pair.

Shadow shifted in Orion's arms but continued to purr against his chest.

Varu's lips twitched at the sight. "Orion, I need a moment. Would you mind if Fara took your friend with her?"

Her eyes sparkled. "Oh, yes, please."

Orion let her because Shadow liked her, and because Varu had asked. His kitten had a thing for fae creatures and happily climbed into Fara's arms. They both watched as Fara walked away, presumably to join the others.

With everyone suddenly gone, only Orion and Varu remained in the kitchen.

"What's wrong now?" Orion waited, pretending indifference when he was actually on edge. Varu felt much more powerful than he had before. A true master with not one but *three* Bloode Stones at his disposal, he might very well be able to rule the Bloode Empire.

And destroy Orion pretty damn easily.

Varu pursed his lips. "I'm glad you're back, even if you are annoying."

"Thanks so much."

Varu grinned. He did that a lot since mating Fara. "I didn't want to mention this in front of the others, but the Bloode Stones make me more sensitive to the bloode. And yours is still tied to someone else."

Orion paused. "Hecate said I'm fine now."

"You're not under a spell. This is more a bloode issue." Varu paused. "And it's the first stone that told me, but Orion, you feel the tiniest bit... mated."

CHAPTER
SEVENTEEN

Tired, Kaia took an extra day off work, her days and nights mixed up. She still grieved the loss of Orion.

She'd only known him for a few days, yet she understood, deep down, that Orion was perfect for her. But life went on. She had more important things to worry about. Like, did her mother know she'd stolen her prisoners, and if so, did Sabine plan to hurt and or *kill* Kaia for doing so?

Though it pained her to consider her mother might be capable of murdering her only daughter, Kaia knew Sabine had done some pretty shady things over the years. Heck, she'd almost killed Sean just for a boost in power. Unfortunately, Sean had disappeared soon after, so Kaia couldn't ask him what else her mother had been up to. Not that she could blame him for not sticking around.

She slept until noon then forced herself to get up. After sitting around her parents' house by herself for a few hours and feeling bored and sad, she'd had enough of her own moping. She called a ride service and had it take her home, where she belonged, then texted her dad and Diana to let them know she'd gone.

Kaia *always* relied on family and friends to feel better. It was time for her to stand on her own two feet. Dad, Diana, and Macy had done enough for her. It was time to fight her own battles now. And she'd start with going back to work tomorrow. She called her boss, who was more than happy to have her, no questions asked.

Then she checked in on her roommates. Apparently, the three of them were working a potential pack war, so they'd be out of pocket for another two weeks for sure.

Stay safe. I'm good, she sent, content when she received goofy emojis from all of them.

She wandered the house, noting nothing to clean up but her own room. She dusted, did laundry, and managed a grocery run for the next week. By five, she'd done all she'd set out to do with nothing to fill her time but thoughts of the stubborn, angry vampire she still missed too much for comfort.

After watching a few Christmas movies still playing despite it being mid-January, she'd had enough. She waited for the darkness to settle and let herself out back, down to the dock, and slipped into Lake Washington.

Surrounded by her element, the warm embrace of life-giving water, she swam and let herself go. Strife, pain, and anger leached out of her, the waters bringing change and movement, flushing the toxic hurts that kept Macy from flourishing.

She flew through the water and decided to move even faster, with a power she hadn't realized she'd had. Before she knew it, she entered the Sound and felt the call of the Pacific beckoning her forward. Kaia pushed, a new form of motion adding to her speed.

She circled Whidbey Island and ran into a pair of Orcas. Joyful, she joined them, and they raced each other and played, skirting a boat with spotlights that pointed at the killer whales in awe while Kaia kept below the surface, out of view of humans.

She felt powerful, no longer a sad sea nymph, but a being who commanded the waters and those who dwelled within them. Until a divine voice shattered her enjoyment.

I am Neptune, and these are my waters. Who are you that you do not pay tribute to my territory? The power in that question should have had her racing for home.

Your *territory?* she thought but didn't say and mentally added, *This is* my *sea, and these are* my *people. Who do you serve, tired Neptune? When this is not your home any longer?* None of which she actually said aloud or to the sea god.

That need to confront a divine presence shocked her into turning around and speeding back the way she'd come.

Holy crap. What was I thinking? She swam faster, a blur in the water as she cut through a school of merfolk who swore at her and interrupted a sea serpent's meal, much to the relief of a group of shapeshifting seals. Finally back in Lake Washington, she paused to consider her uncharacteristic aggression.

Kaia liked being the nice, quiet employee at ADR, checking out books and helping people do research. She enjoyed spending time with her friends and family, always nearby to help out or offer a warm smile or encouraging comment. She didn't play to win; she played to have fun. And she didn't own or claim any territory in the water. She simply liked to swim and be at one with her element.

Had her mother continued to influence her in some way?

Yet that need to claim territory as hers hadn't felt like Sabine at all. There had been no underlying taint of darkness, no pressing desire to conquer and force others to submit. Instead, she'd wanted to hold that water so that others might know safety as well. But to challenge a god?

Was she losing her mind or what?

Worried, she hurried to leave Lake Washington and saw the stars glittering above the surface. How long had she been swimming? But she didn't want to leave yet, so she dove deeper.

She turned and shrieked when she spotted him watching her, a blur of darkness resting in already dark water. Like a shadow rippling before her.

"What are you doing here?" she asked Orion, still several feet below the surface of Lake Washington.

"What are *you* doing here?" he asked, sounding hostile, but not overly so.

"Just swimming."

"You came in so fast I could barely see you." He looked her over, and she noticed him as well, clad only in trousers, his bare chest broad, his arms muscular, tapering down to large hands that waved back and forth as he remained in one place in the water. Still so handsome, violence shining in his dark eyes, but also something else. Something that tugged at her.

She floated toward him for a better look but stopped with plenty of distance between them. "I needed to swim. I feel better in here, away from everything and everyone."

"Yeah, I do too."

Surprised he'd share that with her, she didn't speak, just watched him bobbing in the water, tendrils of her power unfurling to slyly kiss the currents holding him fast. He tasted of dark power and need. A need for blood? For sex? For dominance? She wished she knew.

Orion frowned. "Did you call me here?"

"To my house? No. Frankly, I thought I'd never see you again."

He watched her. "Macy is coming by to get you later. Varu, my patriarch, needs to see you."

She swallowed. "Is he going to kill me?"

Orion scowled. "Of course not. If anyone was going to kill you, it would be me."

"*What?*"

"I'm not going to kill you." He wiped a hand over his mouth. "I just mean no vampire gets between a vampire and his... prey."

"Oh."

"Yeah."

They continued to float, just looking at each other.

Kaia stared at him with hunger, having missed him terribly despite just a day having gone by. Orion seemed fascinated by whatever he saw, and she didn't have the heart to ask what he wanted from her. She just wanted him to stay close.

"Did you put another spell on me?" he asked.

"What? When?"

"After Macy removed your spell at the lake. Did you put another on?"

"Why would I when I did everything I could to make sure you went free?" She flushed. "Though in hindsight, I probably shouldn't have let you drink from me. Blood can be a magical tie, though I hadn't thought about it at the time."

"I drank your blood?"

She blinked. "You don't remember?"

"Not all of my time with you is clear. I remember the sea witch. Your mother."

She flinched and couldn't be sure, but he seemed to take pleasure in that.

"But I don't remember all of my time with you," he continued. "I see us laughing or playing cards. A few times I remember kissing you." He stared at her mouth, bemused, the anger fading. "I took your blood," he murmured and moved closer.

Which had her automatically moving back.

He stopped and watched her, his gaze calculating. "What can you tell me about Sabine Belyaev?"

"Aside from the fact that she's my mom and captured a bunch of magir to steal power, not much." She sighed. "She got that island from a warlock who died. I don't know if she killed him or she just got lucky, but she snagged it and it became hers."

Warlocks were human, witches who had turned to dark arts,

intent on sacrifice and pain to bolster their power. But sea witches surpassed humanity, "sea witches" an odd, technical term for those magir tuned to water who also had power. Kaia had always wondered why her mother wasn't called a sea sorceress, because the term fit better. She was a mage gone wrong, turned sorceri.

"Why is your mother the White Sea Witch?" he asked, mirroring her thoughts.

"Because she's one of the most powerful sea witches born in her generation, I think. My dad might have a better answer. I only know my mom is pretty old, a few hundred years at least, and power is her drug of choice. She'll do anything for it." Kaia shrugged. "She tried to sacrifice my ex-boyfriend. And you, my ex-mate, er, ex-friend, I guess."

He considered her, just watching with that intent stare. She felt pinned under it, unable to leave until he told her she could. Weak, as always.

That thought had her baring her teeth at him. "It wasn't my fault what happened to you," she blurted, surprising him, she could tell, though she couldn't see any change in his expression.

"Oh?"

"I had a bad feeling after talking to my mom on the phone. I just knew she was up to no good. So when she left for her conference, I went over to the island just to look. I had no idea she'd have anyone there in chains."

"I wasn't in chains."

"You might as well have been." She frowned, wishing he wasn't so darned handsome in the water, his dark hair floating like a crown of night around his head, his eyes piercing yet clearly visible despite the darkness all around. In the water, Kaia was queen, able to see and hear clearly. "When I saw she had you under her thrall, I did my best to save you. Unfortunately, that translated to a swap of power, mine for hers. I had no idea how I even did it or that I could do it. But with me, you didn't suffer. I did everything I could to leave you still you."

"But am I me?" He snarled and swam up to her in a blink, grabbing her by the shoulders. "I still feel a connection, Kaia. To you, to the beauty with eyes that bind, a soul that beckons, and blood that makes me thirst." He licked his lips, and she saw his fangs, bright in the midnight waters. "I want you to tell me something, honestly."

"I haven't lied to you, Orion."

"Did we have sex?"

"I already told you we didn't." When he just looked at her, she blushed. "Not technically."

"I *knew* it. I know what you feel like inside. I tasted you."

So embarrassing. "Well, yes, but just with your hands and tongue. And lips." She felt flustered and couldn't meet his gaze. "I didn't mean to, but I'm attracted to you. And you're attracted to me."

"So no sex."

"No, not with anyone." She huffed. "I guess you don't remember that embarrassing conversation about my V-card with Macy then."

His eyes widened. "Oh yeah. Now I remember." He watched her, still holding her shoulders, though his grip had gentled. "You fit me, little nymph."

"I'm not that little."

"Compared to me you are." He smiled, no doubt liking that fact. "If I asked for a kiss to remember, would you?"

"If you promise not to hurt me."

He scowled. "I would never hurt you." He blinked and scowled even harder. "I mean, I would never hurt such a weak creature unprovoked. I'm too good for that. We Night Bloode only accept worthy opponents."

"Whatever." She rolled her eyes, used to the arrogance of a vampire.

"Good." He kissed her before she could blink, and she closed her eyes, missing this so much. Missing *him.*

ORION HADN'T REALIZED how much his lack of a connection to the beautiful nymph had bothered him. But now, with her in his arms, everything felt right. Nothing mattered but keeping her close, protected, a part of him tucked away, deep inside.

She sighed into his mouth, and he deepened the kiss, memories of their time together at the lake house filtering in. Of watching her smile, making her cocoa with those silly little marshmallows. Of seeing her naked, sliding his finger inside her and watching her come.

She yanked herself out his arms, staring at him with wide eyes. "Wh-what did you do?"

"Do?"

"Y-you put images in my head."

"I did?" He hadn't realized he'd done anything. At least, not on purpose.

"I bet you did too on purpose." She glared at him with accusatory eyes. "I tried to help you to the best of my ability before. Nothing I did was to hurt you." She blinked hard, and he realized she was crying. "I tried to help, and I gave you all I could."

"Hush, female. Your tears are useless in the water and useless with me."

She had to stop crying. Her unhappiness was pissing him off.

"I'm not crying."

Such a terrible liar. He felt a great warmth in his chest, his heart pumping harder, then easing, calming her the way a mate should.

With shock he refused to show, he realized he'd been hearing her thoughts and had inadvertently sent her visions of his memories.

The way vryko mates did.

He didn't think her aware of it either, that they were still tied.

What did that mean? And why did he feel so much better knowing they remained connected? *My prey,* he told himself. *She's mine until I decide what to do with her.*

Satisfied for the moment, he pulled back before he went in for another kiss. The water made her clothes cling to her, and that in addition to a clear recollection of her naked form had him longing to fuck her. Right here, right now. To claim and possess. His, forever.

He shook his head. "I may need to talk to you again. But for now, I think Varu won't need to."

"Okay." She watched him, as if unable to help herself.

"Tell me if your mother contacts you. She hasn't, has she?"

"No. I'm supposed to have tea with her this weekend. I don't know if she knows it was me that set you free. I need to go so she won't be suspicious. And she's my mom. She won't hurt me."

Yet Orion didn't think she truly believed her own words. "Fine. Just keep me updated. Let me know if you need protection."

"I'll let Macy know."

He frowned. "No. Let *me* know. Your sister is busy with other things. You will talk to me."

She studied him then nodded and shyly said, "If that's what you want."

He swam with her to the dock, and with no one watching, he hopped to dry land with her. "Remember this number." He rattled off his phone number. "Call me as soon as you get inside. And if anything happens I should be aware of, you will let me know." He added a dose of hypnotism to his words, pleased when the hypno-suggestion took root.

"I will."

Before he left, he said, "I'll be back again tomorrow, and we'll talk more."

She lifted her chin in challenge. "What if I have nothing to say?"

Oddly, her defiance lifted his spirits. He grinned, showing her his fangs. Flirting, though she likely didn't recognize the action. "You'll talk to me, sweet. We have much more to say to each other." He looked her over from top to bottom. "Bet on it."

CHAPTER EIGHTEEN

O rion frowned, unsure of his whereabouts until he spotted
   Spiro laughing as they raced the dolphins under the
moonlight. They had been told by their patriarch, a huge dickhead
named Leo, to leave the Black Rock Clan alone.

But the Black Rock vrykos had been encroaching on Water
Cleave territory, and someone needed to teach them a lesson. So
he and Spiro had desecrated one of their tributes to a fallen
comrade, because if the Black Rock had the audacity to show
their weakness to others, they deserved to be crushed. Regret and
grief were for other magir, not death-bringers. Those Of the
Bloode were better than everyone else because they put unimportant matters to the background, acting as true predators.

Only the weak-willed cared about love and loss. Orion had
lost kin before. But that was the way of life. The Sea gave and it
took, a plentiful playground full of fat prey and outstanding
battles.

The roar they heard told them they'd been found out, and they
laughed as they swam back to their stronghold on the shores of
Thira. But they hadn't counted on a scouting party of Black Rock

vampires coming from the south and got pinched between the angry group behind them and the scouts.

Up for a good battle, Orion fought. Stronger than most of his kin, even at the tender age of fifty, he defeated many of the enemy, not hampered by the water as many fledgling vryko were. Spiro didn't move so well, and Orion hurried to his side.

But he was too late. Spiro fell under a massive attack while someone speared Orion's side, not with fangs or claws but with a bone trident. It hurt, the pain another reminder that he lived, and he laughed and fought back, enjoying the skirmish.

He must have blacked out, for when he came to, he was held down, forced to kneel before the Black Rock patriarch in a large room on land filled with moonlight, fae torches, and marble everywhere. It looked like a Grecian temple, one not built to honor gods but vampiric ancestors. He recognized a bust of Alecta, the mother of all vrykolakas. A sea witch mated to one of Ambrogio's direct descendants, she'd written of a brutal history where she'd founded the vrykolakas in southern Greece after the true-death of her mate.

Though the Water Cleave clan didn't cling to the notion of female idolatry, they accepted their humble beginnings while still worshipping no one but themselves. Water gave life, thus it made sense a female ancestor had given rise to their powerful tribe.

"You do grave injustice to the fallen of our clan." The male was bigger and stronger than Leo, and a lot angrier. The bastard laughed. "Such youth. Ah, I wonder if your fangs will grow back faster than your nails."

He nodded, and one of the Black Rock next to him smiled. Wearing mermaid scaled gloves, he used a pair of silver pliers to extract Orion's nails.

The pain was excruciating, and he screamed despite not wanting to show a reaction. When they'd taken all the nails from his left hand, they moved to his right. He took the opportunity to look around for Spiro but didn't see his kin.

"My father will make you pay," he bit out as they worked through his right hand before focusing on his mouth.

Orion didn't like the shakiness he felt, not wanting to lose his teeth.

"Really? Tassos of the Water Cleave? *That* father will make me pay?" Everyone in the large room laughed. "Who do you think told us to torture you more than the whelp still clinging to life in the other room? Your clan's lieutenant, *Tassos,* has washed his hands of you, fledgling. You will live or die, and life will go on. Are you strong enough to survive? I fear your kin is not. And we have no patience for frailty."

After losing his teeth, including his fangs, and having his fingers broken one at a time, Orion was tossed into a cramped, dark room that smelled of death and rotting magir. Moans and pleas for mercy meant nothing to him, but the dim rattle of Spiro's heart he recognized.

He crawled over the broken and the lost, spearing his leg on a sharp rib bone, and found his best friend. "Spiro?"

Spiro tried to talk but had to spit out mouthfuls of bloode. "G-good r-run."

Not familiar with the panic crawling over him with the tread of a thousand prickly legs, Orion did his best to be strong, though the pain of his regrowing fangs and claws stung. "Take my bloode. We need to escape."

"C-can't." Spiro's organs had spilled over the floor, his body dark with bloode and other black stains Orion couldn't identify. Runes had been carved into the bits of flesh left on his body, though the eyelid over his left eye had been torn out along with the orb. Like Orion, he had lost his nails and teeth. But Spiro was also missing his limbs.

Orion just stared, wondering how long he'd been out that

they'd had the time to carve into his kin this way. He frowned then wished he hadn't, his mouth on fire. His gums throbbed as his new teeth cut through healing flesh, the pain nearly taking him under until he shook it off. "Come. We have to escape if only to go back and beat my father."

It was an unwritten rule that prisoners in vampire clashes remain sequestered, beaten but able to fight when the clan came to their rescue. At any given time, the Water Cleave clan had a good dozen prisoners in holding cells awaiting their kin to get them. Then the clans would battle, good training for them all, and go their separate ways. Why had Tassos left him and Spiro to fend for themselves? His father had always been a cold but just bastard. Orion respected him a hell of a lot more than their weak patriarch. Or at least, he had.

"Take my bloode to heal," Spiro offered, his voice faint. "I see darkness gathering close." His voice grew clearer and softer at the same time. "Death comes for me, brother. I seek its embrace."

Before Orion could try to force his bloode into his kin, or even turn to fight the near-dead and battered group of lamia and lone medusa, a tall man with dark hair approached, glowing in the darkness. He wore a toga that clung to one shoulder and exposed a broad chest corded with muscle. His dark eyes and aura stank of power, and he had the handsome good looks of a hero or god. Orion watched him with a wary readiness.

"That had to hurt." The male nodded at Spiro, now fading to dust.

"It did."

"What about that?" The male pointed to a spot over Orion's shoulder, and Orion half turned to keep the male in sight while staring at the most beautiful woman he'd ever seen, no longer buried in the dark but illuminated by an artificial light.

She wasn't wearing any clothing, and Orion watched himself, his own head buried between her legs on a kitchen counter, of all places, sucking her into an orgasm that had him hard in a heart-beat, the pain from his earlier beating no longer present. The female had an aura of neon blue around her, and they laughed and dove into the floor, which turned from tiles to water, dark yet clear, filled with magic and lust and love.

"Now that looks painful," the male with him said, both of them floating, their hair waving around in the water, while they watched Orion and the woman—Kaia—swimming together.

Orion knew this for a memory, one of many coming back to him.

"Painful?"

"To be such a jackass to the woman who made you smile like that." The male pointed at the image of Orion and Kaia having so much fun together. Orion had no idea he could feel so free or laugh so much.

Then he saw her crying, and his heart felt torn from his body. She looked awful in her grief, beautiful and terrible, like a piece of life too early snuffed out.

"Who the fuck are you?" Orion growled at the male now standing with him on dry land, staring at the back of Kaia's house in Lake City.

"Really, the lack of education in you people is horrendous. I'll be talking to your mistress about this, don't think I won't." The male sniffed and brushed back his long black hair. "I'm Morpheus, Orion, son of Tassos. You can call me Mr. Morpheus." He grinned. "The way that lovely female calls your sexy magician Mr. Mormo."

Orion blinked. "You mean Bella and Mormo? Wait, you think Mormo is *sexy?*"

"He's running scared, but never fear, I'll tag that sexy bastard if it's the last thing I do."

"Good luck." Orion sobered as he stared at the back of Kaia's house. "Why are we here?"

"We're studying truths, of course. Let's go take a look." Morpheus changed into normal clothes but looked as powerful as he had before, his eyes no longer human, gold light pouring from his eye sockets. "Follow me, vryko."

He reluctantly followed the male through a richly appointed domicile, up to a third floor where he heard familiar sounds and a breathy moan that put his back up.

Morpheus wiggled his brows. "Sounds like someone is having fun. Let's take a look, shall we?" He pushed open the door, and there lay Kaia, fornicating with a being full of darkness and power.

Orion would have stopped the obscenity because Kaia looked to be in real pain.

"No, wait."

He was forced to watch as Kaia, looking old and with white, not black hair, rode her lover, facing away from him, straddling his waist while the male splayed his legs wide on the bed. He had ink-black skin and leathery wings that fluttered as he pumped into Kaia. His face remained hidden behind her though his arms kept her in place, his hands huge, talon-like, as he scored into her flesh and dragged handfuls of her blood to his mouth.

The licking and sucking sounds added to her misery, until Orion was frothing at the mouth to help her and destroy the abomination she mated with.

"Wait and look," Morpheus ordered, holding Orion back with just one hand, his strength ridiculously impressive.

Kaia lifted herself from what could only be a demon, and as she lay back on the bed next to him, offering herself, he saw her face subtly shift, becoming that of the bitch who'd caught him in the first place—Sabine, Kaia's mother.

Relieved, he couldn't help grimacing at the full sight of the demon. As much as he looked human with a handsome face and muscular body, his wings and claws said demon. Not to mention the serpentine dick that was about three feet long and barbed had to be painful in the extreme. Dear Night, what had Sabine been *doing* with this creature?

"You mean, demon, not creature. That's P-A-Z-U-Z-U," Morpheus spelled out. "We try not to say his name too often in dreams."

But the demon looked up at them anyway and smiled. "Ah, Morpheus. I have missed you."

"Sorry, it's not mutual. Can't you put that thing away?" Morpheus pointed to the snaking phallus slithering in the air. It caressed Sabine as if it had a will of its own.

Orion had seen a lot of things in his time on earth, but this one he really could have done without.

"Oh, I will." The demon locked eyes with Morpheus as the scene changed. He stood before an altar on which Sabine had been tied down, naked and splayed wide. Then he slid his monstrous cock near the mouth of her sex. "Do you accept me witch? Do you want what I can give you?"

"No way she says yes," Orion said.

"Five bucks she does." Morpheus held out a hand, and they shook on it while Pazuzu laughed.

Sabine moaned. "Yes, Paz. Yes."

"Sucker bet." Pazuzu shoved himself inside her, too large to fit yet he did, and they watched as the sea witch's belly stretched and her skin writhed, overtaken by something new inside her.

"This is fucked up." Orion scowled. "Are we done yet?"

The demon laughed then groaned as he released inside her. "Yet it has already come to pass." He stepped back, his body now clad in a pair of gray trousers. A suitcoat, shirt, and tie clothed the rest of him, his wings vanishing, so that he looked like a high-powered CEO.

"Remember, Sabine. A soul is owed. A soul I shall collect."

"You'll get what I promised." She turned and glared at Orion.

"I will. Or else." Pazuzu saluted Morpheus then vanished.

The next thing Orion knew, he stood with Morpheus in his room, looking down at his body. "What the fuck?"

"Tell the magician he owes me a drink. I'll meet him in the usual place." Morpheus looked at him and shook his head. "You are blessed yet too thick to realize it."

"Hey." Orion took a step in his direction, but the male pushed him back with one finger, shoving him bodily into the wall and leaving a dent. Orion rose to his feet. "Nice. Try that again." He felt the hunger deep inside him, a stirring of danger. It was an end yet to be delivered, a pledge of divine storms gathering in wait, a gift from the Great Mother, Alecta.

Morpheus gaped, looking surprised for the first time that night. "Are you kidding me? Gods-touched? No one shares information around here," he yelled, to whom, Orion had no idea. Then he looked back at Orion and grinned, and his face and form changed, from Morpheus to the CEO-Pazuzu.

"What will you do with the treasure you've been given, vampire? When I can take it all away in a snap?" The demon had a screaming Kaia in his arms.

"Orion? Orion, save me," she yelled, crying in terror as Pazuzu kissed her then pulled away, and a familiar barbed, black appendage circled over his shoulder and aimed for her mouth...

"*No.*" Orion shouted and sat up in his bed, ready to kill.

Kraft and Khent burst through his door, looking recently risen.

Khent glared. "What now, vryko? It's barely sunset. I had been hoping to sleep in."

Kraft sniffed. "I smell brimstone." He frowned. "What's with the dent in the wall? That's new."

Khent went still. "Now that you mention it, there's a faint trace of brimstone in the air, and something else. I smell the ocean, blood, and... the divine?"

Kraft continued to sniff. "Oh, yeah, that hint of bubblegum and cherry. Why do I know that scent?"

"I had a dream."

Kraft stared. "A what?"

"Vampires don't dream," Khent stated.

Orion's heart raced, a need to check on Kaia overpowering. He rushed from the house down toward the pool.

Varu and Fara were talking in the hallway outside the spa.

"Orion?" Varu asked.

Orion ignored him and the vampires following and dove into the pool, past the tunnel leading beneath the house into the lake. He raced to see if Kaia was all right, not sure what he felt as he hurried, his heart pounding, a feeling akin to fear surging in his bloode.

He found her dragging a foot in the water, sitting on the edge of the dock. When she saw him, she gave a shy smile. "Hello."

He just watched her from the water, and it took him a minute to realize a boat filled with his kin had followed, waiting some distance from the dock.

Kaia looked beyond him and frowned. "Is that Kraft?"

"Are you all right?" Orion forced himself to calm down. What the hell was wrong with him? He'd panicked, something only humans or weak magir did. Vampires didn't know fear. Why then did he worry for the sea nymph staring at him in confusion?

"Um, Orion? We're going to head back now, okay?" Rolf asked.

"It's always a female that mucks up the works," Kraft muttered. "Get your head out of your ass and come home when you're done pining for the nymph," he jeered. The look he shot Kaia was anything but friendly, and after the—not scare, but the odd fantasy—Orion had had of Kaia, he didn't appreciate a threat from his kin.

"Fuck off, Kraft. Leave or I'll make sure to rip off something you can't grow back."

"Oh, nice." Rolf nodded. "That's a real threat. Kraft, you can't regenerate can you?"

"Wouldn't you like to know, draugr?" Kraft flipped him off, then turned to Orion and deliberately rolled his eyes. "Not scared, vryko. When you're done flirting, hurry home. Varu's got stuff for you to do."

"I do?" Varu looked amused.

"Come on. This was a huge waste of time." Kraft fought with Khent to drive the boat back, but eventually they left, and Orion felt like a fool as he floated, watching the female he could feel inside him, pulsing like the bloode in his veins.

K raft didn't know what the hell had happened, but hearing Orion's roar of terror had been enough to have him and Khent nearly colliding as they raced to the threat coming from Orion's room.

How had they scented demon, ocean, and a god where only a vampire should be? And why was Orion's first thought to head for the sea nymph he should have been over by now? Kraft didn't like the female's influence over his kin. Over his brother—his friend.

Unlike the others, he knew and accepted that their clan had started forming the bonds of real friendship. Because he spent so much time in his wolf form, he made connections with others easily. The animals in the woods to the north of the city. The lycan in the basement, who had proven to be a decent enough creature for a lesser being. Even Onvyr, their resident murderous elf, amused Kraft and no longer made him long to crush the male's skull when he lashed out.

Something was coming. He could sense it. Danger had a feel and smell to it, and he knew it traveled on the wings of the damned—demonkind.

He went in search of Macy, who had been shacking up with Duncan for the past month, her shifts at MEC now during the night, so Duncan and the Night Bloode could defend her if she needed it. During the day, she had Hecate's protection at the house. He thought she might soon permanently move in with her mate, as it should be. But would she stick around after she eventually gave birth to their young?

From the way Varu acted around Fara, the strigoi had no intention of ever letting his mate go. Perhaps Duncan would also be unconventional and keep his witch around. Then again, she was the clan's Bloode Witch and had a job beyond bearing Duncan a child.

He wished he knew why his kin were acting so strangely lately. Orion especially.

Ever since moving in with these odd vampires, Kraft had been itching to belong. His old clan had been happy enough to be rid of him, not comfortable with his ability to destroy. Weak, pathetic. They hadn't been admirable. He and the wolf he called self knew this.

Here, in this mortal city, he'd found pack. The vampires from all different tribes each had their own strengths. But together, they were a true power. Their patriarch had become a master at just a little over a thousand years of living. Duncan could move through time and space, circumventing supreme spells, though he didn't think anyone but he and his mate knew it. And Orion could move through water as if born a creature of the sea. No other vryko that Kraft had ever seen or heard about was so fast and powerful in any element other than air. He had no idea what Rolf and Khent had buried beneath the respective veneers of annoying draugr and snippy reaper. But for Hecate and Mormo to bring them, specifically, here, meant they were no mere death-bringers. But something more.

He found Macy kissing her mate in front of their bedroom doorway. She was dressed. Duncan wasn't.

"I'm seeing a lot of white skin," Kraft complained. "Too much."

Macy blushed, but Duncan only grinned and shut the door behind his mate, forcing her to deal with Kraft while Duncan went back to bed, from the sound of it.

"Hey, Kraft." Macy smiled.

He nearly tripped over the kitten meowing at his feet. The feline refused to believe himself in danger from Kraft and continued to sneak into his room when Orion wasn't around. He lifted the gray menace and tucked it in his arm so it would stay out of his way. He also ignored its abominable purring, though the furry part of him kind of liked it.

"Macy, your sister is beguiling our vryko."

"What?"

He told her what had happened.

"You're telling me Orion raced after my sister because he was *worried* about her?" She goggled.

"I know." He didn't like it either. Then he told her about Orion's room smelling odd. "And he had a dream. But our kind don't dream, Macy. What does it mean?"

They walked together to Orion's room so she could look it over.

"Kraft, I know you don't want to hear this, but I don't think the spell Sabine placed on him has anything to do with Orion's connection with Kaia."

"What connection?"

She just looked at him.

He scowled. "What?"

She put a hand on his arm that felt... nice. Like kin-pack. "I think they might be mating."

"No way."

She paused and turned around in the room. Then she closed her eyes and murmured under her breath, her impressive magic lighting up the room in a soft, red glow. "Morpheus," she muttered. "Ha. I know it's you."

"Who?"

"I need to talk to Hecate." She left Orion's room, Kraft trailing behind her.

"But what about Orion?"

She turned. "If he's smart enough to grab my sister and hang onto her with both hands, he'll be the luckiest vampire alive. Well, next to Duncan of course."

While she went in search of the goddess, Kraft went downstairs to confront their lycan prisoner. But when he reached the living space, he realized he still had a content kitten in his arms and held the creature up to show his fangs.

It hissed back at him, then blinked, yawned, and just hung from its ruff, watching him.

"You have no sense to be afraid," he growled.

It growled back. He hated to admit he found it adorable.

"Go wait for Orion upstairs. He's gone to flirt with a sea nymph." Kraft snorted. "Maybe you'll get lucky and play familiar to a witch, like your brother, because the sea nymph cast some kind of spell on my kin."

He put Shadow down, unprepared for the kitten to laugh at him and dart away, as if the little thing understood what he'd said and approved.

Then the battle cat—who didn't belong in this house filled with vampires—stalked past him, snapping and roaring, clearly annoyed with the owl hovering too close to the giant beast and hooting.

"This place is fucking weird." That said, Kraft stomped down the hall to play checkers with a lycan. With any luck he'd get the fucker to finally play *Apex Legends*.

He was sick of losing to some asshole middle schoolers who kept stealing his loot.

KAIA DIDN'T UNDERSTAND why Orion was looking at her like that, or why he stayed in the water several feet from her while she sat on the dock. Without thinking about it, she cast a light obfuscation spell to keep them hidden from any passersby.

She had an odd revelation that she no longer needed that borrowed camouflage charm to protect her and chalked up her new power to Becoming. Excited yet nervous, she hoped she got more of her dad's powers than her mother's.

It wasn't uncommon for young magir to "level up," as Macy called it, when a second puberty of sorts hit. A magical growth spurt in mages happened anywhere from twenty-five to thirty years after birth. Her father's aging had slowed and he'd risen from novice to exceptional mage, way before most mages grew in power. He'd also had an affinity for demonkind, which explained his close friendship with her Uncle Anton—a full demon very unlike his evil relations. Personally, she'd thought her father partially responsible for Uncle Anton's kind side. But no one had ever believed her when she'd mentioned it. Just something she'd always sensed.

Kaia didn't mind being lesser in power than her contemporaries. She had a great life, wonderful friends, and if she hungered for a romantic partner, well, she could always turn to books or movies until that special someone came into her life.

Yet here he was, floating while staring at her as if annoyed with her very existence.

But beneath the irritation, she sensed worry, fear, and... relief?

"Orion, are you okay?"

He nodded to the spot beside him. "Come in with me. I want to talk to you."

Giving orders rather than asking, she noticed. The old Orion would have gently requested her company or moved to the dock to join her. But the real vampire, she supposed, was used to giving commands.

She shrugged. "Okay." Not that she needed an excuse to swim, or even better, to swim with Orion. Sliding through the water, she drew abreast of him and let herself sink.

He sank with her, and they watched each other, the light of her special vision kicking in so she could see the handsome vampire scowling at her.

In a deep voice, he said, "You look all right."

"I'm fine."

"Good, good." He continued to watch her, and his attention caught on her hair waving in the water around her. "You look pretty."

She'd swear she felt him cussing in his head, *acting stupid for a female of all things.* Confused, because it felt like his thoughts, she nevertheless ignored her imagination and smiled at him. "Thank you."

They continued to float, staring at each other, and she gasped when she looked down his body, her vision clearing the darkness, to see a naked Orion in all his glory. As she stared, his dick grew hard, pointing at her.

"It does that around you." He gave her a hint of a grin.

She laughed, though she could feel her cheeks heating. "I remember that."

His smile faded, his gaze intense. "Tell me."

"What?"

"Tell me what our time together at the lake house was like. I can't remember all of it. The sea witch's actions are clear in my mind, though some of her questions are fuzzy after she used that dagger. But my time with you is coming in bits and pieces."

She swallowed. "What do you want to know? And before you ask, for the twentieth time, no, we did *not* have sex."

"But we did other things. I know that." He swam closer, and she refused to back away. "I want to know how I held back. Even now, I hunger for you. Not just your blood, but your mind and body." He looked her over. "You're small but put together well. Soft and slight, not as curved as most sea nymphs I know. You're sexy but standoffish. You don't put out a vibe."

"A *vibe?*" She hated the stereotype about nymphs being nothing but lusty females needing to pleasure sexual partners—men, women, other, it didn't matter. If you were a sea nymph, you obviously wanted sex. Sadly, for all the sea nymphs she'd met, that held true. But not for her.

"You don't have it." He caught a strand of her hair and let it trail through his fingers. "Or do you? You've seen my kin. You have male roommates." He seemed to surprise himself with the information, and his brows drew close in a scowl. "Do you want them too?"

"No. Just... " She caught herself. "I don't want anyone."

"Just me."

She didn't like his smug tone. "We're no longer together like that."

We could be. No. We should *be.*

His hunger was impossible to miss, but those couldn't have been his thoughts, could they?

"Tell me. Please," he tacked on in gruff voice. "What was it like before? Tell me what we did at the lake. You can skip the sex parts if they make you want me more."

She rolled her eyes and had the satisfaction of seeing him laugh. Grudgingly, she told him, "We played games together. We had fun. You were always trying to take care of me, though I tried to get you to stop. I didn't want to take advantage of you, but you kept saying that it was normal for a vampire to care for his mate."

He gave a slow nod, watching her as she spoke, and she wondered if he was remembering.

"I enjoyed being with you." She swallowed. "I told myself not to, because you were under a spell, but I... "

His eyes narrowed. "What did you do, Kaia?" She bit her lip, and his gaze turned red. "Tell me." He wiped his thumb over her lip, taking away the sting of her bite. "What did you do?"

"I started to have feelings for you." She felt like an idiot, the confession slipping out. "I didn't mean to. I even knew you weren't exactly you, vulnerable from the spell. But you were so kind and sweet. And you made me ache in places I had never let anyone touch." She put a hand to her heart and looked at him, and his red-eyed stare was so familiar it hurt to see.

He covered her hand with his and listened to their hearts beat in sync.

They floated there, just like that, his hand over hers, beating as one.

After a while, he lifted his hand and drifted away, back into the darkness of the lake.

"Go inside to safety, Kaia," she heard him say. "I'll see you tomorrow night."

"Okay." She felt him move until he'd put plenty of distance between them. Then, feeling lonely, she went inside.

To her surprise, she didn't dream. And if she did, she didn't remember the next morning when she woke to a dark and stormy day. Instead, she felt nothing but peace and a male acceptance that she shouldn't have been able to sense, with the psychic feel of the gruff vryko she'd seen just the other day.

O rion didn't know what to think. His memories of Kaia were rushing back to him in sleep *and* while awake. Saturday night, after his swim with Kaia, he was riding with Kraft into the city for a little recon on some warlocks Mormo wanted them to survey when another memory hit him, this one of Kaia and Orion watching a home shopping channel together, laughing and making fun of some of the stranger items on TV.

Had he ordered cat pajamas for Shadow? And pink "Dogs Do It Better" slippers for Kraft?

"Okay, that's it." Kraft pulled the Land Rover to the curb in front of a small gym that looked as if it supplied drugs to half of Seattle. Not a great area, and not a great human population either, apparently, as a trio of large, seedy, muscular men left the gym toward their vehicle.

"We have visitors." Orion nodded to the humans growing closer. One of them carried a bat. The other two wore suit trousers and white undershirts, their pupils dilated. The tallest man had white powder under his nose until his friend pointed it out. He wiped the powder with his thumb then licked it clean. Likely part of the major drug dealer outfit known to be in the area.

"I'll get to them in a minute." Kraft glared at Orion, who wanted to glare back but couldn't, still too peaced-out by remembrances of his happiness with Kaia. "You are seriously weirding me out." Kraft swore in German. "What the fuck is wrong with you? Where is my angry friend? We should be kicking ass together, Orion. Yet you smell of sea nymph and continue to daydream when we should be hunting down and roughing up witches."

"Warlocks."

Kraft ignored him. "Where's the fun in daydreaming about sex?" He looked down at Orion's obvious arousal with disapproval.

Orion chuckled, not caring that he looked as if he had little control. "If that's what you think, you haven't had great sex."

"I've had plenty of it." Kraft looked annoyed, more so when Orion laughed at him.

"Hey." The man holding a bat stood near the hood of the car. "What the fuck are you doing in our neighborhood?"

"It's Seattle. Go get yourself a latte from the nearest Starbucks and chill out," Kraft said in a loud voice. "Look, Orion, we found hints of a god in your room. So maybe you're not really mating this female. She could be using a god-spell on you."

"Do you really think Macy would allow that to happen?"

Kraft's expression darkened. "The female in question in her sister."

"I'm talking to you." The human pounded the bat in his hand.

"Hold on," Kraft yelled. "We're talking here." He turned back to Orion. "I don't think Macy would intentionally lie, but she did hide you from Varu before. And her own mate, don't forget that."

"I think Duncan knew."

Kraft's eyes widened. "He lied to me?"

"Probably." Because a vampire would do anything for his mate. Yes, they were pretty dysfunctional after a child was born, but before a vampire's female got pregnant, vampires were the soul of courtesy. Poems had been written about a vampire's great willingness to appease his mate, written not just by other vampires, but by the magir as a whole.

Orion didn't want to admit it, but he thought he might really be mating the little sea nymph. Adorable in her pique, gorgeous inside and out, with a pesky tendency to want to be kind and help out strangers. Except for all that niceness, she fit him perfectly, right down to her need to be surrounded by water.

It hadn't escaped his notice that his entire tribe typically took water-magir to mate. Kaia was his type in so many ways.

And why can't I forget what she looks like naked?

"That's it!" A loud boom hit the car, and Orion and Kraft glanced through the front windshield to see the big guy with the bat and his friends pounding on the vehicle. Apparently, they'd found a tire iron and lead pipe to add to the damage.

"I'll handle this." Kraft's eyes flashed red then back to normal too quickly to be noticed.

"Now I feel bad." Orion huffed. "There's no challenge out there."

"Well, there's no challenge in here," Kraft snapped back.

"Fuck you."

"No, fuck *you.*" Then, instead of wrapping his hands around Orion's neck, Kraft jumped from the vehicle and leveled the three humans in seconds.

Orion left the vehicle and glared at the one human who looked to not be breathing. "You broke his neck. Great job."

"Hey, not my fault they're so fragile." Kraft cursed Orion in German before turning to meet the horde of men running from the tiny gym. "And where are these warlocks we're supposed to spy on?"

Orion looked around and noticed movement from a second floor apartment to the left of the road. "Up there I think." He saw one of them point at Kraft and say something. So he grabbed one of the downed humans and threw him at the warlock on the second floor, having no patience for witches turned evil.

The female screamed while two of her conspirators yelled at Orion and waved wands.

Kraft laughed as more humans joined the fray. One of the men tried to hit him and lost the use of his left arm for his efforts. But at least this time Kraft didn't break the limb off. "Wands, really? What is this, Harry Potter?"

Orion would have laughed, but he hadn't forgotten Kraft's comment about him being no challenge. He shoved a bulked up female face-first into the concrete before she could stab him. "We finish this, I challenge you. Right here, right now."

"Yeah? You think you can do something besides pine after a sea creature that spreads her legs for everyone?" Kraft said.

Orion took the insult personally, as the bastard had intended.

Kraft laughed at him. "If you could see your face."

"You're a real shit, you know that?"

"I know she's ruining you, asshole." Kraft turned as a human shot him. "I'm done with this." In seconds, he mowed through the humans pouring through the gym and disappeared inside it, with screams, gunshots, and shouts following.

Orion had had enough of the warlocks trying to break him, and the last volley of burning arrows had scorched his favorite shirt and put a hole in his brand new jeans. "That's *it.*" He used his anger to rush the building. And rammed it.

He pushed through brick and stone, bursting pipes, and saw a small coven with dead animals and a few dead humans hollowed out and carved with dark symbols he recognized from his time in Abaddon's hell plane.

"Oh, fuck no." Orion went to both floors, leaving only two of the senior members alive for Mormo to question. The other nine he killed with prejudice. After knocking out the last two and tying them up with magic-sealing rope, courtesy of Mormo, he shoved them in the trunk then turned to face Kraft.

Who started ahead of him by slamming a rock-hard fist into Orion's face.

Orion crumpled, his head ringing, and looked up into the dead eyes of his kin.

"She has made you *weak*. Look at you." Kraft growled, his wolf close to the surface, all that tasty rage burning in his red eyes. "Why, vryko, do you revel in the soft touch of a female when your power is all you have? Your true worth is not in your emotions," Kraft sneered, "but in your fighting spirit. Varu and Duncan mated, but do you see them getting beaten up? Pathetic? Less than the humans I just crushed with one hand?"

"You caught me by surprise." Orion knew he shouldn't have said that the moment it came from his mouth.

"Oh, I'm sorry," Kraft said in a sweet voice. "Should I warn you next time I try to kill you? Who's the fledgling? I'm less than half your age, yet I could kill you here and now." He leaned closer, the wolf present and waiting. For what, Orion didn't know. "And then I'll go after that pretty morsel in the water. She'll do whatever I say before I drain her and feed her to my wolf. All that magir blood, so tasty under my tongue."

Orion lost it and grew larger. He launched himself at Kraft and didn't back down, barely aware of Kraft laughing with delight. "There you are," the nachzehrer said.

But he'd threatened Orion's female, and that could not be allowed to stand. Orion let go of the hold over his deepest rage, needing to make a point Kraft would understand. "She does *not* make me weak."

"No, *you* make yourself weak," Kraft yelled to be heard over the sound of an approaching storm. "Take her or not, but stop wallowing in a state that will get you killed, you fuckhead."

A dark cloud gathered over them from out of nowhere, and

shocks of lightning accompanied the deluge of rain that fell from the sky. Orion's upper chest grew hot, the mark he'd been born with flaring to life.

He looked up at Kraft, the world bathed in blue.

"Yes, yes, there you are," Kraft repeated in a deep growl more suited to a wolf than a vampire. He howled and shifted into a giant wolf, one bigger than Orion had ever seen him assume. *"Let's have a taste of your power, puny vryko."*

Orion wanted to warn him, but he also wanted to teach Kraft a lesson he would not soon forget. The threat to Kaia hovering, as well as the taunt to the true power inside Orion from that partic-ular voice not quite Kraft's, made the decision for him.

The bolt of lighting that hit Kraft dead in his heart should have killed him. The crack of that boom killed the electricity all around them for at least a good mile, even as the storm dissipated as if it had never been.

Orion shook his head and pressed a hand to his chest, tracing the familiar burn of the trident, a symbol of the first vryko's true power. When he looked down at Kraft, he didn't see the giant wolf but a woozy nachzehrer laughing his fool head off.

"That was *wunderbar.*" He giggled like a child, and Orion stared at him in concern, spotting the melted soles of his shoes, the scorch marks on his chest, and the smoking tatters of his shirt.

With a sigh, Orion returned to his normal size and lifted Kraft in his arms. He shoved the unsteady vampire into the passenger seat of the dented Land Rover. With the warlocks tied up in the trunk, they'd accomplished what they'd been tasked for the night. And if he didn't soon get moving, they'd have to deal with MEC, which Mormo had strictly told them to avoid.

On the drive home, he wondered what tonight had been about —Kraft's challenge, his own feelings about Kaia, and why he kept referring to her in his mind as his mate and not his prey.

She's not my mate, he continued to tell himself, ignoring the fact that they'd shared thoughts. That he grew way too possessive and angry over a slight directed at her. Or that the thought of Kraft taking a taste of her blood made Orion want to rip his head off and give him the true-death that thought deserved.

I'm not getting mated, not now with all the crap we're dealing with and living with Mormo and Hecate. He put his foot down on the accelerator.

Kraft giggled again. "Sorry. Can't help it. That really tickled."

Orion shot him an incredulous look. "What is wrong with you?"

Kraft groaned. "So much. We don't have time for that talk tonight." He squinted at the dash in the vehicle. "Only another hour to sunrise." He rubbed his chest. "That's one hell of a punch you've got there."

Orion couldn't believe he'd let it out, and at his kin no less. He hated to say it, but he owed Kraft an apology. "I'm sorry."

"I'm not. Finally! It's good to have you back."

Orion laughed, relieved—and surprised—he hadn't done Kraft permanent damage. "You're an idiot."

"Yeah, but it's good to know you're not the lesser being I thought you were becoming."

"Fuck you."

"Didn't we already have this conversation?" Kraft sat up, still rubbing his chest. "You're mating the nymph. Go with it or kill her. But you can't stand in the middle anymore. Not when we need your power to face what comes." He paused, his voice growing quieter. "The things Varu has are talking." He glanced behind him at the backseat, reminding Orion of the warlocks in the trunk.

"Huh?"

"You know. The talking *things* that sometimes sing," Kraft snarled.

"Oh, right." The Bloode Stones.

"They warn of the Darkness. It's not all the way gone the way we thought it was. You know, when you danced with those goblins."

"Wait, really?" Orion had helped take down goblins and minor demons in a hell realm not long ago. The threat then had been to open the world so that the demon lord, Abaddon, might have dominion over mortals. Then, when the predicted Darkness came, it would have a toehold in the living worlds, because the mortal plane would always be connected to the other realms, no matter how much fae and gods wished otherwise. "I thought we took care of the demon threat when the big guy died." When Macy and Duncan had killed Abaddon, also known as the Lord of Doom.

"So did the rest of us. But the boss says no. It's connected, she thinks, to demon-kin. Something about you-know-who's mom and that guy she slept with and the other guy who's his dad and—"

"I'm going to stop you right there, Kraft. You're confusing me, and I need all my brainpower to drive." He yawned. "That took a lot out of me." He hadn't talked to Kaia yet tonight. But did he have to? She wasn't *really* his mate. Or was she? Make a choice, Kraft had said.

Well, Orion was making one by not making one. Not about Kaia. He didn't have the energy, frankly, and he'd never admit to anyone that he was so unnerved about a female.

"That lightning was massive," Kraft said as they pulled into the driveway of the house. "And I'm thinking it's not something Mormo or Hecate know about."

Orion frowned.

"Well, they're not going to hear it from me."

Orion parked in the garage and sighed. "Thanks."

"No problem. But now you owe me."

Orion groaned.

"The next time Onvyr loses his mind and tries to attack us, and Mormo puts me on elf-sitting duty, you take my place."

As far as debts went, that one seemed fair. "I suppose I did try to kind of kill you."

Kraft glared and pointed at the scorch mark still healing on his chest. "Kind of?"

Orion flushed, embarrassed to have lost control. "Fine. I'll elf-sit when he loses it. But you don't mention any of this to anyone."

"Scout's honor."

Orion frowned. "Since when were you a Boy Scout?"

"I've eaten a few."

Orion raised a brow.

Kraft scoffed. "Oh please. Not kids. I mean mature, used-to-be Scouts. Does that count?"

"I guess."

Kraft said in a low voice, "Now let's get our stories straight before we're interrogated by 'Mr. Mormo.'" They snickered at the stupid name.

As if they'd conjured him by saying it, Mormo appeared, annoyed as usual.

"What the heck did you two do? I saw that lighting, and it wasn't natural." His steady gaze went from Kraft's bare, healing chest to Orion.

"We got the warlocks." Orion popped the trunk, and Rolf appeared to carry the unconscious warlocks away.

"What happened to the Land Rover?" Mormo blinked. "We just got this fixed!"

"Drug gang," Orion said quickly. "Oh, and I wanted to tell you, some guy named Morpheus said you owe him a drink."

Mormo's face took on a blank expression.

Kraft looked intrigued. "Mormo, who's Morpheus?"

Orion grinned. "No, wait, he told me he had plans to 'tag that sexy magician.' He meant you. So who is the guy?"

Mormo shot him a scorching look before vanishing.

Kraft blinked. "Oh, wow. You have to tell me what that's all about."

Orion slung an arm over his kin's shoulders and tugged him toward the door to the house, where Shadow sat waiting, taking a cat bath. "Sure thing. But let's do it over drinks. Because it's a lot more involved than it seems." He paused and in a lower voice admitted, "I think I had a dream."

Kraft frowned. "Vampires don't dream."

"Exactly."

CHAPTER
TWENTY-ONE

Sunday, January 16

Kaia had thought about it for days, but she refused to be scared of her own mother. It might have been nice to talk to Orion about it last night, but he hadn't shown up before midnight, and she'd been too tired to wait up for him.

Disappointed but trying not to be, she forced herself to not care about seeing him again as she took a boat taxi to her mom's island. She would have swum the whole way, but she still felt odd after that last bout of power swimming in addition to going too near a god's territory. It all felt like a dream, honestly, and she preferred to keep it that way.

Dressed in a cute blue dress that made her feel pretty and gave her a boost of confidence, she'd also added her best leather boots for warmth and because they worked great in the snow. But when she left the dock for the trail leading to the keep, she found it devoid of snow or sludge, the weather also warmer than she'd expected. Still cold, but not bitterly so.

She didn't see Lord Ruin guarding the front gate. Instead, a new minion, this one an ogre, waved her in. He had a blank look, obviously someone her mother had brainwashed. So far so good. And then she entered the front door and froze.

Two of the lycans she'd set free that fateful night stood in the entryway, like the ogre, with blank stares. They wore fancy suits, looking so out of place in finery when she'd recently seen them barely clothed and nearly wild.

Her heart raced, and she wondered if she should leave now, while she still could.

"Oh, Kaia, there you are, sweetie." Sabine waved from just a few steps beyond the foyer.

"H-hi, Mom." *I have to get out of here, stat!*

"Oh, don't mind Len and Bill. They're harmless... but not in bed. Know what I mean?" Sabine tittered. "Of course you don't. You can use them if you want. In fact, consider it my birthday present to you."

"Mom. That's okay." Too late to leave, Kaia stepped forward to receive her mother's hug. It felt a little too tight, but then Sabine let go and tugged her inside.

The smells of apple and cinnamon and the sunlight streaming through the many windows overlooking Puget Sound showed a bright and cheery day, raging against the terror filling Kaia from head to toe. The lycans followed, seating her and her mother at the dining table.

"There we go." Her mother smiled at her, no hint of malice or suspicion darkening her eyes. Her white hair had been pinned up in a sophisticated twist meant to look casual, her makeup artfully applied to enhance but not overwhelm her mother's strong, beautiful features. Sabine wore jeans and a dark purple blouse. The crystals on her necklace winked at the light streaming through the windows.

Nothing about this visit felt off or ugly, though the presence of the lycans made it impossible for Kaia to relax. "Great to see you, Mom. How was the conference?" She accepted a kiss to the cheek while a handsome young satyr took her coat and hung it up for her.

He smiled, bowed his head to Sabine, and walked away. This one not bespelled, apparently.

"I would have gotten you flowers, but they die so easily." Sabine tapped her long nails on rare plates made of kraken bone worth three thousand dollars a place setting.

Her mother had really gone all out. On an early birthday celebration or her last meal, Kaia couldn't say.

Sabine studied her closely. "How are you feeling? More powerful? I had thought that maybe with your father's mage blood in you, you might be on the verge of Becoming."

"I, ah, I'm not sure. I don't feel any differently."

"Well, you never know." Her mother smiled, though the expression didn't reach her eyes. "You could become more powerful than me."

They both laughed, but Kaia felt overly hot and stressed out. The lycans remained in the dining area, standing against the wall like servants ready to fetch for their queen—the White Sea Witch.

She tugged at her collar.

"Are you okay, sweetie? You look a little pale."

"I'm fine." She studied the gloriously set dining table before her. The circular wooden table had a grand winter arrangement of flowers set back to allow room for the tower of finger sandwiches and treats, and to not crowd the small pots of tea they'd be drinking. "This looks amazing."

Above, a chandelier cast a prism of light over the ceiling, making Kaia feel as if in a rainbow winter wonderland. One presided over by the Queen of Hearts from Lewis Carol's *Alice in Wonderland.* At any moment, Kaia expected her mother to say, "Off with her head" and follow through.

Sabine nodded to the wall, and one of the lycans came over to place an assortment of treats on their plates and tea in their cups. He didn't spill a drop.

"Thank you, Len."

He nodded and stepped back like a robot.

Kaia wanted to leave. Despite how amazing it all looked, she had no appetite for cucumber sandwiches, macarons, and her favorite, witch's pat—a strawberry licorice flavored dessert the consistency of marshmallow that paired well with a chocolate biscuit. Instead, she moved her food around on her plate and sipped at her tea while her mother regaled her with stories from her conference.

"So there I was, trying my best to refuse service to the drunken gremlin who didn't need my help to attract a third wife— she was hanging on his every word, a sad little human who wanted *so much* to be magir that she bargained with me—when his first two knocked him over the head and dragged him and the human girl back to his suite, where his twenty-four children wait- ed." Sabine grinned. "Rumor has it he got his third wife pregnant despite the infertility potion his first two wives bought from me. The problem is humans are extremely compatible with gremlins."

Kaia cringed. "Don't gremlin females have litters of up to two dozen babies at a time?"

Sabine chuckled. "Yes, they do. But his new wife got what she asked for. And yes, she's now knocked up with two dozen babies and probably close to death. Gremlins are small when born, but when they start fighting in utero, it takes a special kind of body to handle that kind of trauma." Sabine's wide smile unnerved her, all malice and greed. "I made a killing. Literally." Her mother snorted with laughter.

Kaia had seen her mother like this a few times in her life, and it always made her more than a little uncomfortable. Especially today.

"Oh, there I go talking about myself. What about you, Kaia? Have you been having fun with my vampire?"

"*What?*"

Sabine relaxed, not looking so angry anymore. "I'm kidding. I had a break-in while I was gone."

"Oh, Mom. I'm so sorry. What did they take?" *Please say your computer or silver. Don't mention lycans or a vampire.*

"Some extremely valuable pieces that aren't easily replaced. But I left my marker on them, so I'll know when they turn up soon enough."

Kaia waited for her mother to lower the boom, ready for accusations and shrieking and a major guilt trip, the way she'd reacted upon discovering Sean gone and Kaia left holding his bonds.

But Sabine changed the subject back to the gremlin. "That human girl knew he already had two wives, but she just had to go being number three, or rather, number one." Sabine huffed. "And she wanted him for his money too. Gerhavlin-Staz might be the richest gremlin in Washington, but child support for his nearly two dozen children is going to cost him. His wives are suing for divorce and incompatibility with their husband." She leaned closer and mock whispered, "I gave them that advice for free. But you know what's even better?"

"No, what?" Kaia asked weakly.

"The infertility potion they gave him tampers with his genetic code enough that any children he has with the human wife will be little monsters. I mean, more than they already are. We're talking mini mutants not likely to bond with mother or father."

"Wait. So you helped the husband ruin his marriage with his first two wives and made sure his human wife will have two dozen monster babies?"

"Sadly, he'll probably eat them when they're born. Instincts, you know."

"That's *horrible.*"

Sabine waited a moment before she laughed and laughed. "Oh my gosh. If you could see your face. I'm kidding."

"Oh, good." For a moment there, Kaia had thought her mother really might be a horrible person. Well, more horrible than she already was.

"They won't be monsters, and she will only have one baby unless she has twins."

"Geez, you almost gave me a heart attack."

Sabine's eyes narrowed in thought. "He probably won't eat them until they hit puberty. With any luck, the human girl will have left by then after cleaning out all his money. She was pretty shifty." Her mom winked. "You're so gullible. Honestly, Kaia, I'm a sea witch. We make deals for souls and magic. It's what we do." She tittered, and Kaia swore she saw something nasty in her mother's expression directed at her. But then Sabine blinked, and Kaia saw nothing but motherly affection.

"So what about you? Any new men in your life? Rumor has it you were seen with a handsome charmer the other day."

"Really?" Kaia forced herself not to leap from the table and run away. "Well, maybe Drake. I saw him briefly before he, Jack, and Web went out on another classified mission." She forced a laugh to cover the lie. "I swear, I live with the best roommates. They're perfect men—they're never home."

Sabine appreciated that, Kaia could tell. She'd always thought her mother disliked men, despite going through hordes of them at a time. "Mom, why did you marry Dad? You guys never seemed to get along."

"Now there's a question." Sabine looked thoughtful as she sipped her tea and sighed. "I'm partial to oolong, but this Kashi tea has a lovely bite. Like the spirit for which it was named, it's got two sides. A spicy flavor that eases into a sweet, peppery taste after a bit. Goes very well with a honeyed ricotta cake."

Kaia tried a sip at her mother's urging and broke down coughing. "Quite... a kick."

Sabine chuckled. "So's your father. He's powerful, which I love. But his moral streak leaves something to be desired. You think like him but you're more like me than you'd care to admit. I respect that side of you, you know." Her mother looked proud of her. "You're powerful, Kaia. Or you will be at some point in your future. With your father's genes and mine, you have to be. Rumor has it your father has a demi-god somewhere in his family tree."

"Really?" Her dad had never mentioned that.

"That's a big reason why I married him. To my surprise, we married and got pregnant right away. Or rather, *I* got pregnant. Your father didn't do much more than provide the ingredients, if you know what I mean."

"Mom."

Sabine snickered. "Anyway, nine months later, you popped out." She grabbed a sandwich and followed that with several more, surprising Kaia with her appetite. "Your dad and I had been at each other's throats my entire pregnancy. It was tough." Her eyes shone. "I loved you so much and you weren't even born, but your father nearly ruined the entire experience with his hostility."

Kaia had seen a few videos to prove otherwise, and she knew her mother. Bless him, but her father should be sainted for dealing with Sabine at all. Her mother hadn't been very nice to him. Not like she was to Kaia.

"But then I had you, and I loved you."

Kaia waited for it. The sigh.

Her mother sighed. "Except Rán came for me with her nets, trying to drag me to death at the bottom of the ocean because she mistakenly thought I'd slept with her boor of a husband, Aegir. As if." Sabine snorted. "I left you with your father while I dealt with her."

"How did you deal with her?"

Sabine gave a dainty shrug. "I gave her the woman he'd really slept with, a rival of mine the world was better off without. Rán was happy and finally left me alone, but by then five years had gone by. You were happier with your father, more stable, so I left you there. That's why you didn't live with me, sweetie."

"I know, Mom." *I also know you're full of crap.*

"But I do love you." Her mom kissed her on the cheek. "Just think, you might one day become more powerful than me. Wouldn't that be a kick if you had a Becoming like your father did when he turned twenty-five? It's something to think about, Kaia. You do have mage magic in you."

"No way. I like working at ADR, Mom. It's a great job. I don't want gobs of power or riches or tons of boyfriends. I just want the quiet life I have now, but yeah, maybe with a boyfriend at some point." Kaia smiled then laid it on thick. "I'm so proud to have a grand mage as my dad and *the* White Sea Witch as my mom. I mean, you're famous."

Her mother blushed. "I am." She sipped her tea and looked at Kaia over her cup. "So you really didn't get together with some tall, dark, and handsome stranger while I was gone? No lycans or vampires for you, eh?"

Kaia forced a laugh. "Yeah, right. If I found a vampire, he'd go for my throat. They're not supposed to be friendly. And lycans scare me. They're too rough, at least the ones I've met, minus Jack of course." She smiled at her mom. "More like *you* found some hunky guy at the conference."

"Guy? You mean, guys."

"Ha. Figures."

"No, just one guy." She gave Kaia an odd look. "I really like this one. He's more my type than anyone I've ever met. I think we might have a future together."

"That's great, Mom."

"Do you mean that?"

"I do. I wish you every happiness."

"Thank you, sweetie. With any luck, my dreams will come true." She gave Kaia an intent look that made Kaia distinctly uncomfortable.

"You deserve it. You've worked so hard your whole life."

"I really have." Sabine seemed more than pleased as Kaia continued to compliment her and ask about the classes she'd taken at the conference.

As they wrapped up, Kaia felt a sense of relief to have made it out alive. She glanced at the lycans, still staring into space near the wall.

"Well, I'd better get going." She saw her mom watching the lycans, a sly smile on her mouth, and Kaia's palms grew sweaty. She stood. "I have a lot to do this week. More cataloging, you know how it is."

"Yes, I do. Best of luck, dear." Sabine stood to hug her. "Do me a favor."

"Sure, Mom." Kaia tried to pull back, but Sabine held tight, staring at her eye to eye.

"Don't be a stranger." She walked Kaia down the dock and watched her board the boat taxi manned by the third lycan.

Holy crap. He's going to eat me on the way home. I know it.

"Safe travels." Her mom winked. "Scott will get you where you need to go. Home or wherever."

Kaia gave her a weak smile. "Thanks. Bye."

The lycan said nothing, staring blankly like his friends as he drove away from the island.

CHAPTER TWENTY-TWO

S abine watched her lying daughter leave. She'd known that Kaia had been in the house at least once since her last visit. Not only had the lycans spilled their guts before she'd trapped them in a spell they'd never break, but a small spot of trace magic remained on her daughter's cheek, put there when she'd intruded during Sabine's absence. Though it hurt to know her daughter would be betray her like that, Sabine had a grudging respect for the girl.

"Lied right to my face like a champ." She shouted, "Yeva."

Her nyavka drifted inside, looking uncomfortable. The spirit longed for the open forest and air around her. "Yes, mistress?"

"I want to hear it again. You said you saw me, plain as day, with the vryko when he escaped?"

Yeva nodded.

"My own daughter. You're sure?" It wasn't just that Sabine didn't believe Kaia could do such a thing, but she had a tough time believing Kaia could be so stupid and clumsy about it.

"I am. The vampire carried her with a speed I could not match, but in doing, a piece of her hair fell behind. A single strand which I ate. It tasted of youth and potential, a female unblooded, your daughter." Yeva looked at the lycans standing behind Sabine. "Your wolves testified to the truth. May I have one? I'm hungry."

"Not yet, dear. Thank you, Yeva. You may go." Yeva turned, exposing her fleshless back, still red and wet and plumped with organs since she'd ingested a few fishermen with the bad fortune to run into Belyy Zamok yesterday. The nyavka left, and Sabine stared unseeing after her.

How best to handle what she now knew? Paz had been very clear. Either she delivered the vampire to him, or she would pay his soul price. She'd lost Orion and had been waiting for a visit from the Bloode Empire, fearing the worst case that hadn't come to pass, curiously enough. Which meant that though Kaia had the vryko, she hadn't been able to break the spell on him.

That meant her sly daughter had the vampire in her clutches. No. Wait. Could she?

The girl had lied so well just now. A hint of nerves though she'd stuck out the tea, and she had to know she traversed a thin line between living and dying.

Sabine didn't know what to believe. But she did know the Night Bloode hadn't arrived to take her down. Nor had the Bloode Empire, and if either of those factions knew what she'd done, she'd already be dead.

That meant Orion of the Night Bloode was a still a possibility. She'd gladly trade him to Paz. Yet... Kaia might be coming into power. The girl could say what she wanted, but her twenty-fifth year approached and she remained a virgin. Sabine could sense it. That untapped energy would continue to grow inside Kaia, making her a more than worthy sacrifice than the vampire.

Maybe. What to do? On the one hand, Kaia as a power reflected well on Sabine. On the other, the girl would become a rival. But not if Sabine had a vampire at her beck and call. The perfect answer would be to offer Kaia up to Paz instead of Orion, take the power Paz offered, as well as work her way to becoming his wife. Then offer him Orion as a sacrifice to open the gates to the mortal plane.

That could work, especially if Paz left Orion alive. Then she could chain her vampire for an eternity, using all that glorious bloode in spells and to keep her demon husband happy.

Or she could go with plan A and sacrifice the vampire instead of her daughter. A useful strategy if Kaia proved to be as useless and powerless as she'd been the past twenty-four years.

Only time would tell. Sabine would have to wait and see. Although... a test to prove her daughter's worth might be interesting. After planning something in time for Kaia's birthday, Sabine sat back to relax. Such a creative way to spend the day, she thought, and smiled.

I deserve a treat. She crooked her finger at her new servants, loving their internal struggles with the notion of an eternity of helpless servitude. "Boys, time to service your mistress. Come, little doggies. Let's play."

ORION HAD BEEN WRACKING his brain about what to do with Kaia. The fact she hadn't answered her phone or talked to her sister after tea with her mother bothered him to the point he couldn't think about anything other than the fact Kaia might be in danger.

He swam from Mercer Island to her home, a big idiot in the water watching like a stalker. But when he heard a muffled scream and the scent of her blood reached him, he lost all control.

Racing into her house through locked doors and up the stairs into her bedroom, he found three lycans enshrouded in shadow along with a half dozen ghouls trying to drag Kaia away with them.

The ghouls hadn't bitten her, but the lycans kept nipping at her and laughing, and he caught the scent of brimstone over everything.

Kaia slapped one of the lycans so hard he flew across the room.

Shocked, everyone stopped moving and stared at her while Kaia stared at her own hand in astonishment. Then she spotted him. "Orion! Help me!"

He tossed the ghouls out the window, startled to see them vanish into smoke despite feeling real in his hands. But when he turned to confront the lycans, he paused.

"Welcome back, vryko," one of them said in Sabine's voice.

Another snarled and snapped at him, biting so fast before he leapt through the window that Orion missed him leaving. Odd. The other two watched him but didn't attack.

He clenched his fist at the sudden pain in his hand. A glance showed traces of something black spreading from the bite but stopping halfway up his forearm.

One of the lycans smiled, his eyes empty of anything but darkness. "See you soon," he promised before he and his companion departed.

Orion started to follow when Kaia went into a convulsion.

"*Kaia.*" He put her down on the bed, doing his best to hold her steady so she didn't fall off and bang her head or hurt herself.

The air felt oppressive, a layer of energy spreading throughout the room. The subtle scent of ocean water and a sweet floral essence coated everything and stole the pain from his hand.

He watched as the blackness inside him dissipated. His hand healed, now coated in a bright blue light that slowly vanished.

Kaia arched up once more then sagged to the bed. She didn't move.

Orion leaned close, not prepared for her to open her eyes and scream.

He winced. "Damn. You okay?"

She grabbed him to her in a hug and burst into tears.

He had no idea what he was saying as he patted her back and comforted her, but it seemed to work. She sank into oblivion once more, but this time she looked at ease.

With no idea what the hell was going on, Orion gathered her in his arms and walked her down the stairs to the ground level, past the back porch to the dock and into the water.

Feeling much better, he swam with her back to the house and walked her in through the pool. He didn't see anyone on his way inside, fortunately, the rest of them out on missions except for Kraft, who was still messing with the lycan in the basement. But Orion had a feeling Kraft had given up on torturing the wolf since he continued to lose to him at *Mortal Kombat 11*.

Swiftly returning to his room, Orion locked the door behind him, setting a special vryko lock to keep the nosy fuckers out— namely, Kraft. Then he cleaned both himself and Kaia and settled her under the covers in bed.

She seemed even more beautiful than the last time he'd seen her, something about her different. He frowned, not sure what to think by the fact her skin seemed paler, her hair darker, and when she'd opened her eyes earlier, there had a been a soft blue light in her pupils for the briefest second.

He needed to talk to Macy about it, but agitated at letting Kaia out of his sight, he decided to keep her close instead. *Safe. Mine. My prey,* he told himself and relaxed. He slipped into a pair of shorts then eased next to her in bed and watched her sleep, her heart beating in time with his.

"So, what are you planning to do about her?" Morpheus asked.

Orion groaned. "Who the hell let you in here?" He glanced around and saw Kaia in his bed. "I'm not dreaming."

"Are you sure?" Morpheus smiled. "What did Mormo say when you told him I'm waiting for that drink?"

Orion recalled and grinned. "He can't wait to see you."

"Really?" Morpheus looked surprised

"No. He turned sheet-white and vanished."

"Wimp. Him, not you." Morpheus disregarded him with a wave. Then he looked closer at Kaia. "Oh, this is interesting."

Orion curled around her. "What?"

"Relax. She's cute and all, but she's been tagged as demon bait."

"*What?*"

Morpheus pointed to a spot on her neck just under her nape. "See that? She's been bought and sold. Might want to fix that before her owner comes calling." Morpheus shook his head. "Shame too. She's on the verge of Becoming."

"What does *that* mean?" Orion couldn't stop looking at the tiny black dot on the back of her neck. *Shit.* Had her mother done that to her? Or had it been the possessed lycans and ghost ghouls, or whatever they were? He needed Macy's help. Or Mormo's. Maybe Hecate's?

Morpheus cocked his head. "Sorry, boy-o. Gotta motor." He vanished.

"Bastard." Orion gathered Kaia to him, concerned. And then the strangest thing happened. The dot disappeared, and he blinked up at his ceiling, now lying flat on his back next to Kaia, who remained asleep.

Careful, so as not to wake her, he shifted her head and lifted her hair. And breathed a sigh of relief to see nothing marring her skin. He lay back beside her and watched her eyes open. No blue in their depths, just a deep, dark brown that looked black, her eyes shadowed by thick lashes, her lips the richest rose.

"Orion?" she whispered then struck him right in the feels with a smile that grew. "Orion." She sighed, cupped his cheek, then went back to sleep.

My mate. He heard her say and jumped out of bed, worried she'd bewitched him somehow.

For a second there, he'd almost said something schmaltzy, near poetic about the moonlike glow of her skin, or the bloode-red kiss of her lips.

"Shit." He waited as he watched her, prepared for some other weirdness. When nothing happened, he left the room, relocked it, and ran into Hecate. It was all he could do to contain a tiny jump of surprise.

She looked up at him, small in this incarnation. "Have you seen Kraft with our prisoner?"

"He was downstairs playing *Mortal Kombat* with the guy."

"Really? Because he's not there now, and Varu wants a word with the lycan."

Orion shrugged. "No idea."

Hecate stared at him. More like through him, but whatever.

"I sense a water mage about." She smiled. "Is Kaia here?"

Orion cleared his throat and glared down at the nosy goddess. "She's resting."

"Oh, good. When she wakes, bring her to me in the basement, if you would." She took his hand in hers. "Hmm. What's this? A smudge, I think." She rubbed the exact spot where the possessed lycan had bitten him earlier. Then she dropped his hand and turned to go.

"Hecate?"

"Yes?"

"Can a magir or human be tagged by a demon? Sold without knowing it?"

"Of course. It's only too common in the slave markets, in particular in Galla-Ahtma, a stone's throw from Irkalla."

"Huh?"

"The Mesopotamian underworld, also known as Kur." She frowned. "Pazuzu has been known to frequent such places."

"The same demon Sabine's been messing with," he murmured.

"That's just an example. Heck, if you run into the wrong person, you can come back from Pike Place Market with a demon tag." She snorted. "Steer clear of the fish market if you're smart." She laughed. "I'm kidding." She continued to chuckle at her own joke, which Orion didn't find at all funny. "Did you have something else you needed?"

"What? No. I'm good." He took a step back. "I'll bring Kaia when she's awake."

"Do that." She left.

Orion didn't know what to do. Hecate didn't seem bothered by his hand, and he'd been dreaming that bit about Morpheus and Kaia's demon mark. But it couldn't be a coincidence that Hecate mentioned Pazuzu and Galla-Ahtma in the same breath.

He heard Kaia stirring and let himself back into his room.

Unfortunately, she'd sat up, the covers pooled around her waist.

She didn't seem to realize he'd put her to bed without her clothes.

He really should look away. *But I can't.*

Kaia glanced at Orion, seeming confused about how she'd come to be where she was.

He couldn't stop staring at her breasts, a bit less than a handful, tipped with hard, rosy nipples just begging for a bite.

It took her a long moment to realize she was naked. "Oh." She grabbed the covers and held them over her chest, a pretty blush coloring her cheeks. "Thanks a lot."

A little sarcastic there, Kaia. "For saving your ass from demonic lycans? You're welcome," he growled.

She blinked. "That wasn't a dream?"

He leaned against the back of his door and crossed his thick arms over his chest, bursting with muscle. The shorts he wore came to just above his knees and only emphasized his powerful thighs and trim waist. And that bulge between his legs grew as she stared.

He wished he couldn't read her thoughts, but her need was obvious. Hell, he could smell her creaming for him as she watched him, her gaze zeroed on his cock that felt like steel the longer she stared.

Orion cleared his throat, wondering how far to take her game.

She whipped her gaze to his. "What?"

He wanted her to want him, needed her like he needed blood. And the feelings, emotions cascading through him as he looked at his pretty, frail mate. It felt like a trap, so much pressure to protect her, to be what she needed. Fuck, he couldn't handle it and not want her so desperately.

None of which felt remotely *real* to him but like that fucking enslavement spell cast by her mother and then Kaia.

He snarled at her, not buying for a minute her cringe as real. "*You* did this."

"What?"

"You get off on me wanting you."

"I do not." She bit her lip, and he smelled a more intense desire emanating from the sea nymph. What would be natural coming from her sister nymphs, but what had never been normal from Kaia before.

"Cut it out."

"I'm not doing anything," she cried and clutched the coverlet in front of her.

"So this intense need is all my doing, huh?"

"No. Yes. I don't know." She did the vulnerable bit a little too well.

"Come on. Let's just get it over with. We both know you want this." He cupped the raging erection his shorts couldn't hide, so he dropped them. "It's not a spell. It's normal need." Bullshit, but he wanted to see if he could get her to admit the truth. "You want sex. So do I. How about you give that V-card you've been saving up for a rainy day? Maybe then I'll believe you're not putting a spell on me."

"How does that correlate or make any kind of sense?" she asked, her temper high.

Not so frail now, eh, princess? "It doesn't. But maybe I want to know that the woman I'm going to sleep with is real. That she didn't use magic to get what she wants. You give me that V-card you've been saving up. I'll give you the best sex of your life, because it will be real, not a spell." He paused. "And maybe I'll forgive you for putting me under your spell the last time."

She turned a bright red with what seemed like shame, not anger. "I never meant to hurt you. I was trying to help."

He hated how he felt. Suffocated by affection and unfamiliar feelings he couldn't trust as his own. Wanting her to the exclusion of all sense. "Damn it. I want to trust you, but I can't, and it hurts," he said, his voice thick with uncertainty, that he didn't know his own mind anymore. Afraid. A vryko, feeling fear. It was unheard of. "What the fuck are you doing to me?" he yelled, clutching his head, trying to look away but unable to resist her.

"You're acting like this is all my fault. I didn't mean any of it. But I can't sleep with you to prove it, you big bastard." She started crying, and he couldn't tell if her tears were true or not. "I don't want my first time to be coerced. That's rapey."

It was, and he had never in his life forced sex. It went against everything the vryko believed in to sexually assault one who could give birth to young, the act of conception a sacred one first born by Alecta.

Orion cringed deep inside while taking refuge in anger. "You're right. It is! So get the fuck out. Go stay with Macy or your dad. Or hey, I know. Why not hang with Sabine so you can share stories of how you take advantage of ensorcelled males?"

Kaia stared at him, that blue in her eyes returning, so beautiful he felt ensnared and hated himself for it.

Waiting for her to just cast her spell and be done with it, he wasn't prepared when she burst into tears and turned away from him, sobbing her heart out as she cried. "I'm so sorry. It's all my fault. I'm sorry."

CHAPTER
TWENTY-THREE

Kaia had lost it. She couldn't stop crying, all of Orion's blame settling firmly over her shoulders, where it belonged. She'd never meant to enslave him. And the fact she had showed she was just like her mother, a woman who did evil things to get power at the expense of everyone but herself, only proved he was right to distrust her.

"I'm sorry, Orion. Please, forgive me. Forgive me." She continued to sob, wishing she'd been better, stronger like her father. Then maybe she could have cut the spell her mother had made without hurting Orion. Because she heard his pain. Hell, she could feel it, as if his confusion, longing, and self-loathing belonged to her.

Lost in her head, she jumped when he took her in his arms and hugged her. "Damn it, stop crying," he said, his voice harsh, his hold gentle. "Okay, I was kidding. I don't want you. I'm just hard up, that's all. Any woman would do."

Stop crying, Kaia. You're killing me.

She imagined him cradling her with tenderness, and it was no fantasy. He held her in his arms and rocked her, his big body hard and strong, yet never harmful. Safe.

"I don't want you, okay? I just want to stop craving you. It's my fault. Not yours. I'm just mad at myself." He stroked her hair and kissed the top of her head. "I'm going to take you home after Hecate says it's okay. Just relax. No one's taking any V-cards." He sighed. "No coercion. No rapey vampire. It was all nonsense. Go back to sleep."

He tried to move away, but she clamped her arms around his neck and held tight.

And the cover dropped between them, her bare breasts grazing his naked chest.

They both froze. He didn't so much as breathe. Then again, he didn't really need to.

But she could feel his heart racing, and she felt hers hurry to match his. Not consciously changing her body chemistry, yet she sensed it responding to the perfect male in her arms.

His mate. Her mate. They belonged together.

Then she realized she was picking up on his thoughts again. Images of him sliding inside her causing a fever to burn.

"Sorry," he said in a voice so low she had to work to hear him. "I can't help it."

"Because I'm your mate," she said. "I'm yours. And you're mine. And no spell can make that happen."

She took a chance to glance up into bloode-red eyes. "Orion?"

"Kaia," he whispered. "I'm a killer. I hunt for pleasure. I'm not soft. I can't be what you need." But he wanted to with everything he was, and the waves of need in his bloode reached her without having to try.

"Orion, I—"

"I need to go." He pulled away from her, standing on shaking legs. He snarled again, facing away from her, but he didn't take a step.

Kaia stared, seeing the same vampire she'd fallen in love with. A little coarser, a little more violent. Okay *a lot* more violent. But the real essence of him remained the same. She didn't know why it had taken her so much effort to see that truth.

"Orion, do you want me?"

"Fuck yeah, I want you," he snapped and turned around. "What the hell do you think this is?" He pointed at his huge shaft, and like before, he seemed to grow. Not just his cock, but all of him. Bigger, broader, taller.

"No. I mean me." She dared to look into his eyes. There she saw and felt it all, his hopes and needs, the loneliness he refused to admit to having, and that hint of fear that he'd never be worthy of a female like her. "Do you want a sometimes timid water nymph with a witch of a mother? A girl—a woman—who loves books and kittens and home shopping on TV?"

He quivered but didn't look away from her eyes. "I'm not gentle. I'm a vampire. We're cruel and we kill. I love blood. The color red. And maybe hot cocoa. But not with marshmallows." He let a fang show when he gave a small grin.

"How about carrot cake?" She smiled, wiping away the rest of her tears.

"Never. It's disgusting."

"I'll never drink blood."

"I can handle that."

"I, um, might be turning into something else."

He frowned. "Like what?"

"My parents and sister think I'm Becoming. It's like, a level-up for mages."

He stared at her. "Am I supposed to care? Kaia, I want you. I can't think for wanting you. So if you want me to go, it needs to be now. Right now."

She stared at him, letting go of old hurts and old insecurities. She'd been waiting for the right man her whole life. So what if this one wasn't a man at all, but a dangerous predator who looked at her as if he'd never look at another?

I won't once I have you.

She heard what he didn't say. "I'm new at this, so you'll have to be patient with me." She held out her arms, expecting him to pounce on her.

But he walked carefully, like a cat stalking prey. No sudden moves, and then he was sliding into his bed with her, rolling her under him as he pushed aside the covers.

"You sure?" he asked one final time. "Because once I start, I might not be able to stop." He brushed her hair off her neck. "I don't want to hurt you."

"But if I'm your mate, not because of a spell or magic, but because I'm truly yours, will that hurt *you?*"

"Making you cry already hurts. Not being with you pains me. Thinking you might be in trouble has me raging to protect you." His voice grew lower, the rumble from a large predator. "I crave you. Your smile feeds me, makes my heart pump and my soul bright."

"I thought vampires didn't have souls," she whispered, in awe of her mate, at the love she saw that he dared not admit, so overwhelmed his eyes welled with emotion. "Orion?"

"You talk too much."

He startled her into a laugh. "You talk too much, *mate,*" she corrected.

He groaned. "I give up. You talk too much, mate."

She kissed him, giving him the permission, and the love, she'd been holding back for so long.

Orion kissed her back, his tongue invading, his hands everywhere his lips soon followed.

He suckled from her breasts, biting the taut tips until she couldn't stop writhing, hungry for completion.

"Make me yours," she demanded and clutched his head to her chest, keening when he finally pushed his finger inside her.

He pulled back, his eyes glowing, his fangs sharp. "You're so fucking wet."

"Yes, in me." She pulled him back down, not flinching when his fang tore her lip.

He lapped up her blood and moaned, removing his finger while he replaced it with something much bigger. Then he rose up on his hands and stared into her eyes.

"Watch me while I enter you."

She stared at him, feeling everywhere they touched. He pushed into her slick sheath and kept going, the feeling of fullness so pleasurable she started coming, clamping down on him while he continued to thrust.

His eyes narrowed, and his heart raced faster. But Orion wouldn't be rushed, and while she came, lost in pleasure, he made love to her, his body so slow, his taking so thorough, that she continued to seize as he moved, the overpowering rapture of a sea nymph in love.

The rocking of his body was like an ocean of ecstasy, and she cried his name, lost in the storm of their making.

"Kaia, let me, *yes,*" he hissed and stilled, releasing a flood into her, the climax ongoing as he spilled down her thighs and began to move again, still hard. "Gods and demons and everything in between, I'm not done, mate. Not done," he moaned and took her once more.

But this time he withdrew and flipped her over, onto her hands and knees. He lifted her ass higher and entered her again, feeling huge from behind.

"Orion, yes."

"I'm going to fuck you all night long. Coming with you, Kaia. Over and over. Until neither of us can walk, *agapi mou.*"

This sex felt so different, so wild and raw. He pounded into her, doing everything to make it pleasurable, following her thoughts as she guided him to what she needed, feeding off of what he needed. She'd had no idea making love could be so all-consuming. She could think of nothing but Orion, feeling so full and stretched and pleasured.

He put a hand under her and rubbed her clit, and the climax took her over, her body listening to his, squeezing him with her inner walls into an orgasm that had him roaring. He stayed like that inside her, pumping his seed that seemed never-ending.

Just as she thought they were done, her desire returned.

"Oh no, mate. We've hours to go," he promised.

And the sea nymph buried inside her for so long exploded into being as he withdrew and moved underneath her. "Ride me, Kaia. Let me watch those pretty tits while you suck me dry with that pussy."

She shivered. "Is this normal?" She didn't see any blood from losing her virginity, just the pale pink semen from Orion all over her thighs and womanly curls.

"It's normal for us," he murmured. "Now bring those pretty breasts to my mouth."

"Only if you promise to bite and suck them."

He tensed. "Bite?"

"And suck those pearls of blood you took earlier."

He groaned. "You're making me way too hard too soon."

She licked her lips. "You wanted a sea nymph. Now you have one."

"No. I wanted you. The sea nymph stuff is add-on."

She smiled. "Wait 'til you see what I can do with my lady muscles."

"Your what?"

She showed him not much later, and his eyes rolled back in his head as he came like a geyser, filling his pretty mate with everything he had to give.

Including his love.

Kraft, Khent, and Rolf listened to Orion and Kaia from across the hall in Kraft's room. They'd been going at it for hours, and Kraft had to hand it to his kin for some kind of stamina.

"I think that might be a new vampire record," Rolf said with a big grin. "You're saying they haven't taken a break since they started?"

Kraft made a face. "I've been trying to tune them out, but unless I leave my room, I keep hearing them. How the hell are the others not bothered by this?" Kraft didn't mind his friend finally getting lucky. But by the Night, he was starting to feel jealous. It had been a while since he'd had a female. Maybe he ought to find one and see if he could get one to make him groan that loud.

"Macy and Fara are working in Fara's lab," Khent said. "Duncan and Varu are following up on that odd storm by the nest of warlocks you found."

"Oh, right."

Orion let out another satisfied groan.

"What is that? Six or seven times now?" Rolf asked.

"I can't take it." Kraft took Shadow out from under the pillow where he'd been hiding and headed for the basement. Khent peeled off to his laboratory, no doubt to play with more dead things. Rolf disappeared, to keep listening to Orion and Kaia—*creepy*—or disappear to wherever he disappeared to whenever he wanted to leave.

Unfortunately, instead of his new lycan buddy, Kraft found Hecate and a weird bar that stretched so far he couldn't see where it ended. Which was super weird because the basement only had so much space on the land Hecate had purchased in Mercer Island.

"Hold there, Kraft. I'll be right with you," Hecate called, looking hot as hell in stilettos, a dress that showed some leg with a tight, V-cut bodice, and long, black hair with witch-red lips, her skin a warm brown that smelled like rich earth and mystical female. Hmm. He might just prefer this version of her forms over the others she'd worn. Hel-lo, Goddess.

She was deep in conversation with a dead-looking witch in a flapper dress and bell-shaped hat. Without looking at him, the dead witch fixed him a drink and slid it down the bar, where it stopped directly in front of him.

He took a sip, delighted to find it tasted like rich blood and moonlight with a hint of fae.

"Eh, wolfé, might ye be lookin' fer company?" The giant dryad by his side had muscles bigger than his own and the greenest eyes he'd seen outside fae lands. She sounded part fae and part Irish and had to stand several feet taller than his own height.

Before he could answer, her gaze locked on a tall fae with antlers, a longbow over one shoulder, and a squirrel that kept running from shoulder to shoulder, occasionally scampering into the tall male's spines.

"You evil pile of sticks," the male boomed, and half the glasses near him shattered.

Interesting.

"Who are you calling a pile of sticks, you dead tree?" she boomed back.

They rushed each other and fell through the floor at a wave from a male in a long robe. Mormo? When had he arrived?

"They need couples counseling in the worst way," a sprite near the now vanished couple said.

A few others nearby nodded.

Kraft finished his drink, his thirst quenched. A low meow and a scratch across his belly reminded him he wasn't alone.

He watched as a bowl of milk slid down the bar and stopped

in front of him without spilling a drop. The kitten climbed up his body, using him as a scratching post.

"Ow. Here, damn it." Kraft pulled the clingy thing away and placed Shadow by the milk.

The little kitten drank a lot more than something of that size should be able to ingest, including the second and third bowls that arrived.

"What the hell are you, cat?"

Shadow looked at him then turned back to his meal, ignoring Kraft as if unimportant.

"Bastard." He turned at the sight of Mormo, standing a few people down from him at the bar, arguing with some dark-haired, divine-looking fuck in a toga. Not Norse, but maybe belonging to a Greek or Roman pantheon.

"I do *not* owe you a drink," Mormo snapped. "Stop following me around."

"Sweet cheeks, I hate to break it to you, but we need to talk. And yes, you do have a stellar personality and just the nicest ass, but we've got problems."

Kraft grinned, entertained. He would have settled in to watch Mormo's head explode—if the color of his eyes and scent of his anger was anything to go by—but a commotion from behind him stole his attention.

"Grab him," Khent yelled.

Kraft saw the lycan they'd been questioning for a week slung over the back of a great big, shifted direwolf, this one larger than a typical lycan in shifted form. "Berserker?" he yelled to Khent, who nodded.

Khent's dead crow flew after the escaping lycans, but the giant one turned and ate the bird in one bite before running again.

"You'll die for that," Khent pledged, getting ready to work some death magic, Kraft could tell.

"Khent, *no,*" Hecate ordered.

"Stay here, cat." Kraft ran after the lycans down a hall that emptied of people and just kept going. Had to be part of Hecate's weird border magic, since she was a guardian of crossroads after all.

The berserker looked over its shoulder at Kraft, its blue eyes brilliant in a face covered in ash-gray fur speckled with black. It seemed to recognized Kraft, or at least, the wolf part of him knew something strange centered around that lycan carrying their prisoner. Unfortunately, the pair were sucked away, and Kraft somehow came to a standstill in front of Hecate back in the bar.

He wavered, trying to find his footing. "What the fuck?"

"Watch your tone, nachzehrer," Mormo warned, flipped off the toga-wearing god next to him—who winked at Kraft before disappearing—and turned with Kraft to face Hecate. "My lady, I do believe our lycan prisoner has left the building."

"I know." She sighed. "And I was just getting to like her."

"Wait. Her?" Kraft scowled. "The lycan I played with was male."

"Yes, he was. But that's not who we were after." Hecate drummed her fingers on the bar. "Now Kraft, tell me about Orion and Kaia. Exactly what's going on upstairs?"

"I'd rather talk about the lycans."

Mormo frowned. "Mistress? What's this about Kaia?"

She laughed. "Dear one, we've got another dreamer. Orion has mated the sea witch."

Wait. Sea witch?

Mormo and Kraft said as one, "*What?*"

CHAPTER
TWENTY-FOUR

O rion woke feeling sore but happy. And he didn't do happy.
Not feeling happy sounded right in his head. The need
to tamp down his negativity and present a bright face to his mate
wasn't there, not like it had been before.

He sighed with relief, turned, and stared at a very naked Kaia.
He froze.

She smiled and traced a finger down his abdomen to his belly,
where his cock stirred and stiffly pointed at the creature he
wanted like no other. Still. As if they hadn't spent the entire night
fucking until the sun had sent him into a death sleep.

But now, as the sun set, he stared into eyes pricked with blue
and smiled. "I feel crabby about life."

"Good." Her smile widened. "I'm still not drinking blood and
killing people because it's fun."

"Uh, okay." Had they agreed she should do that? He couldn't
think because she followed her finger with her mouth, which
settled on that very happy part of him pointing at her.

She took him between her lips and started sucking.

He held her head, dreaming, obviously, but rode out the pleasure as she blew him, taking him to the back of her throat while

she cupped his balls and dragged her nails up and down his thighs.

The need to fill her wouldn't leave him, and he yanked her off him before he came and flipped her to her back then shoved inside her pussy, pounding hard to fill her while she seized around him and moaned his name, milking him dry.

"Fuck, Kaia. Oh man, I can't..." He jolted, coming again, the pleasure unrelenting.

Finally able to function, he blinked his eyes open and stared into Kaia's beautiful face. At least, he thought it was Kaia.

"That was amazing." She smiled, then frowned. "Orion, what's wrong?"

It sounded like her. It still looked, smelled, and—

"You *bit* me." She gasped.

—tasted like her. But... "Kaia. You're different."

"Huh?"

"Your hair."

She touched her head. "What about it?" She lifted a strand and stared. "What the heck is happening?" She pushed at his chest, and he withdrew, sad to leave her warmth but way too concerned to have another go.

Or so he told his randy dick.

He followed her into the adjoined bathroom and stared over her head at the mirror.

"I'm whiter than a ghost." Her hair glowed.

"You're still you." He felt weak with relief but refused to show it. "Thank the Night. I thought I was having a sexy night-mare. Not cool."

"Vampires dream?"

"Apparently." He ran his fingers through her hair. "Okay, I'll say it. You do look a little like your mom. But you're different enough that I know it's you. And not just because of your kind eyes."

She softened. "Thank you."

"Or because of your sweet ass."

She rolled her eyes.

"But because I feel you inside here." He put his hand over his heart. She turned, and he took her hand and put it where his had been. "Feel me. I'm in you."

We're one.

She smiled.

"I'm still cranky too." He felt really happy about that, more so when she laughed at him. "I know, I sound like a dope. But I need to be me with you."

"I understand." She twirled her hair around her finger and stared at it. "And I guess I need to be me around you. I think I'm Becoming, Orion."

"You mean you Became. All night long." He felt pretty proud about that fact and laughed when she blushed. "Sorry. That was crude."

"But that's who you are, yeah yeah," she grumbled, adorable.

"Oh crap."

"What?"

"Smoky—I mean, Shadow—is going to be really mad at me. I kept him out all night." He sighed.

"I'll talk to him."

"Will you?" He knew it sounded goofy, but Shadow understood him. The little cat had been his companion for the last few months, a balm to his lonely nights feeling apart from his kin. "He'll like you."

"Don't worry."

"I should be saying that to you." He hugged her. "The white hair is sexy. It's the new you. Accept it."

"I need to see my dad.'"

"Okay. We'll go together."

She paused.

"What?"

"What happens now? My mom still wants to sacrifice you. She tried to kidnap me." Kaia paused. "And I think I might be turning into her."

He hugged her. "No, *agapi mou*. You're you. You're just getting new power. You said it's a thing that happens to mages, right? Let's go talk to Mormo. He'll know more."

She blinked at him with a shy smile. "What does *agapi mou* mean?"

He hadn't realized he'd said it. "Ah, it's an endearment." It meant *my love,* but he felt it too soon to admit how he felt.

They cleaned up and dressed, Kaia having clothing in his armoire, because apparently that thing was magic too. Orion shook his head but couldn't complain about Kaia in tight jeans and a cute top that showed off her slender curves. She put her hair back in ponytail, and it accented her oval face and ruby lips.

He frowned. "Are you wearing makeup?"

"What? No."

He hated to say it, but he had to. "Don't take this the wrong way, but I'm an expert on Disney movies. And you are rockin' the Snow White look minus the dark hair. You're pale, with white hair, blue-black eyes that have a blue glint in the light, and those red, ripe lips." He had to kiss her and would have gone for a second round of lovemaking had Kaia not pushed him back.

"Mormo first."

He sighed. "Yeah. And Shadow. Then I fuck you some more." He sighed again. "When you blush, you look like a straight-up princess. *My* princess," he growled, feeling possessive.

After a quick kiss, because Orion had no discipline when it came to *his mate,* he thought with satisfaction, they searched for Mormo and found him in the kitchen pacing.

He wore normal clothes for once, jeans and a long-sleeved tee-shirt like the rest of them, looking almost human.

Mormo took one look at Kaia and stopped. "Well, well. What have we here?"

Kaia blushed.

"A true beauty." Mormo bowed, and Orion growled, not liking Mormo playing the gentleman.

"Flirt on your own time, Mormo."

"Ah, the gentle bridegroom. I hope you were gentle with him, Kaia."

She laughed, her cheeks pink, so incredibly pretty. Orion's heart beat just for her.

"A good match," Hecate said, appearing out of nowhere. "A sea witch for a vrykolakas." She smiled. "Do you see, Orion? The heart is more powerful than the brain or the body."

"Whatever, Hecate."

Kaia's eyes widened. "H-hello, um, Goddess Hecate."

Hecate's smile was full as she put a hand on Kaia's head. "You have some growing to do, young nymph. But you'll get there." She glanced at Orion. "With any luck, you'll have a positive influence on your mate."

"Hecate," he growled.

Kaia's smile faded. "Am I nymph or a witch? Am I going to turn evil?"

Mormo blinked. "What?"

"I'm like Sabine now. I can feel myself getting stronger, more powerful. Will I do bad things to people?"

Orion would have laughed, but Kaia looked serious. "What? No." He could feel the truth of her in his bloode, and though yes, she had become more powerful, she was nothing like Sabine.

"We have need of your father, I think." Mormo shared a look with Hecate.

She vanished.

Mormo turned to Kaia. "Can you call him and ask if he'd meet us somewhere?"

She nodded. "I need a phone." Mormo handed her one out of thin air, and she dialed. "Hello. Dad? I'm fine. I'm okay." She paused and turned pink. "I'm sorry. But, well, I need your help. Can I—can we meet you somewhere?"

Orion heard her father more clearly and smirked.

"Yes, and the damn vryko. Mormo wants to meet you too."

Over the phone, Will Dunwich sighed. "Fine. Swing by the house. I'll be here all night."

Mormo nodded. "Let's take the express lane."

KAIA HAD no idea Mormo could open a gateway right in front of her father's house. Wow. She trembled, trying to stop the dizziness as she stepped out of that funky void he'd produced in the kitchen back in Mercer Island.

"You okay?" her gruff mate asked, looking concerned.

The affection inside him flared bright for her, and she knew that no matter what came next, she could honestly say she'd known a perfect night. It had started with tears and ended with a connection that went soul deep—for both of them.

He frowned then slowly smiled, reading her mind. "Pretty perfect, yeah."

"Kaia?" Her dad left the front porch and met them halfway across his front lawn.

She couldn't read his face as he took in her new hair color, but he swept her into a tight hug without hesitation. Grateful for that acceptance, she hugged him back until a familiar growl made her smile.

She pulled back. "Dad, you know Orion."

"Honestly. I'm a good person. I'm not sure how I keep getting involved with blood-suckers," he muttered.

"*Dad.*"

Her father reluctantly released her and gave Orion a sweeping onceover. "The vryko. I'm not surprised."

Orion yanked her close, glaring at her father until she cleared her throat and subtly stepped on his foot to get his attention.

"What?"

She frowned. "Be nice, please."

He gave an exasperated breath but nodded to her dad. "Mage."

"Vamp." Then her father turned to Mormo and smiled. "Magician, welcome to my home."

Mormo shook her dad's hand and pounded him on the back. "Good to see you, Will. How's Diana?" The two turned and swept into the house, leaving Kaia looking at Orion in surprise.

"They seem pretty friendly," he said as they followed.

"I know. That's weird."

"Not weird," her dad said and closed the door behind them. He gestured to the dining room, where he'd laid out some food. "After we fought with Mormo in the Chaos Coliseum, and Macy joined his cult" —Mormo's raised a brow, and her father amended — "I mean, *clan*, it made sense to keep tabs on the new power vampires in the city. But I found that Mormo's a pretty sensible guy. And Diana got to meet Hecate, which checked off one of her bucket list items. She had a thing at work or she'd be here, Kaia."

"I know." She did. Diana had always been there for her, and Kaia loved her unreservedly.

Orion squeezed her shoulders, standing behind her like a rock she could always rely on. She felt him hum with satisfaction, pleased to be useful and protective, which was new. She'd been hearing his thoughts on and off but not sensing his emotions. She didn't know if she liked that. Did that mean he could read hers too?

He leaned down and whispered, "You okay?"

"I'm fine." She smiled over her shoulder at him.

"Well, that's to be determined," her father said, drawing her attention once more. "Mormo, you don't sense any demonic energy in her, do you?"

"No."

Kaia heard a question there.

Orion lifted her hair and stared at the back of her neck. "Nothing here."

"What?"

"Never mind." He let her hair go and stepped back while her father flashed a net of golden energy over her. Awash in mage magic, she relaxed into his psychic touch, feeling at ease with her growing power despite not yet knowing what she could do.

Her father finally stepped back. It felt like a warm bath of power that took no time, but when she looked at the clock on the wall, she realized an hour had passed.

"Well, you're definitely more than a sea nymph now. I mean, the white hair confirmed it."

"What does that mean?"

He smiled tiredly. "It means you're the new White Sea Witch in town. And your mother is not going to be pleased."

CHAPTER TWENTY-FIVE

O rion hadn't wanted to leave Kaia with her father, but he had some important things to do back at the house. Namely, let his patriarch know he'd taken a mate without asking permission first. But then, he was only following in Duncan's footsteps. They weren't a true bloode clan by definition. None of them were into all the posturing and respect-is-due shit that the rest of the bloode clans employed. In the Night Bloode, respect had to be earned, not automatically deserved.

But he did respect Varu, so he needed to talk with the strigoi. And honestly, ever since the male had mated Fara, he'd become a lot easier to deal with.

He and Mormo stepped back through the portal into the house. *His* house, Orion figured he could admit, because no way would he return to the island he'd once called home and leave behind his new freedom and his new mate. In Santorini, he'd be expected to get a child on Kaia then take it away to raise if a boy. Kaia would be forced to leave. And if a girl, the child would leave with her mother.

The thought of never having Kaia in his life didn't work for him. And if Varu didn't like his vryko mated, then Varu could go fuck himself, and Orion would find a new place to live.

The strength of that thought, of his acceptance of his new sea witch mate, pleased him enough to leave him smiling when he met with Varu outside on the back deck under the sliver of moon trying so hard to shine.

"So, Macy's sister?" Varu said without emotion after some moments of silence.

As good a way as any to break the ice. "Yep."

Varu stared at him. Orion stared back.

"If I tell you I don't accept the mating, what will you do?"

Orion flashed his fangs in warning. "I don't need your permission. I'm letting you know it's done."

Varu just watched him. "Her mother's a problem."

"Tell me something I don't know. If it wouldn't hurt Kaia, I'd kill her myself."

Varu nodded. "I figured." He gave Orion a slow grin. "Congratulations, you big idiot. You got yourself mated to a powerful witch. Fara and I were talking, and the Bloode Stones—all three of them—gave us a huge shine of approval at sunset. It's a good pairing, you being a vryko with a water-magir."

"Yeah. I hadn't planned on it, but back home, most of us mate with those bonded to water in some way. I... She's mine. I won't let her go."

"Good. I think it's healthier for us to decide what we do with mates than go off what our fucked-up ancestors decided was right for us. I can tell you if Fara and I do have a child, and it turns out to be female, it won't matter. My kin belong with me."

"I agree." Orion hadn't realized Varu could be so personable. "Why are you being nice to me?"

Varu chuckled. Another shocker. "Because you finally took your head out of your ass and are behaving sensibly. You still have the bloodlust, aggression, and sheer meanness of your kind, but you're balanced now." Varu cocked his head. "Yes, he is. Much better."

Orion cringed. He hated when Varu communed with the Bloode Stones.

"Now, what are we going to do about this demon Sabine's been talking to?"

Good, something Orion *wanted* to talk about. "Kill it, of course. I'm not happy that she used me to tell it our secrets. That bothers me."

"Mormo and I have been talking about it. Pazuzu can't cross into this world without help. We think he'll use the Bloode Stones, or your bloode the sea witch already stole, to somehow allow him to cross planes. But he won't have the power to stay here without a sacrifice." Varu paused. "There's been a lot of discussion lately about whether or not we have souls. We don't."

"We don't?" Huh. Orion had started to think that maybe he did since coming to love Kaia.

"No, we have something else that functions in the same way, but a lack of a soul is why Hecate has no power over us in death. Why the gods can't affect us unless we let them, not when it comes to free will. The only way Sabine was able to get through to you was your willing taking of her blood. Then, while you were drugged on her poisons, she used demon energy to bind you."

Mormo appeared and nodded. "Yes, your kind has more in common with those from the hell planes than you want to admit, but it's true. That's why Hecate's ancient grimoire had been sealed with vampire bloode to keep a demon imprisoned. And why Sabine is trying to use you, Orion, to pull the demon Pazuzu and his father, Hanbi, from Irkalla. Make no mistake, Pazuzu wants to be here, where he can gobble up human souls and living magic from the many magir in this world. And that will translate to the other worlds as well."

"A repeat of what Abaddon wanted?" Varu asked.

Mormo nodded, his expression grim. "Macy's been research-ing, and several clairvoyants at MEC have confirmed a darkness gathering, once again. A link to Abaddon has been suggested. Hecate and I think Pazuzu and Hanbi, Pazuzu's nightmare of a sire, plan to take up where the Lord of Doom left off—creating chaos large enough to destabilize us before the Darkness comes. We cannot allow that to happen."

Orion sighed. "When can we get rid of this Darkness gig? I'm in the mood for some local battles. Fights to save the cosmos are gonna be draining."

Mormo glared at him, though Varu's eyes crinkled in amusement.

Before Orion could say anything else to needle the magician, Duncan ran up to them. "We have a problem." He looked at Orion. "Your mate is gone. Her dad, Macy, and their angry demon friends are waging a war on the White Sea Witch. I'm planning to head over to help."

"Heading where?" Mormo asked.

"To that mystery island Orion found."

Everyone looked to Orion. He turned to Varu and raised a brow, refusing to panic—*vampires didn't panic*— because the link between him and Kaia remained strong. He felt no fear or pain from her. Not yet.

Varu nodded. "Duncan, go. But the rest of us will stay with Orion and plan. The witch is too smart to be so obvious."

"Agreed." Orion felt a hunger for battle, and his fingertips itched, his nails growing sharper and stronger as they pushed past their normal length. "She's not the real threat."

"Right. The demon is," Khent said, appearing with Rolf and Kraft behind him.

"No, I am," Orion smiled, his fangs sharp and his appetite keen. "I'm ready to kill the unkillable."

"Now *that's* what I'm talking about." Kraft chuckled and rubbed his hands together with glee. "This is going to be epic, *ja?*"

KAIA HAD TAKEN one small step outside the house, waiting for her father in his safely protected driveway, when Jack, one of her roommates, drove up and waved from the driver's side, his window down.

"Kaia, thank God. I was worried. I couldn't get a hold of you." He blinked. "Nice hair."

"Thanks." She glanced around, prepared for a trap or her mother to pull a fast one using one of her friends as bait. "Jack? I thought you were working on a project for MEC."

"I was." He grimaced. "I need your help. I think your mom did something to Drake and Web."

She hurried over to him, her new power still growing, still shifting inside her, calling for her to return to the sea, a lake, any type of water so that it might swell and settle. And then, according to her dad, she could start to feel for what she could do. Not every sea witch was the same. Though all could make deals with humans and magir, the extent of their power to make wishes come true varied. Unlike the djinn, who were a similar yet very different level of Wish Master.

"How did she find you guys?"

"She has some lycans we were sent to look for. They've been missing for over a week and they have a connection to some artifact we're after." He rubbed a hand over his eyes, his worry evident.

She looked over her shoulder, needing to get her father involved. That's when Jack struck.

The needle to the back of her neck didn't hurt, but it stole her will to resist.

"Get in the car, Kaia," Jack said with a smile. "No one wants to hurt you. I just want to talk to you about a problem I'm having."

But when Kaia stared into Jack's eyes, she didn't see him at all. She saw her mother.

The trip to her mother's house in Magnolia happened without incident, the music in the car something she hummed along with as they drove, the streets not crowded at all due to the late hour. She felt a need to scratch the back of her neck but didn't, irritated but not hurt in any way by the pressure at her nape.

Once past a long driveway to the grand home sitting on an acre of land and overlooking Elliot Bay, Jack parked then went around to her side of the car and opened the door for her.

"Thanks."

"Sure, Kaia." He tucked her arm in his and walked her into her mother's fancy home. Worth several million and decorated with no expense spared to give the house an ornate interior design, filled with white or near-colorless walls and blue and green accents, it fit Sabine Belyaev. But Kaia didn't care for the expensive pieces making the house feel like a showplace instead of a home. At least in Belyy Zamok, the castle felt authentic, not as if her mom were trying too hard.

Jack walked her to her mother then sat down on a plain white chair, no doubt worth more than Kaia made in months, and stared at nothing. Oddly, she felt relieved that she'd been right; Jack wasn't working for her mother of his own free will. He'd been enthralled.

"Is he okay?" She should have been more worried about her friend. But she liked keeping calm, and the roiling seat of her power relaxed, the frothing waves no longer fighting to storm free.

"Your friend is just fine." Sabine smiled, walking forward with her wine glass half full. She took a sip, looking Kaia over, and frowned. "I'm not sure I like your new look." She fingered her own white hair, worn down. "But I sense something else different about you."

"I mated with Orion," Kaia announced, too happy to keep the truth a secret.

Her mother's mouth dropped open, and she set her wine down then hugged Kaia hard. "Oh, honey. I'm so happy for you." She pulled back, clasping her hands with her daughter's as she studied her. "You've gained so much power." Sabine looked delighted, not at all as angry as Kaia had expected.

"You're not mad?"

"Why would I be mad? You're perfect. As you were meant to be." She guided Kaia with her up the stairs and out onto a large patio on the rooftop overlooking the bay. Overhead, a storm gathered, the clouds constantly shifting to block what little light the crescent moon reflected.

It was then Kaia saw the marble altar and table next to it filled with sharp instruments, a few daggers, and a large black statue, half as tall as Kaia, presiding over it all. The altar was slightly tilted and solid, beautifully crafted with thin red lines, no, rivulets, carved in a pattern that led to a hole at its base. And underneath, a flat black bowl sat, ready to gather whatever flowed from the altar's lines.

"Mom?" Kaia turned, and her mother stabbed her just above the heart with an athame that smelled of cinnamon and ash. Brimstone. Kaia couldn't move, frozen. The pain was nothing compared to the horror that washed over her as the statue came to life over her mother's shoulder. And grew.

"Ah, but what is this?" a deep, sibilant voice hissed. "The sacrifice I was promised is not here."

"Not yet." Sabine nodded to Kaia. "She mated him. He'll be here soon."

"And so we wait." The man, no, *demon,* drifted closer. Handsome and human looking, if not for the large, black, leathery wings behind him, or the tail that whipped around and slashed her cheek. The sharp tip of his tail flicked over his lips, and he licked her blood off it. "Oh, lovely." The creature—Pazuzu, maybe?—stroked her mother's cheek with a long finger ending in a sharp black nail. "But not what we agreed upon, my love."

"*My love?*" Kaia couldn't believe her mother was cavorting with demons. "Mom?"

"I'm sorry, Kaia." Sabine sounded genuinely apologetic, which made the chaos around her even more confusing. "But there can only be one White Sea Witch."

Then her mother flicked her hand, and Kaia was yanked back and slammed onto the altar, her head higher than her feet, her wrists and ankles bound with chains of black bone. Sabine shifted Kaia's hands in place, moving them over the red grooves in the marble. Her mother took the athame from Kaia's chest and slit each of her wrists, the cuts deep yet small, allowing Kaia's blood to drip constantly from her body.

Kaia screamed as the burn in her wounds intensified, the marble under her sucking her blood into the mapped lines carved into the altar.

"Slow and steady." Her mother smiled. "You're beautiful, almost as pretty as I am. But your blood is tainted. Time to purify it."

"It's not." Kaia couldn't help crying, especially when Sabine ground the slits in her wrists over the marble, keeping her injuries fresh. She shrieked when slender bone picks shot up from the altar through her wrists, keeping open the flesh that tried to heal itself.

A roar echoed deep inside her, and she knew Orion would come.

It's a trap. Stop, she tried to send him as hard as she could. But she knew nothing she said would keep him from coming.

Her mother stepped away to fiddle with her ringing cell phone.

The black statue now moving around as if alive stood over Kaia and smiled. "Yes, child. I am Pazuzu. Soon to be your new sire." He leaned down, studying her and said in a lower voice, "Or your new husband. I feel that your mother will not be enough to satisfy my needs."

She cringed. "I'm already mated."

"Not for long." He tapped her forehead, and her pain stopped. "Now, that's better."

"What are you doing?" Sabine asked, looking up from her phone. "Oh, Kaia, your daddy says hi."

"Leave him alone." How could she have been so wrong about her mom? Sabine had always been dark, a little bad. But not out and out evil. Or had Kaia only seen what she wanted?

Sabine laughed. "You hear that, Will? Come to Belyy Zamok if you want her. But be prepared for a fight. The door's open." She disconnected and tucked her phone away. But the look she shot Pazuzu was nothing that could be called pleasant. "I've brought you a soul."

"But not the one I was promised. If I can't have the vampire, I'll have you sweet." Then he ripped through his clothing, and Kaia saw something she wished she could unsee. A phallus that was in no way human. The thing was several feet long and moved like a snake. It touched her leg, and she screamed.

"Not yet, Kaia. But soon," Pazuzu promised and laughed.

CHAPTER TWENTY-SIX

O rion refused to give in to the fear threatening to cloud his bloode. It had no place in a vampire's heart. He would fight to the end, but he would never let his own weakness stop him from battling for what he possessed. His heart and his mate.

At the thought of Kaia, he stiffened his resolve and forced the fear away.

The storm over Seattle grew stronger, clouds gathering, the rain coming down in icy sheets as the wind whipped in a fury.

"We know she's not at her island," Orion told those with him —Mormo, Varu, Kraft, Rolf, and Khent. "Duncan and the others are at Belyy Zamok, and he said the place is crawling with zombies and monsters."

"Oh man. We'd better get something just as good," Kraft complained.

"I feel you," Rolf commiserated. "But I have a feeling the demons we encounter will sate that appetite."

Varu glared at them both while Khent ignored them, gathering his dead servants. He sent two new crows ahead through the portal Mormo had crafted into the floor, which should take them to an area just outside their target in Magnolia. "I'll scout and await you at the witch's home." He transformed into an owl and followed them.

Hecate had felt the presence of a demon god the second the creature entered the mortal plane and directed them to the home Sabine owned in Magnolia. "It's a sure bet Kaia is there," she'd said before disappearing to handle more disasters flaring around the many crossroads she guarded. Apparently, all the demon activity was stirring chaos between the realms.

Mormo looked around at the remaining Night Bloode. "Rolf, I think we need you on the island. There's too much to fight there."

Rolf groaned, waved, and walked through the portal Mormo directed him to. It disappeared.

Mormo continued, "Varu, Kraft, Khent, and Orion, you four will have to handle Pazuzu. I need to help my mistress. The foul energy from Hanbi and Pazuzu's machinations is spreading, creating chaos. That's why Hecate's so busy lately." Confirming what Orion had thought.

Mormo swore and vanished then quickly reappeared and grabbed Orion by the arm. "Do not give it what it wants or it wins. But you may be able to bargain with Pazuzu." He vanished once more and didn't return.

"No idea what that means, but Kaia is hurting." It took everything inside Orion not to fly into a rage and go straight for the demon's throat. Then the witch's.

"Steady," Varu ordered. "We go in. You focus on your mate. We'll handle the rest." He then reached into his heart, his hand disappearing inside his chest, and removed three Bloode Stones.

Kraft gaped. "That's not freaky as shit. No, not at all."

Varu let go of the power gems, which floated in the air before him. "Find Fara. You can't stay with me when we encounter the dark ones. Go."

Orion shook his head. "You keep getting weirder, Varu."

"I know." Varu smiled, showing sharp fangs. "Now let's go kill what needs killing."

"*Finally.*" Kraft darted to the portal on the floor, swearing in German about slow-ass vampires as he crossed.

Orion followed. *Get ready, Kaia. I'm coming.*

He appeared behind Kraft, who knelt while Khent flapped his wings and settled on a tree branch, magnificent in his eagle-owl form. They looked to be in someone's backyard overlooking the water. The scent of demon seemed distant, as did the scent of his mate.

Varu appeared, and Khent shifted back into his human form to report, "Kaia lies upon an altar, being drained of her blood in a ceremony of some kind. The demon Pazuzu is there, as is Sabine Belyaev." He blinked, his eyes completely black, staring through the eyes of his scouts. "I see several lycans inside, all tainted with the sea witch's power. I don't know if they're willing servants or enslaved."

"Try not to kill if you don't have to," Varu said, and everyone stared at him in shock. "Only because we need that artifact the lycans have that leads to the fourth Bloode Stone. After we have it, I don't care who you kill."

Orion nodded. That made sense. But he'd come to the end of his patience. "I'm going after her."

"Go." Varu nodded to the house. "We'll deal with the rest."

Orion followed the source of his heart—his mate—and bounded to the rooftop of a very nice home clouded with dark energy. He spotted Kaia immediately, but before he could rescue her, that bastard Pazuzu, from his dream, was there in his monstrous form. Upon spying Orion, he shifted so that he looked like a man, the darkness of his features fading, along with his wings, tail, and monstrous dick behind a gray suit.

The rain and wind didn't touch him.

"So, my payment arrives." The demon turned and frowned at the empty deck. "Tricky sea witch, to leave when I'm just getting started." Pazuzu sighed. "Ah well. So, Orion of the Night Bloode, you have come to fulfill the bargain the sea witch made."

"I've come to take back my mate and cut your fucking head off."

Pazuzu grinned. "A fight then? Excellent. I haven't had one of those in eons. You have no idea how boring the afterlife is."

"Don't you mean hell?"

"I wish." Pazuzu sighed. "Irkalla is the afterlife, where the dead go to roam. It's nothing but dust and ash at home. I rarely get the chance to come out and play." He spread his arms wide. "Yet here I am, ready to change it up. So here's the deal. I was promised your bloode. If you give it willingly, I'll let your mate go and stop chewing on her soul. If not, we fight. And by the time we're done, I'll have eaten her up. She's delicious, by the way."

Orion glanced at Kaia and saw her wan features and fading essence in danger. "I'll kill you."

"Boy, you can't," Pazuzu said, almost kindly. "I have been alive for thousands of years. Even if my body leaves this plane, it will go back to Irkalla. I am destined to guide and guard the lands of my people. But with Kaia's soul, I'll have enough power for a quick rebirth."

"Why are you telling me this?" Orion had no idea what his kin were up to, but Pazuzu needed to be stopped.

"Because I feel cheated, to be honest." Pazuzu removed a handkerchief from his inner pocket and dabbed at his mouth. "She is tasty." He turned it to show Orion a hint of blood.

Instead of rushing the demon, Orion waited, using his brain for once because Kaia kept shouting in his mind, and he couldn't make out her words or intent, though he could see her blood slowing, her wrists seeming to fuse to the bone spears sticking out of them. This he noticed out of the corner of his eye, not wanting the demon to see.

"Why do you feel cheated?"

"Because I was promised a rather tasty soul, and she left when I wasn't looking." Pazuzu frowned at Kaia. "And this one isn't—" He dodged the fist Orion shot at his face and smiled, his face looking almost canine for a moment, with a muzzle, large eyes, and even larger teeth, before he resumed his human form.

"Excellent. Well, then, vrykolakas, bring me your rage while I consume your female."

Orion stopped, not sure why his kin wanted him to distract the demon when everything he did only gave Pazuzu more time to *eat his fucking mate.* "Take me instead."

Pazuzu paused. "Really? Even if it means your end? Even if means ending *the world?*" He smiled wide, showing sharp teeth. "Fascinating. Very well. Come here, boy."

"Call me boy again and I'll rip your dick off and feed it to you."

"Now that's a knee-slapper." Pazuzu chuckled and literally slapped his knee. "Kneel."

Orion hurried forward and knelt, anticipating the pain. But the agony was worse than anything he'd ever felt when the demon reached into his chest and put a fist around his heart.

And squeezed.

KRAFT DIDN'T LIKE what he was seeing. The sea witch had driven away in her car while Orion battled the demon on the roof. He had no idea what condition Kaia might be in, but he did know the jagged portal in the basement that kept growing could not be a good thing.

"This is what we need to stop from entering our world," Varu growled. "It smells of death and rot."

"And life too." A voice deeper and louder than Kraft's ears could comfortably hear made him cringe and shake his head to rid himself of the pain.

Next to him, Khent grimaced. "A god."

"Yes, and soon *your* god, my children." A massive serpentine tail came through the void, with jagged ridges, what looked like teeth, on one side of it. The thing couldn't possibly fit inside the room, and then it didn't have to, as the cavernous basement became a cavern in truth, several stories in height and deeper than Kraft could see, darkness eating at the endless distance beyond.

Scents and sounds grew muffled, only Khent and Varu any color in the monochrome of gray all around. Except for the demon who continued to move forward.

Another tail with teeth joined the other, acting as legs for the green-scaled and black-furred torso that arrived before the creature's giant human arms, feathery wings, and head finally came through.

"So much to experience," the creature said and shrunk, so that he was no longer fifty feet tall, but twenty feet, closer to its prey —vampires.

"Who are you?" Varu asked, their badass patriarch not taking one step back. No fear, no give, that was their master strigoi.

"I am Hanbi, your father, child. You are my eyes now, my teeth." The jagged spikes between his snake legs chittered, and Kraft stared, mesmerized, at a predator who impressed the hell— no pun intended—out of him.

He shifted into his wolf and sniffed, then sneezed and shifted back. "*Kumpel*, you stink."

Hanbi turned to look down at him, his face a stone mask of evil, dark smoke wafting from the sockets where his eyes should be. He had a man's face with long hair made of black feathers and a mouth with rows upon rows of teeth.

He laughed, and the boom of eternal damnation sang from his throat. "So I do. So will you when we are one, little brother." He paused, and Kraft swore Hanbi shimmered, transparent before becoming solid once more. "I hunger."

He reached for Kraft but had to battle Khent's attack with a white, shining sword.

It hit Hanbi, slicing his arm off, which vanished when it hit the ground. Hanbi didn't bleed. His arm regrew, his hand now equipped with sharp talons, each with four digits, all ending in black nails a foot long.

"Keep him busy," Varu said and vanished.

"Oh, nice." Kraft snarled and avoided the giant serpent teeth trying to decapitate him as he ripped into Hanbi's wing. He made contact and chewed through feathery skin that tasted like ass and melted like snow in his mouth. He spat out the offensive texture only to realize it had vanished as if it had never been. But while distracted by that weird taste, he let Hanbi smack him so far away he could no longer see Khent or the demon god and hit something hard and sharp that caused him to bleed.

"Shit." He listened and heard Khent in the distance, so much gray all around him beginning to blend, no longer the pale outline of trees and villages, animals and people with no life left to give.

And then the real demons ventured forth, drawn to the bloode that poured from his shoulder and wouldn't stop.

"My children, I bring you a present." Hanbi's voice echoed all around, and Kraft raced toward Khent's faint swearing as he called for Kraft to stop dicking around.

With a grin, Kraft shifted into his wolf and ran as if his life depended on it. And when the demons came after him in droves, he knew it did.

KAIA COULD FEEL the pain coursing through Orion as he let that bastard Pazuzu rip into his very core. It felt as if he were tearing her in half as well, tied as she was to her mate. When he tried to sever their link, to keep her free from his burden of pain, she doubled down, gripping him with all the love she had inside her.

Their bond remained, and she gasped as she felt herself begin to die.

She'd been able to seal her wrists when Orion had come, but now she'd healed around creepy—unsanitary—bones that felt like they'd been dipped in acid.

"Now this is interesting," came a low voice that would have scared her into a scream if the stranger hadn't put a hand over her mouth.

She glanced at a tall, dark, and extremely handsome male with red eyes. A vampire, and by the look and feel of his immense power, she sensed he was Orion's patriarch—Varujan. She had yet to meet him, having been so busy having sex and all.

Great *sex and all*. She heard humor amidst the pain radiating from her mate.

Hold on, Orion. I'll get you out.

Varujan watched her while he broke the bones holding her fast to the altar, as if breaking through dry sticks. Once freed, she tried to sit up but couldn't, feeling extremely weak.

Varujan helped her, lifting her from the altar.

"You brought friends and haven't introduced us? Rude." Pazuzu didn't seem bothered by her escape. If anything, he looked happy to see Varujan. "The patriarch. Very good. Once I drain your kin, you will make a worthy replacement. And I see you've met my new bride."

Orion's growl grew louder.

Pazuzu blinked down at him. "Hmm. Something hiding inside

you, boy. Is that what gives you such brute strength?" He squinted. "Now isn't that strange. I feel something of the moon inside you, and the oceans. Many of them."

Varujan looked from Orion to Kaia.

"Take her away. Now," Orion managed to get out and stiffened, still on his knees as Pazuzu continued to crush his heart and absorb more of his bloode. The thick red stuff swam from Orion's chest and up over Pazuzu's arm, past his shoulder and neck up into his mouth. A horrific vision of sacrifice made even worse by the blood he'd already stolen from Kaia, which she could sense the demon using to power him into killing her mate.

Varujan patted her shoulder. "I have to get back. Orion, remember what Mormo said."

He vanished, and Kaia stumbled and sank to her knees. She felt so weak, yet a storm within her woke, and the wind around them whipped in a fury.

"That's what I want," Pazuzu said with a sigh, his gaze on her. "You're Becoming, my beauty."

"Not... yours... " Orion hissed and put his hands on the arm attached to the hand buried in his chest. "My mate," he roared and opened himself, was all Kaia could think.

She had no idea why, but she thought he was yelling at her from deep inside himself to grab hold of him. She crawled to him, ignoring the wind and rain, the throbbing agony where her wrists tore open once more, her blood streaming into Pazuzu alongside Orion's.

"What a lovely pair you make." The demon laughed, his face morphing into that of dog's, his skin turning black as his body changed from human-like to a demon's. "My hunger has awakened," he said, a deeper voice echoing, a new form taking shape from the shadow behind him.

A monstrous beast rose from Pazuzu's shadow, clutching two struggling vampires in hands as large as cars, its scaled arms as long as semis. Then a giant wolf ran up its back and sank its teeth into the beast's neck, and it shuddered and howled.

But not in defeat. In laughter.

"My return has been foretold," it shrieked with joy.

The fuck it has, she heard in her head. *Kaia, hold on.*

Lightning spiraled down from the heavens. And then she saw a bright light, felt a burst of heat from within, and knew nothing more.

CHAPTER TWENTY-SEVEN

Orion had never felt such suffering, not even when he'd been a fledgling and watched Spiro die a true death. Kaia was hurting, and something terrible was coming through to this plane.

He could see the line Pazuzu made, taking his bloode into himself, adding it to the rich life he'd already stolen from Kaia. Orion's fury built, knowing how much his mate endured.

But the evil reaching toward him came not from Pazuzu, but from the shadow now made flesh. From Pazuzu's sire. Hanbi—the king of all evil.

He had no idea where his kin had gone, but now he could see them, both Varu and Khent in Hanbi's giant hands, being crushed to death, like Orion's heart. And there, Kraft trying to bite into the demon and having no luck. Hell, from the demon god's laughter, he thought Kraft might just be tickling it.

Mormo's words came back to him. *"Do not give it what it wants or it wins. But you may be able to bargain with Pazuzu."*

The real threat then, was Hanbi. Not his son.

Orion called upon the storm deep inside him, warned his mate to hold tight, where he'd do his best to protect her, and let himself open all the way up.

Before Pazuzu could touch the power inside him, the lightning, a blessing from several water deities Orion had annoyingly been pledged to at birth thanks to Alecta—Mother of the Vrykolakas—shot down and spread along his bloode into the creatures of darkness and evil holding him fast.

Hanbi roared and struggled as Varu, Khent, and Kraft took advantage of his temporary paralysis to ravage him. Black blood that oozed as if alive welled along Pazuzu's body while divine rains whipped the demon god, the king of all evil, alongside the vampires who worshipped no one but themselves.

He felt Kimbazi, the Congo goddess of sea storms. Nephthys, Egyptian goddess of rivers and the night. Poseidon and Aegaeon, Greek gods of the sea and storms. And even Freyr, a mighty god of the Norse pantheon, of rain and life. Together, they and Orion seized the evil trying to take hold of the world.

Kaia hugged him, awash in love and protection, and smothered the taint of evil still trying to break free.

You're almost there, Pazuzu said, his voice faint though he held on to Orion through bloode and blood—his and Kaia's.

Orion had to ask now. *I offer you a bargain.*

Orion, no, Kaia cried. *Don't.*

Your terms? Pazuzu said. *Hurry, vampire. I cannot hold for much longer.*

You wish for life. I offer you mine if you save the others and sever the tie to your sire.

But yours is not whole. And I cannot, as it's tied to new life, which I am bound to protect.

Orion felt Kaia's fear for him, knew his own confusion. and then he felt it. A small spark deep inside, a tiny meow in question. *What the hell?* He struggled to hold on, feeling his grasp on

Pazuzu slipping, Hanbi regaining a bit of power, siphoned from the idiot gods offering the help he hadn't asked for.

"Meow." Shadow rubbed his fur along Orion's bloode, the connection forged of affection and magic that shouldn't exist yet did. Not real yet real anyway.

He's tied to my magic. Kaia gasped and asked the kitten, *Do I know you?*

The cat purred and put a psychic paw on Orion's mind through to the demon wanting a bargain.

A life, yes, Pazuzu agreed. *It is done. Well thought, vryko. We will meet again.*

Then the world imploded.

Hanbi screamed in rage as the gods tore him apart alongside the vampires continuing to bleed him out. Having been made flesh, he couldn't hide in the shadows, and as the wind blew the clouds apart, moonlight speared the evil until it burned away and the rains washed it back into the earth and out to sea, cleansing them all with the purity of a powerful new White Sea Witch.

Kaia blinked at him. "Orion?"

He grinned. "We kicked its ass."

Sadly, he passed out before he could explain, even to himself, what the hell had just happened.

Sabine laughed as she hid in Belyy Zamok in her plush bedroom in a secret bolt hole, watching through a mirror pond as her zombies and minions made short work of Will and his idiot friends. Such weakness. How had she ever thought she'd make something viable with that man? His morality had skewed so far from hers that they'd never been able to breach the distance between them.

But one thing he had done. He'd helped her create an incredibly powerful daughter, one a little too powerful, to be honest.

Well, now she was Pazuzu's problem.

Sabine thought herself such a clever witch. Giving Paz her daughter's soul and the vryko had cemented their deal. She would have power beyond imagining, no more competition from Kaia or any other sea witch, and an end to her enemies, all in one blow.

Watching Will slowly die next to that bastard partner of his was so satisfying. Trust Will to find the one demon in all of hell who wanted to be nice and help people. "Asshole."

"You called?" Her husband appeared behind her, whole and hearty. And amused.

"You piece of shit," she screeched and ran at him, exploding into her half-kraken form and bursting through the castle.

As everything crumbled, she did her best to crush him but knew she'd missed. She saw him watching her with Anton, that pathetic excuse for a demon, standing on the ground away from her destruction. So close to death...

Then, to her shock, a dark elf was suddenly there, in front of her, holding a sword that felt like dragon and fire. "You," he snarled and sliced her throat before she could blink.

As she clutched her neck, trying to stop the bleeding, she heard him bitching about all the animals who'd apparently died during the skirmish on her island.

"I found baby deer ripped apart," the elf cried, and actual tears trickled down his cheeks. "Squirrels and wolves. And so many birds, so many, forced to endure your cruelty." He bellowed in a foreign tongue she'd never before heard.

She tried to ignore him as she trailed her tentacles toward the water to aid in her healing. But Anton and his stupid halfbreed of a son grabbed her.

"Good hold, Cho." Anton grinned. "Not today, witch."

"There can only be one White Sea Witch, Uncle Anton,"

Macy Bishop-Dunwich said, her eyes sad. "Kaia is worth a hundred of you, Sabine, and you know it."

Desperate, Sabine reached out with her magic.

But the dark elf was there, hatred burning in his eyes. "Your life is forfeit," he said, clear as day, and sliced off her head. As she slowly died, her magic returned to her, just a spark.

But something soft and furry ate it, swallowing her soul whole. In an instant, her new world became one of pain and servitude.

For an eternity.

Pazuzu winked at her through green eyes and lifted a small gray paw to clean his face.

"Shadow?" She heard the elf gasp. "How did you get here?"

ORION WOKE with Kaia wrapped around him like a constrictor, but he'd never been so happy to be smothered in his life. "Kaia?"

She woke and kissed him all over. "Oh my gosh, you're here. You're alive!" She burst into happy tears. "I almost l-lost you."

Orion kissed her and couldn't stop kissing her. Until several disgusted groans told him they weren't alone.

"Get a room," Kraft said. "You mated vampires are disgusting."

"Get a life," Rolf said. "You Kraft, not Orion. He's got one. And a connection to some water gods, if I'm not mistaken. But that's just what I *heard.* I didn't get to *see* it, because Mormo shoved me with the B team." He sighed. "I missed out on all the fun."

"We did kill a lot of zombies," Duncan reminded him, his tone dry. "And we did get to watch Onvyr behead a sea witch turned kraken and take over her island."

Everyone paused.

Kaia realized what Duncan had said.

"Nice, Duncan." Macy glared at him, and to his credit, he looked shamefaced.

"Sorry."

Kaia wiped her eyes. "She needed to go. Maybe now she's at peace."

Orion didn't think so. Sabine had made a pact with a demon, and she owed it a soul. Pazuzu didn't seem like the type to go away emptyhanded.

Kaia blinked and looked around her. "Why are we on the couch?" She kept looking. "In your house?"

Orion hugged her tighter. "My guess is this was the safest place for us to recuperate."

Macy nodded. "You two need time to heal, but we saved the day. I think." She frowned. "Khent still hasn't convinced us the danger is past. How did you stop Pazuzu?"

He wondered if he had. But no, the demon had taken his offer. A life for a life. He put a hand over his healing heart, feeling a slight twinge as the organ continued to repair itself, but no tie to a demon. He didn't think. But he remembered giving the demon something. A life...that purred.

Green eyes came into view, and Shadow licked his nose.

Orion slowly sat up, keeping Kaia in his lap, and took the kitten in hand. Kaia turned with him, staring in awe at Shadow.

"What's going on?" Mormo asked, then froze. "And who the hell let *that* into my house?"

Everyone stopped and stared at Shadow, who chirped and grew small, leathery wings.

"What is that?" Macy asked in a shaky voice and took a step back into the arms of her mate. "Because that's not a cat."

Kraft frowned. "Yes it is. Look at it. He just has wings now." Kraft cocked his head. "And he smells like brimstone."

"He's my familiar," Kaia said in a light voice as Orion placed the kitten back down. "He saved us when Orion had hold of Hanbi through Pazuzu. Don't worry. He's friendly."

To prove it, the kitten rubbed his face along Kaia's, and purred, settling against her breasts with a sigh.

"Hey, watch it, buddy." Orion glared, knowing who occupied the kitten, now Shadow and Pazuzu. Oh boy. Varu was not going to be happy about this.

We made a bargain, Shadow reminded him, still a kitten, yet more.

How is this possible? Orion paused. Had he inadvertently sacrificed his cat? His heart broke at the thought.

Kaia stroked the little guy, and Shadow blinked slowly at him.

Onvyr entered the room eating an apple, battered yet smiling as if he'd been given the answer to everything he ever wanted. "It's simple," he explained. "Smoky was just a *shadow* of Nightmare to begin with. A shell, I think he said." He looked at Shadow and nodded. "Yep. So he's a cat but not a cat. A perfect familiar for a sea witch, because, well, they're usually more on the bad side than the good side. Like vampires." So saying, he walked out with the large battle cat that appeared by his side.

"A perfect mate for a vryko," Varu murmured as he entered the room and nodded. "Mormo, the Night Bloode now counts the new White Sea Witch and her demon familiar as kin." Power settled over the group as new energy added to the collective strength of Hecate's death bringers.

His dusk elf mate looped her arm around his middle and smiled. "Sounds about right."

"I don't know about this." Mormo ran a hand over his head, looking frazzled. "Hecate needs to be told."

"Like she doesn't already know," Khent said with a snort.

But Orion didn't care about any of it. No worries, no problems would ever be insurmountable, not with his kin and his mate by his side. "You think the ADR would let you shift to nighttime hours?" He asked her with a smile.

"I bet they would." Kaia kissed him. "I love you, Orion."

"Ah mate, not more than I love you, *agapi mou.*"

He heard a few groans, felt Shadow's purr of acceptance, and appreciated the sighs from the females in the room watching over them.

But nothing mattered except getting his mate where he could see to her needs in private.

"Told you vampires do it better," Duncan said with a laugh. "Yeah, mate, you did right by her V-card."

Macy laughed with him. "Idiot."

Kraft asked, "What? I don't get it. What card?" After a moment, he laughed. "Oh, her *V*-card."

But Orion was already carrying his mate to their room. Once inside, he paused with her in his arms. "I'm sorry you lost your mother."

"I am and I'm not. She nearly killed us." Kaia sighed. "It's going to take some time, but I have it thanks to you."

"Thanks to us. Without you, I couldn't have held on." He glanced down at the kitten that had followed them. "And *you.* We'll deal with you later." He lowered Kaia's feet to the floor and picked Shadow up by the scruff, his wings nowhere in sight.

The kitten hissed and tried to smack him with a paw, but Orion wasn't having it. "We'll talk about what this means, but not now. And we are not putting on any shows for your amusement or entertainment, buddy. Go fuck with Khent. He needs the practice. Or Kraft." Orion grinned. "He kept calling Shadow dinner, remember."

Shadow seemed to perk up at that and let Orion put him outside the room, even accepting the pat to his head and stroke along his back.

When Orion went back inside, locked the door behind him,

and turned to his mate, he saw her naked and waiting by the door of the bathroom. She winked. "We never did get to shower sex, did we?"

He grinned and stripped, dropping his clothes on the way. "Nope. No time like the present." He took her in his arms and kissed her. "I love you, Kaia."

"I love you, Orion." She paused. "Now let's get in the shower and get busy."

PAZUZU SAT outside the door listening, a little annoyed he hadn't been allowed to watch. He had, after all, done them all a *huge* favor by shoving his father back where he belonged, in the underworld. Not that he could have accepted Orion's sacrifice or killed Kaia, because he did protect pregnant women, and Kaia was due to have twins in nine months. Linked as she was to the vampire, taking him out would have taken her out.

He had to hand it to Orion. The vryko worked fast.

Paz stretched, a little sleepy, bemused by this new form that really did make him feel and behave like a young feline. But everything was so bright and bold. Sounds and scents had texture, form. So much life in this world full of so many kinds of creatures. He couldn't wait to help Kaia learn her new powers. This White Sea Witch promised to be one heck of a power hitter for the Night Bloode, and the old one kept him content, eternally feeding him with the power of death and dying things.

"You're not fooling us, you know," the nachzehrer said, showing some impressive fangs and startling Pazuzu into a jump and a hiss. "Shadow, Pazuzu, whatever. I'll be watching you, demon." He lowered himself to a crouch and smiled. "Don't think I won't swallow you whole if you piss me off." He paused. "Just like you swallowed the sea witch."

Startled the nachzehrer knew that, Pazuzu took a hesitant step back.

"But hey, if you're bored, I know some fun stuff we can do. You interested in tracking down a lycan gone missing and a possible artifact we really need to keep the Darkness from killing all the worlds as we know them?"

Now *that* sounded interesting. Pazuzu leapt onto the vampire, scrambling with his claws to balance on the male's shoulder.

"Let's go. And remember, you do anything to endanger the clan, I'll eat you." Kraft chuckled and rose to his feet.

Not if I eat you first.

THANK you for reading Orion and Kaia's story. There's just something about a stubborn vampire… Just wait until you read about Kraft and the strong wolf who ties him in knots. You can find Kraft's story in ***Between Bloode and Wolf***.

And to read **special bonus scenes** and sneak peeks into Between the Shadows, join the newsletter on Marie's website!

GLOSSARY

INTELLIGENT BEINGS CLASSIFICATION:

- **Demons**—creatures from any of the hell planes, tricksters, evil-doers, and powerful beings with a bent toward dark desires, associated with fire
- **Divinity (gods and goddesses)**—those of a divine nature and whose power is derived from creationism and worship
- **Humans**—mortal beings from the mundane world, not born with magic though some can harness its power
- **Magir**—an all-encompassing term to describe those supernatural creatures living among the human population in the mundane realm (e.g. lycans, witches, druids, mermaids, gargoyles, etc.)
- **Monsters**—animalistic creatures that aren't human or magir but do have magical properties/abilities (like fox spirits, gryphons, dragons, manticores, etc.)

Vampire Terms:

- **Ambrogio**—the first vampire ever created, born from a curse given from the god, Apollo. Father (Primus) to the vampire species, husband to Selene, the mother of the species.
- **Blood-bond**—the psychic connection a vampire has to a blood donor
- **Bloode**—that intrinsic vampiric essence within a blood-drinker that makes him a vampire, as opposed to a demon or other dark-natured creature
- **Bloode-debt**—vampiric debt incurred by a member of one's clan, passed on through familial members until fulfilled
- **Bloode Empire**—the name for the vampire nation created in 727 BCE
- **Bloode-magic**—magic in a vampire's bloode, manipulated through the Bloode Stones or a deity with power over blood and the dead (i.e. Hecate, thus Mormo)
- **Bloode Stones**—six droplets of Ambrogio's blood or tears (split mythology on origin) congealed into power gems when they made contact with the earth. It is rumored that only a Worthy vampire can handle a Bloode Stone and instill peace within their species.
- **Bloode Witch**—a witch who uses bloode to power herself, serves his or her vampire clan and is considered kin. Very rare, more common in older times.
- **Clans**—groups of vampires within a tribe that act as family, led by a patriarch, comprised of kin (brothers/fathers/sons), anywhere in number from ten to sixty members

- **(The) Ending**—the period of time before vampires came into existence
- **Guide**—also known as bloode-guide, someone not related who mentors a young vampire through adulthood
- **Kin**—family, those vampires who do not instill an urge to kill. Another word for vampire brother, father, or son
- **Kin Wars**—legendary vampire civil war, thought to have been fought several thousand years ago, brought about by a foul curse from the gods, turning vampire against vampire and forming the ten tribes
- **Master**—vampire leader of an entire vampire tribe
- **Mate**—a vampire's bonded female partner, with whom he can sire offspring
- **Of the Bloode**—another term for vampire
- **Patriarch**—vampire leader of a vampire clan
- **Primus**—the first vampire, the father of all (Ambrogio), also refers to a pureblood vampire leader
- **Sire**—a vampire's father, also sometimes used as a term of respect for the Master of a tribe
- **Tribes**—the ten large factions of vampires, bound together according to particular traits. The tribes are as follows: Strigoi, Upir, Nachzehrer, Reaper, Draugr, Revenant, Jiangshi, Sasabonsam, Vrykolakas, and Pishachas.
- **Upir Gold**—term used to denote vampire bloode and brains, a divine delicacy
- **Vampire**—a blood-drinker and descendant of Ambrogio, always male, always naturally born. "Vampire" is also a generic term in reference to describing a blood-drinker from any of the ten tribes. Other names for vampire are: Of the Bloode, blood-

suckers, blood-drinkers, vamps, fangers, and death-bringers.

- **Worthy**—characteristic of a vampire who is the quintessential essence of the Bloode, who has the true heart of Ambrogio in his body, courageous and powerful, a leader who will do what's best for his people

THE REALMS:

- **Celestial**—the homes of the gods, no matter what pantheon
- **Death**—also called the afterlife, the plane that harbors the dead, looked after by Hecate and several other deities, not to be confused with the hells; also sometimes referred to as the Netherworld
- **Fae**—home of the fae, to include the lands of the elves, dwarves, and faery, as well as elemental spirits
- **Hell**—the underworld planes, of which there are many, usually inhabited by demons, devils, and dark spirits, not to be confused with the Netherworld
- **Mundane**—earth, the mortal plane where humans dwell
- **Pocket**—small planes, or "pockets" of reality, created by powerful magic-users

SPECIES:

- **Dark Elves**—Fae creatures who prefer the night, they

often live in the caves and underground with dwarves in Nidavellir, which is part of the fae realm

- **Demons**—those who live in the hell plane, tricksters, evil-doers, and powerful creatures with dark desires, associated with fire
- **Druids**—humans who can do natural magic and commune with fae spirits
- **Dusk Elves**—rare (and often hunted, unwelcome among the elves) blending of light and dark elf parents, live in fae realms. Also known as mrykálfar.
- **Dwarves**—also known as dvergar, fae creatures who live in Nidavellir
- **Fae**—those who live in the fae realm, an alternate world comprised of elves, dwarves, sprites, and other creatures from a multitude of pantheons
- **Light Elves**—fae creatures who live high in the mountains in Álfheim in the fae realm
- **Lycans**—shapeshifting creatures who can assume the form of a human or large, magical direwolf
- **Mages**—magir-born, long-lived mortals who practice magic for good (also sometimes used as slang for magic users of all kinds)
- **Nymphs**—beautiful magir partial to water, generous in spirit, often sexual creatures in tune with nature
- **Necromancers**—humans who can harness death magic and command of the dead
- **Shapeshifters**—rare creatures who alternate between human and animal forms at will
- **Sorcerers**—magir-born, long-lived mortals who practice magic for evil purposes
- **Warlocks**—humans who perform magic for evil purposes, typically utilizing sacrificial magic

- **Witches**—humans who perform magic for good purposes, typically utilizing celestial or earth magic

ALSO BY MARIE

LIFE IN THE VRAIL

Lurin's Surrender

Thief of Mardu

Engaging Gren

Seriana Found

CREATIONS

The Perfect Creation

Creation's Control

Creating Chemistry

Caging the Beast

CONTEMPORARY

WICKED WARRENS

Enjoying the Show

Closing the Deal

Raising the Bar

Making the Grade

Bending the Rules

THE MCCAULEY BROTHERS

The Troublemaker Next Door

How to Handle a Heartbreaker

Ruining Mr. Perfect

What to Do with a Bad Boy

BODY SHOP BAD BOYS

Test Drive

Roadside Assistance

Zero to Sixty

Collision Course

THE DONNIGANS

A Sure Thing

Just the Thing

The Only Thing

ALL I WANT FOR HALLOWEEN

THE KISSING GAME

THE WORKS

Bodywork

Working Out

Wetwork

VETERANS MOVERS

The Whole Package

Smooth Moves

Handle with Care

Delivered with a Kiss

GOOD TO GO

A Major Attraction

A Major Seduction

A Major Distraction

A Major Connection

BEST REVENGE

Served Cold

Served Hot

Served Sweet

ROMANTIC SUSPENSE

POWERUP!

The Lost Locket

RetroCog

Whispered Words

Fortune's Favor

Flight of Fancy

Silver Tongue

Entranced

Killer Thoughts

WESTLAKE ENTERPRISES

To Hunt a Sainte

Storming His Heart

Love in Electric Blue

TRIGGERMAN INC.

Contract Signed

Secrets Unsealed

Satisfaction Delivered

AND MORE (believe it or not)!

ABOUT THE AUTHOR

Caffeine addict, boy referee, and romance aficionado, *New York Times* and *USA Today* bestselling author Marie Harte has over 100 books published with more constantly on the way. She's a confessed bibliophile and devotee of action movies. Whether hiking in Central Oregon, biking around town, or hanging at the local tea shop, she's constantly plotting to give everyone a happily ever after. Visit https://marieharte.com and fall in love.

And to subscribe to Marie's Newsletter, click here.

facebook.com/marieharteauthorpage

twitter.com/MHarte_Author

goodreads.com/Marie_Harte

bookbub.com/authors/marie-harte

instagram.com/marieharteauthor

Made in United States
Orlando, FL
21 April 2022

17039633R00171